Sweet
Medicine

Also by David Seals

THE POWWOW HIGHWAY

THIRD EYE THEATRE

THE POETIC COLLEGE

Sweet ▲▲▲
Medicine
David Seals

THE LIBRARY OF THE AMERICAN INDIAN

Herman J. Viola, Editor

ORION BOOKS / NEW YORK

This book is a work of fiction. Names of characters,
places and incidents either are the product of the author's
imagination or are used fictitiously, and any resemblance
to actual persons, living or dead, events, or locales
is entirely coincidental.

Copyright © 1992 by David Seals

Published by Orion Books, a division of Crown Publishers, Inc.,
201 East 50th Street, New York, New York 10022. Member of the
Crown Publishing Group.

ORION and colophon are trademarks of Crown Publishers, Inc.

Manufactured in the United States of America

Library of Congress Cataloging-in-Publication Data

Seals, David.
     Sweet Medicine / by David Seals. — 1st ed.
          p.   cm. — (The library of the American Indian)
     1. Indians of North America—Fiction.   I. Title.   II. Series.
     PS3569.E1725S93   1992
     813'.54—dc20   92-4069
                                                                   CIP

ISBN 0-517-58801-3

Book Design by Shari de Miskey

10 9 8 7 6 5 4 3 2 1

FIRST EDITION

DEDICATED
TO
MY FATHER, GREAT SPIRIT
WALTER J. SEALS,
1919–1991

Preface

THE RETURN OF THE QUEEN

YOU WON'T KNOW ABOUT THIS STORY UNLESS YOU'VE AL-
ready read *The Powwow Highway*, or you've seen the movie,
but that doesn't matter. You didn't miss much. It was a real
disrespectful story, anyway, and I can explain it to you in
about two easy sentences. It was all made up by Mr. David
Seals, and everybody knows he never tells the truth or has
any respect for anything. There are a number of people
who are scouring the countryside looking for him right
now, and if they catch him, they swear they'll murder him
on the spot, just as the old Cheyenne Indians swore they'd
kill Sweet Medicine if they could ever catch him.

For this tale is not unlike a continuation of the Quest to
rescue the Sacred Woman, which we had to endure in that
first idiotic and badly written book, and Philbert and Buddy
are not unlike the warrior-knights of yore. If you were un-
lucky enough to have stumbled upon one of those original
ratty copies, you would have discovered a tale that was supposed to have been full of all kinds of allegorical signifi-

1

cance and a lot of other literary tricks to make you think it was good writing, but I'll tell ya, I think he was winging it as he went along. Seals didn't know what the hell he was doing. He probably smokes marijuana too! There we were, bouncing along in a stupid 1964 Buick LeSabre that had been burned, rolled, and inhabited by skunks, and this total idiot fullblood Cheyenne named Philbert thinks it's a war pony, which he calls Protector. No wonder the college professors sneered. And Buddy Red Bird joins him in Montana to go rescue Buddy's sister Bonnie in New Mexico because she's been busted for selling every kind of drug imaginable, and cavorting through every kind of sexual aberration possible, and we're supposed to believe she's a sweet, innocent young thing. I'll tell ya, this girl is about as innocent as Madonna.

And there's a lot of hooey about exalted visions of Spirits in the Other World and all that drug-crazed Carlos Castaneda crap. I've never seen a Spirit, have you? Or a Flying Saucer? No, I didn't think so. That stuff's for New Age crackpots.

But oh boy, is it profitable. So I guess we'll have to wing it through another goddamn allegory full of significance, because the publishers are hoping to make a few bucks on this, and the movie's gone into video and pay-TV distribution, with worldwide rights, and the author is sick of sleeping on the sidewalk.

In case you may be wondering who I am, I'm the Storyteller, and I don't like it one bit. Seals is manipulating the hell out of me, too, just like you, and turning Bonnie into some kind of Queen from Avalon and Philbert into King Arthur and Buddy into Sir Lancelot. Next thing you know he'll be comparing me to Merlin. So I hope you'll stop reading this shit right now so we can put this clown out of business once and for all. You're just encouraging him if you keep reading.

1

HOW THE KING AND QUEEN CAME TOGETHER INTO SACRED UNION.

PHILBERT AND BONNIE WERE MADLY IN LOVE. NO GREATER nuptial ceremony had ever been performed in the sacred halls of the Heavenly Palace than had been seen between these two. Nobody had ever been in love as much as they were. They loved each other so much that it made them sick to their stomachs, so powerful and intense were their destinies intertwined. It was as if acid was eating away at their bowels. Love ran through their guts like water flooding unto a mountain canyon after a spring rain, washing gravel and sagebrush off the slopes and down into the normally placid little creeks and gullies with all the rampaging force of a Flash Flood sent from the Great Goddess above, devastating all ordinary life in its path.

That is the kind of Power the Queen's most sacred gift—Love—has. It is supernatural.

Philbert was still pretty much the same big fat slob that he had been when he busted Bonnie out of the Santa Fe city jail yesterday, but he was more imbued with the essence

of the sacred fertility king than ever. He had slimmed down
to about 290 pounds. He didn't quite have the same goofy,
moronic expression on his fat brown face, but almost.
Maybe he was a little smarter than he had been a week ago
when he left the Lame Deer Reservation of the Northern
Cheyennes in Montana, and maybe he was a little more
confident, but not much. These miraculous transitions from
comic idiocy to heroic parable take time. And Philbert was
still in mourning for the death of his noble steed Protector.
Never had a Sacred Pony executed his duty so valiantly as
that rattletrap old Buick LeSabre, freeing his master of the
Indian dependency on the American machine, and also
tearing down the fucking walls of the tower where the Princess had been imprisoned. So what that the State Pigs had
an APB out for them in ten states? Philbert and Bonnie
and Buddy and Rabbit and Sky and Jane and Jennifer were
hiding on the Picuris Pueblo up in the mountains, watching
themselves on the local TV news.

"Terrorists who destroyed municipal property, shot up
La Posada Inn, injuring a number of law enforcement offi-
cials, stole an estimated one hundred thousand dollars from
the City and County treasury—"

"It was only twenty-two thousand," Philbert interrupted.

"Yep," little nine-year-old Jane confirmed confidently. "I
counted it."

"But in the movie they changed it to only four thousand,"
Sky remarked. He was only seven and was puzzled about
these discrepancies of the media (not to mention Time and
Space).

"Huh?" Philbert inquired dumbly. "What movie?"

"Powwow Highway," Sky replied.

The TV continued, paying them no attention at all. "—are
still at large. The FBI and numerous SWAT teams of
United States Marshals have been called into the state, and
there are reports that the terrorists have links to Iran or
Libya and—"

"Oh, bullshit!" Rabbit swore in her twangy Oklahoma
accent.

Buddy angrily turned off the TV. "They just make up
all these fucking lies, fucking Veho whitemen!"

While Buddy and Rabbit ranted and raved about the pigs

and turkeys and spiders and sheep that described for them the various mammalian and bestial qualities of the various kinds of American people, Philbert and Bonnie snuck off to bed.

Because, as I have said, they were very much in love, which means that they were also very much in need of their own kind of profane animal expressions and they were content to leave the politics and the plot to their friends. Philbert and Bonnie were content to let madness and irresponsibility sweep over their sacredness and profane the divine destiny waiting for them on the horizon: they tore off their clothes and crawled into the cold sheets and forgot about cops and manhunts and escapes for now. For now, they both had a lot of sex to catch up on, and sex, as most of us over the age of ten know, is a pretty good way to escape from the clutches of The Law. Oh, I know there are a lot of people under ten years of age who are hoping I don't go into too much detail about just exactly what these two naked animals were doing to each other under the covers, and what kind of filthy juicy things and other untamed and brutish acts they were performing upon each other, but you would also be surprised to learn that there are a great many people who are actually over the age of ten who would object to any graphic descriptions of the sucking and slurping that was going on. Ours is a very moral and religious age, in which pornographic filth is not appreciated. I personally would prefer to skip any talk of hot, pounding thighs and various types of erections, but, as I have said, the author of this earthy tale has no respect for propriety or people's feelings. He panders especially to the lowest common denominators of the reading public, and has been egged on by his editor and agent, a woman. Women, as is well known, are particularly fond of eroticism and other displays of naked wanton Power. Whereas a man asks only for gentleness and consideration, women in this new pagan age are demanding Orgasm Rights in the very halls of government. They seem to think that the very Deity argues for orgiastic ritual in the performance of Worship! Yes, I can see that culture and civilization are in the final throes of deterioration.

So there they are (in my bed, by the way, as everybody

is staying at my house, and I have to sleep on the couch), and it's a pretty strange sight, as you can well imagine. I have to imagine it, too, since I am not privy (as some peeping tom authors I might mention) to the scene. Although I wouldn't mind just a peek, as I am after all only human, since Bonnie is the real genuine classic Indian beauty and we can almost be sure that her butt looks real good naked. Boy, I almost envy that ol' Philbert, the son of a bitch. But he deserves it. Even though he's gotta look like a walrus in my creaky old double bed, Bonnie must surely be an antelope beside him . . . Well, all you ten-year-olds know what I mean. I don't want to go into any more lewdness. This is after all a love story, so I'll just say that anybody who has seen the way Bonnie looks at Philbert knows how she feels about him. There's no doubt about it. And there's really no doubt about why she loves him, if you could see his big, warm, brown elk eyes. He's a really warm human being, he really is. *Dumber'n* hell, but the nicest guy you ever will meet. I confess to a prejudice—I really do like him. If you're looking for an objective yarn in which Philbert's enemies (in the ivory bastions of Academia) are drawn with precise, polished prose, you can forget it. This is gonna be a love poem, dammit, and you can look for rational explanations in the sociology textbooks or somewhere. The know-it-all professors and preachers don't like me, and I don't like them.

But you and I can imagine what lovers say to each other in the privacy of their pillows.

"I love you," he might say.

"I love you too," she groans politely in the grip of a sweaty, impassioned delirium. (That's all women want. When a man seeks a meaningful relationship, they run the other way.)

He smiles, looking up at her with adoring eyes, as she thrashes away, blinded by desire. "You're so beautiful."

She replies, playfully clawing at his legs. "Unnnh . . . ahhhh."

Is my romanticism too bold? Am I a naive dreamer, fantasizing about the ecstatic realms where dwell the hearts and souls of lovers? Maybe.

"My love," he sighs.

"Ohhhh, Philbert: OH, AH!"

"Yes?"

"Oh . . . uh . . . what? Did you say something? Did I say your name?"

He allowed a fleeting, wistful smile to cross his enraptured face, as hers was red and covered with her long black hair (wet with sweat). "I remember when we were kids but . . . that was a long time ago."

"Yeah," she gasped, and opened her eyes momentarily. "I don't remember you too well."

"I remember you," he continued conversationally, thrilled beyond belief, sure that he had died and gone to heaven. "I can't believe I'm here with you now, like this, Bonnie Red Bird."

"Yep, that's me."

"Bonnie Red Bird. I can't believe it."

"Yeah, it is CRAZY aHhhhHH!!"

If it was left up to me, I would have a delicate kiss right here, to see if it's real, if they can believe it. Have you ever kissed like that, Gentle Reader? Just to see if she's real, if you're awake? As Indians, maybe Philbert and Bonnie wondered which was their dream world and which the real world. Have you as Irishmen and African women wondered about this too? Kiss your sweetheart, and close your eyes, and you will see Philbert and Bonnie.

She was crying and carrying on in a way that scared him. He was sure that he must be hurting her, but she quickly and inarticulately assured him that he was not, and then he felt a most inexplicable and unprecedented urge surging up through him.

"Gosh," he gulped, unsure of himself.

Tears came in her eyes as she wildly stiffened and screamed. He lost sight of all reality in that moment, too, but it didn't worry him anymore. He wanted to ask her what was the matter, but it seemed impossible, or at least irrelevant. He didn't care. She didn't care.

Blinding light flashed all around them, and Thunder Beings exploded. They couldn't tell each other anything; she pulled herself close to him and comforted him, into her cheek, his eyes wet with her hair, and he cried. She marveled as she trembled on top of him, protecting him, hold-

7

ing him together as if he would fall apart without her arms
and legs around him. She listened to him sniffle. He tried
to stop but he couldn't. Her ears felt his breath blowing
lightly into her, into her like his hot sperm, but the more
he tried to control himself the more his giant chest trembled. And the more she said, "It's okay, it's okay, My Darling," the more he clung to her. He couldn't breathe
anymore; it was all inside her now.

She remembered what a lonely and abandoned boy he
had been back home, always the butt of the jokes of the
other children because he was fat and stupid, an orphan
whose father no one knew, and whom nobody wanted. She
had always felt a little sorry for him, like most other people
had, but they had their own gut-wrenching problems on
the desperately poor reservation and they couldn't dwell on
poor Philbert's problems for long. They had to find their
own livelihood in a place where there was eighty percent
unemployment, where they didn't have even minimally adequate health care or education, where they had to see their
religion and cultures systematically destroyed by the prevailing society. Everyone had drunks in the family and dead
children in the graveyards, everyone felt helpless as they
watched strip-miners and lawyers destroy their beloved
Mother Earth and Her honor, everyone was almost as bad
off as Philbert. And Indians are human beings, too, just
about like everybody else, so they couldn't help but laugh
at him a little because he was at least a little bit lower than
everyone else, he was a little more foolish, a little more of
a loser. And Philbert himself even compounded the ridicule
of his tribe because he would smile at their insults like they
were jokes, he acted like he almost knew some Comic Tickle
was at work. He took the cruel mockeries with magnanim-
ity; his innocence counterbalanced the guilt everyone else
felt. If no one ever saw him sob (until now, beneath Bonnie), alone at night where he slept in abandoned and
wrecked cars, then that wasn't their fault. If no one knew
that he often didn't eat for days at a time or even weeks,
except for garbage from the hospital trash cans or handouts
at the Senior Center, then how could they appreciate the
fact that he was a Contrary who had grown fat from half-

stale beans and potatoes? Philbert was obese but he was undernourished.

When Bonnie asked him softly, "What's the matter, Darling?" he gave her a sharp, startled look and turned away. "Have I done something wrong?"

He looked back at her, even more startled and scared than before. "Oh, no, no. Not you, no. Don't ever think that."

"Then what? I didn't hurt you, did I?"

He was embarrassed, but he told her anyway. Slowly at first, but then as he saw sympathy in her eyes the story of his life poured out of him as involuntarily as the seed and the sorrow of his lonely race had poured into the ground where the great buffalo herds had once roamed. The more he told her of the death of his mother, the more she loved him, and washed him. The more he saw the love upon her, the more he wanted her, and the harder he got. They talked, and then made love, ferocious sexmaking, and they didn't come out of the bedroom for three days.

"Hey, you two," Buddy shouted through the locked door the first morning-after. "Jesus, you goin' for a record?"

"We're okay," Bonnie shouted. "Go away."

"Damn," they heard him mutter. "I thought I was the champion tipi-creeper. 'Til now."

Then the kids burst through the door and the lovers hastily covered themselves up. Sky and Jane didn't seem to notice the proximity of the two adults. "Merry Christmas!" Sky shouted.

"Christmas?" Bonnie muttered. "I forgot all about it."

You may recall that the first episode of this epic involved a four-day journey that culminated on the Winter Solstice, which is the night before the night before Christmas. As I said, this story is just full of all kinds of mythological significance like that. In the movie the screenwriters got that all screwed up, and therefore the story lost a lot of its power and flopped at the box office. But don't get me started on movie assholes.

"Santa Claus was here," Sky bubbled. "And left me a Nintendo with Mario Brothers and Kung fu and Wrestlemania, and I'm already up to the fourth level of—"

"Whoa, whoa, Partner," Philbert interrupted, laughing. "Santa Claus was here? I didn't know anything about it."

The kids piled on the bed, and Buddy and Rabbit came in the room, too, grinning.

Rabbit said, "Yep. I thought from the commotion we heard in here you saw the magic old gent, too, last night."

"Uh . . ."

"And I got the lavender jogging suit and fifty bucks," Jane explained proudly.

"Okay Troops," Buddy ordered, "let's march. These two have got their own presents to unwrap."

"What presents did you get, Uncle Philbert?" Sky asked.

Philbert looked at all of them, and especially Bonnie, curled up in his big arm. "I got all of you, my friends. This is the greatest gift any man could ask for."

"C'mon, Kids." Rabbit smiled.

They ran out and Rabbit whispered as she left, "We snuck into town and got the presents yesterday."

"Great. Thanks, Rabbit," Bonnie said. "I love you."

"Yeah, well . . ." She smiled, and closed the door quietly behind her.

Bonnie and Philbert smiled at each other, kissed lightly . . . and then went right back into it. This time Philbert even ventured to assert himself and Bonnie expressed her pleasure that he was coming along very well in his sexual instruction.

They snuck in the bathroom and took a shower together. It only had one or two pathetic little trickles dripping from the cockeyed old nozzle, but eventually it did the job, and the two people managed to get each other clean, in between some more shenanigans. It was getting a little embarrassing how often they went at each other, as if they had nothing better to do.

Back in the bedroom it started all over again, and Bonnie experimented with one or two new variations on an old theme that, for most people, has served very satisfactorily for countless eons.

The aroma of cooking meat wafted through the cracks in the walls—and there were numerous such ventilations in the quaint old adobe shack—so that Philbert started to suds over (in a more normal expression of human desires: I'm sorry, I couldn't resist making the vulgar comment), and said, "Christmas dinner."

He started to get up, but Bonnie stopped him. "No. No dinner."

"Huh?"

She explained. "You have to go on a diet, Philbert. I'm sorry."

"Well, yeah, I know that. I'm embarrassed. But this is, uh, don't you smell that? It's like a goose or deer they're cooking. It—"

She grabbed his you-know-what and added persuasively, not really understanding it either, "Something tells me we should make with a fast, as of the Old Days when dreamers and visionaries pursued sacrifices. For the people."

Well, that spoke to Philbert. You may recall he was particularly fond of the poetic expressions of the Old Ones, his traditional ancestors, who saw the world differently than you and me. They didn't know who the hell christ was, for instance, or his christ-mass. Why should he celebrate a savage feast? His great grandfathers wouldn't. They saw this time of year as the Extra Day of the Year, when the sun stood still, when the days and nights turned around and started to get long again (sort of like Philbert, under Bonnie's ministrations: I'm sorry, I did it again). Did Bonnie see this as an omen of Philbert's status as the fertility chief? Did she think, as her great grandmothers did, that it was planting time?

There was a knock on the door. Buddy said, "Come and get it, Boys and Girls. Roast buffalo, yams, squash, corn, homemade biscuits with sausage gravy, pure honey, choke-cherry jam, preserves—"

Philbert looked imploringly at Bonnie. She was firm. He looked at the closed door, closed to him now forever from all the ordinary happy pursuits and appetites of mortal men. "Uh, no thanks, Buddy. We're fasting."

"What?"

"Uh . . ."

"Oh, c'mon, you guys. Jesus, we have pumpkin pie and fresh peach ice cream with homemade chocolate fudge syrup and—"

Bonnie said, "Thanks anyway, Buddy." She didn't understand it at all. It was as if something supernatural was working through her. She smiled wanly at her compeer. "I'm

11

sorry, Honey. I just feel like something is working through me, and we have to do this. Didn't you say something about me sewing a medicine bag for you out of my prison dress?"

"Oh, yeah," he remembered, and jumped up. He reached in the pockets of his smelly old jeans laying crumpled on the plain wooden floor where Bonnie had torn them off and thrown them, fishing around to find something.

She sat up in bed and lit a Winston. "I . . . it's crazy. I don't know why I feel so strongly about this all of a sudden, but—"

"No. It's good to trust the Powers," he said. "I have to learn about making sacrifices, you're right."

"Is that it? I feel so good and strong right now."

"Here they are," he said. He showed her two small stones and the old cigarette lighter from his dead pony. "These two stones . . . I didn't notice before, but they're white."

"Like white crystal, maybe."

"Yeah, or . . . I don't know much about rocks. This one is from Nowah'wus, the Sacred Mountain Bear Butte in South Dakota. I got it on our trip down here to rescue you. And this one is from Fort Robinson, in Nebraska, where Crazy Horse of the Sioux was killed, and Dull Knife's Cheyennes were massacred in 1879. This came to me from the Powers there. And this is the token of my Sacred Pony, who gave his life that we may live."

She touched them and looked at them. "I feel dizzy. There is a strong . . . spiritual . . . ."

She blew tobacco smoke on the objects, and then leaned back on the pillows.

"What's the matter?"

"I don't know. I just had to lean back. Something went through me."

He felt something powerful surge through the room at that moment, like a fluctuation in electricity, and a whisper, like static in his ears. He thought he heard voices calling from far, far away. He put the two stones and the lighter on Bonnie's belly, just above the triangle of her womb, and they grew warm. She groaned, her eyes closed.

She began talking in a quiet voice that was almost not hers. "When I was a girl I had a vision. I dreamed I saw a woman with Yellow Hair, the color of corn, and she was walking toward me. I didn't know her. I was sick for a long time and my parents thought I was going to die. But I recovered. I heard that woman's voice often over the next few years, but when I asked people around me they looked at me like I was crazy. They didn't hear the voices. My stepmother wanted to put me in a mental hospital when I was sixteen. No, I was seventeen. So I ran away. I took a bus to New York City and hid out, and fell in love with a whiteman, but he was killed in a wreck. I got married and . . . well, it was pretty bad, except for my kids. I love them very much, Philbert. But it all got screwed up and I ended up in jail, and men were just bastards. Until you. And until now, I forgot about the Sacred Woman and the voices. I haven't thought about her for years. I thought I was crazy too."

"But now you know it was a vision?"

She opened her eyes and looked at him. "Well, what else could it be? What do they mean when they say you're mentally ill or something? That's bullshit."

"Yes."

"The Woman . . . I wish I could remember what she was saying. She was saying something to me. She's always been trying to tell me something, but I've been too stupid to listen or know. Oh." Tears ran down her cheeks, and she turned over and sobbed into the pillows. Philbert watched the three objects of his medicine slip beside her, and her naked womb covered them under her.

He laid beside her and hugged her. She sobbed uncontrollably for an hour in his arms, and all he could do was wonder why, and how, this great woman had come into his arms. Why me? Philbert thought. Why her? He always thought of Bonnie, when he was a boy, as the most beautiful girl in the tribe, and the most special. There was almost an air of tragedy around her, as if, for all her seemingly normal and girlish activities and laughter and games, she carried a burden around with her, a sadness. He saw her one time walking alone in the pine hills above Lame Deer, and he could have sworn there was a glowing light around her; faint and dim, as if she was only walking in front of the setting sun silhouetting her on the horizon, on the crest of that hill. He thought he was looking at Is'siwun, the

13

goddess who sent the buffalo Power to the Cheyenne through Sweet Medicine's twin, Erect Horns. The tipi of the Sacred Buffalo Hat of Is'siwun had once held divine authority over his people. But now, today, something was wrong. They had done something very, very wrong to be going through so much hell and suffering and destruction as a nation.

Impulsively, Bonnie sat up and looked under her. "Oh, I dropped your medicine objects."

"It's okay—"

"No, no. I have to sew you a medicine bag out of my dress." She jumped up and found her prison dress on the floor. "I need scissors and needle and thread . . ." Her face was streaked with tears and distraction, and Philbert was alarmed. For the first time he saw that Bonnie was in pain, and that she was not all that she appeared to be.

He got up. "I'll go ask—"

"Oh, here's a pair of scissors. And some leather. That's okay, Darling. I can do it with these."

"You don't—"

She suddenly smiled and hugged him ferociously, squeezing him tightly. "I want to do this. Oh, Philbert, thank you for being so sweet."

She rushed to her task and he sat on the bed, watching her. "I just thought the bag could be the fourth token of—"

"Oh, yes, yes, you're absolutely right."

"You know," he offered, "maybe we could ask a medicine man or somebody about your vision, and he could help you find out what the Yellow-haired Woman is saying to you. I bet we could do that."

"Oh yeah? That's a good idea. How do you want this bag? Fancy or small with some ribbons—"

"I don't know."

She worked for a long time, sitting naked on the floor. He covered her up with a blanket, as it was cold outside, and the shack wasn't too well insulated. It was cold outside, and gusts of sleet blew past the one tiny window looking out over the Pueblo compound. She laid the blue cloth on the floor, and he put the medicine objects on it, singing an old song his Uncle Fred Whistling Hog once taught him. It was simple, but seemed appropriate. Bonnie was very

14

particular that the pouch be made right, and once she put on a robe and went out into the other part of the house and came back with a leather sewing needle and brown thread. Philbert could hear that the house was full of people, laughing and watching a football game on TV, but he didn't feel right joining them. Something else very, very important was happening to him, and Bonnie, today. It was strange, and wonderful too.

He listened to a strong wind blow outside, and it scared him, and made him feel safe too.

When it was done, she handed it to him. "What a strange turn of events."

"Yeah."

"Wear this medicine as a Great Warrior, and make us proud of you."

He had a thought, and handed the pouch back to her. "Will you carry it for me?"

"Me? Why?"

"If it wasn't for you, I would never have gone on my journey with Buddy, and I would never have this power in the first place. It is your power, I think."

She looked at him, and held the pouch between her breasts. She pulled him into her, and this time they truly made love. It was not just sex this time. The Sacred Bundle lay in between them and made them feel like their Spirits had joined as their bodies joined, and it was intoxicating. There are special moments like these in all our lives, so we all know that they are true and possible, if only we would listen to the voices far, far away that whisper in our ears. If they imagined a dim aura wrapped its otherworldly light around them at that moment, and that the light came from the bundle, then who is to say it is not true? Who is to say that there are not sacred men and women on this earth, and that love is not as real as sex and happiness? I am too much of a fool to admit to such wisdoms. I dream of virtue and justice too often to deny their existence, no matter how naive that may sound to you. Forgive me, as I hope you may forgive Philbert and Bonnie, for being dreamers, and lovers, and believers in Magic.

"Hey!" Rabbit yelled later through the door. "You guys comin' up for air?"

15

"Go away."

"Mommy," Sky asked a little later, "when are you going to open your presents?"

"A little later, Honey."

The world did not exist outside. They knew that the children were being taken care of, that food and clothing and shelter were being taken care of, but none of that *Out There* was real. It was only a shadow of reality, a darkened dream. In here in bed, inside Bonnie and Philbert, another day and night went by, and this was reality.

"Fourteen times," Bonnie joked at one point.

"Huh?" He couldn't tell if it was day or night anymore.

"That's fourteen times we've done it."

He sat up weakly on his elbows. "You mean—"

"Yep."

"You've been counting?"

"I think we're going for a record, Philbert," She smiled seductively, a fresh twinkle in her eye.

"Oh," he groaned.

"Yep, a goddamn record. It's gotta be. I've never felt so strong. Hey, you asleep?"

He felt like a piece of raw bacon. He couldn't move his eyelids. Here she was acting like a spring chicken and he was already the rooster on the dinner table. "I'm cooked."

"Well, I'll see what I can do about that."

And she went right to work on him. She was a regular farmer at it, too, and before long the henhouse was squawking and feathers were flying like the fox had just come to town. Everyone in the rest of the house decided to go out for a walk, until the barnyard might quiet down a little.

"Help," he shouted almost inaudibly.

"Sixteen."

He was sure his brains had drained out his ears. In the rest of the Pueblo community hushed tones descended upon the people, as they sensed they were in the presence of a new and awesome spiritual greatness, of history, and that this mysterious gift sent from the Powers would be discussed and argued over for years to come.

"They were in there making sacrifices on their vision quest for a solid week. Grampa told me."

"No. It was only three days."

"Uh-uh. No food or even water for seven sacred days. Not since the time of the old Holy Ones have such sacrifices been made for the people."

"I heard they did it an even one hundred times."

"That's an exaggeration. Gramma says she knows for a fact that they only did it seventy-seven times."

"Is that right?"

"She knows it for a fact."

"And they say the Great Spirits descended upon and into them."

"That pore feller. It musta killed him."

"Yeah, I heard he died."

"And went to heaven!" One of the other men laughed.

Whatever the truth of these sacred myths may be, about sacrificial kings like Dionysus and Jesus and Arthur, there are indeed documented accounts of high priestesses like Athena and Mary and Viviane behaving like queen bees or queen spiders. They select the strongest and best male of the tribe, fuck his brains out, and then kill him. It's a very solemn form of religion.

"Nineteen."

"God," he sighed, sure that he had shriveled to the size of a raisin. "Mary Magdalene," he gasped.

There are, of course, many documented accounts of witches, too, and various assortments of vampires and sorceresses as well. A bonfire was built outside in the ceremonial plaza, and dozens of traditionalists gathered for a solemn vigil. If a few backsliders happened to pass around a few jugs of Thunderbird wine and a few joints of primo michoacan sensimilla flowertops, then you'll just have to realize that not even Indians are perfect. Most of the other grass-roots worshippers there did not permit the heretics to sit in among the inner circle, where they were circulating stories of the Old Days along with thermos jugs of coffee. Couples held hands, lingering with the thoughts of their own hopes and fears. Children threw the bones of poached deer at each other, and dogs watched the directions of the bones with intent interest. Some people were telling lies about vampires, and predicted that whoever was trapped in there with that screaming banshee would probably be found

17

later, and that there would only be a little pile of ashes left. One old woman swore she saw fire coming out of the bedroom and that she heard a ghoulish cackle of triumph from some nymphomaniac *powaqa* who was known to haunt these mountains at certain times of the year. As people ate some venison stew and frybread they admitted that such a witch had been known to terrorize poor helpless men, and the children stared with delicious horror at the bonfire.

"Yep," one Old Codger with long gray braids hanging down his chest said, "you get messing around with stray women and you might never be seen again."

"You should know," his Old Girl snorted beside him.

"They've been known to turn ya into animals."

"Like dogs and cats?" Sky and Jennifer asked at the same time.

"More like coyotes and jackrabbits."

"Girls too?" Jane gulped.

"Yep. Stray boys and men—well, you never know who they are or where they been."

Sky stared with wide eyes. "They might be monsters?"

"Yep, especially white people."

It went on and on, lies piling up on lies, until they seemed to burn like the firewood of the bonfire, blazing with their own light.

"I think they mighta just caught fire in there. They mighta just burned up. Maybe we should just go check 'em. I'm worried about 'em."

Old Girl poked Old Codger, and the other women giggled in their shawls. Somebody started up singing an old-time Indian chant, and a coyote joined in from somewhere far off. The dogs perked up their ears, and sparks flew up into the sky from the fire. It was a cold, dark night in the beginning of winter, and the adobe village was as quiet as the piñon forests all around it, except with the music of nature.

"Twenty-three."

The Sacred Chief lapsed off into euphorigenic dreams, and he saw his old dead, destroyed car shining on the horizon of the spirit world like a new model flying through that great big Showroom in the Sky. Protector gleamed like moonlight, a silver horse flying at a gallop through the clouds, a playful young pony, happy and healthy and clean once again. And on him rode a Great Chief who spoke without making a sound, and he said, "My Son." He rode the proud new stallion, and they were as bright and light and mystical as the music outside flowing through Philbert's ample mind.

2

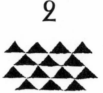

HOW THE KIDS
COME UP WITH A PLAN,
AND OF A FEW
VISITORS WHO STOP BY.

BONNIE LIMPED OUT OF THE BEDROOM ON THE FOURTH morning of her vision quest and actually found the bathroom open and the shower available. She stood under the two trickles of warm water and let the purification rite cleanse her of all the sacred ceremonies she had been performing. She felt strong and good. There's nothing like a little good, honest naked fertility ritual or two to make a woman feel like she's in touch with the holiness of her spirit. There was a fine purity to the sore flesh she washed with a little piece of old soap; it was like a sacrifice she made to the *màiyun* powers that govern the world, and if she was chafed raw and her skin stung then that was proof of the sanctity of her sacrifices. She found a couple drops of cheap shampoo at the bottom of an old bottle and scrubbed her beautiful hair until it shone with a brilliant ebony sheen. She dried off with one dirty towel she found on the floor, and she had to hold her legs apart a little because she was a little . . . well . . . maybe she had overdone the performance of her duties somewhat. It is not easy for a true priestess of the Goddess these days: many of them labor under the false mythology men have perpetrated that she is just a piece of meat to be cut on some Aztec altar to male gods. Oh no, that's completely backward. A true priestess like Bonnie knows that flesh and blood are offered in honor of higher ideals.

She went back into the inner sanctum of her temple and found some clean panties. Slowly slipping them up and over her raw ass, wincing a little as she touched her thighs (which were red and scratched from some unremembered episode of worship), she let out a deep breath and sat down for a second. Wow, she thought, I definitely overdid it. What had come over her? It was as mysterious to her as the origin of feminine orgasms and menstruations. Every time was different, and came from different places. One even began in her lunar plexus and washed down over her in waves of delirium like tidal waters. She looked at the man still asleep on the bed, tangled up in the covers, with his mouth open and a little drool soaking the sheet. What a Dear he was. What an Elk he was!

She slipped on a ribbon shirt hanging in the closet, with brown and green Picuris designs on it, over her sore breasts. Her nipples stung, even at the touch of the soft cloth. She brushed her hair for a long time. It was hopelessly tangled. She longed for some good conditioner and a mirror and some makeup, but none was available. Impossible tangles tore at her hairbrush (and her understanding), and she tried not to complicate the moment by thinking about things like love and purpose. Women are so stupid, she thought. We should just fuck and leave it at that. Fucking is complicated enough.

She walked out into the rest of the shack in her bare feet, brown with red paint scaling off her toenails, and proud of the blueness of her beautiful hair. She had always liked her hair. She stepped over half a dozen Indians sleeping on the floor, but she didn't know any of them. She didn't see her children or her brother. Finally she wandered back to the bedroom end of the place and found Buddy in bed with

Rabbit; or rather it was a crummy single mattress on the
floor with no sheets and one old blanket from some old
giveaway.

"Well, looky here," Bonnie said with a giggle.

Rabbit opened one eye and rolled over off the bed onto
the floor, butt naked. "Huh? What the . . ."

"Good morning."

Rabbit cleared her throat and wanted to spit. "I don't
believe it." The whitewoman stood up and grinned girlishly,
utterly unabashed about her nakedness (she had always
liked her nice big, round tits). "So you're still alive?"

"Yes. And I feel wonderful."

Rabbit eyed her. "I'll bet you do. I'm surprised you can
walk."

"Now whatever do you mean?"

Rabbit hurried into the bathroom and sat on the pot.
"C'mon, you can tell me, Sugar, how many times did you
do it?"

"Don't be crude. Twenty-seven, for him."

"Twenty-seven!" Rabbit exclaimed, wiping herself with
the last three-inch shred of toilet paper. She went back in
her bedroom and Buddy made some disgusting noise as he
rolled over. "I'm lucky if I get three or four out of this
peckerhead brother of yours. Hey, whadda ya mean, 'for
him'?"

"Oh, I wasn't counting, Sugar. Let's get some breakfast."

"Not on yer ass, not 'til I hear."

"Oh, I don't know. Hundreds anyway."

"*HUNDREDS!* You had *hundreds* of orgasms!? Oh, I'll kill
ya! I love ya, Bonnie rabbit, you're the rabbit, not me."

"Oh, what is an orgasm anyway?"

"Yeah," Rabbit snorted, and went back in the bathroom
and spit in the sink. She found some toothpaste and a couple
of brushes, and they brushed their teeth. "He's a regular bull,
huh, that Philbert?"

"You're so rude."

"Rude and crude." Rabbit grinned, going back in the bedroom. Bonnie followed her. Rabbit eyed her friend envi-
ously. Bonnie was so pretty and girlish this morning. Rabbit
had been worried about her when she was in jail, and after
the jailbreak—she had looked sallow and forlorn, but today,

boy, what a gorgeous chick. Rabbit suddenly hugged her, stark naked and all.

"Hey, what will people think?" Bonnie teased.

"Who cares? Say, now tell me the truth, you really like old two-ton Phil in there?"

"Yes, I think so."

"This sex orgy ain't just some kind of gratitude for him bustin' ya outa the hoosegow, is it?"

"No," Bonnie replied slowly, thoughtfully. "Maybe it was a little bit at first, and he is awfully fat, but then I got to know him better—"

"I guess you did."

"And he's so sweet. He's . . . I don't know. I never met anybody like him."

"No, probly not."

"And you and Buddy?" Bonnie grinned.

Rabbit smirked, pulling on her cleanest pair of dirty panties. "Yeah, how 'bout that? He's got a long way to go, I'm afraid. Let's get something to eat."

Philbert was awake by now and heard the last of their conversation. It made him smile. His nuts were sore and he was still weak as a kitten, but boy, what a miraculous occasion it had been. He had never really been with a girl before (let alone a woman), he was almost like a virgin in a screwed-up kind of way, and now to have caught up for all those horny years with these three sex-crazed days was just too mysterious and sacred for one man to handle. His stomach suddenly roared so loudly and so angrily that it seemed a little unnatural.

Buddy opened his eyes at the sound. "What the hell was that?"

Bonnie smiled. "I think Philbert's hungry."

"I think Philbert's inhuman," Rabbit snorted, pulling on some muddy blue jeans.

Buddy rolled over and looked at her bare breasts. "Now, hmmm, I think I remember those."

"Dream on, Peckerhead."

He laughed. "Ahhh, life is hard. Well, Sis, you through tipi-creeping for a few minutes?"

"A few. Where's the kids?"

"How the hell should I know?" He yawned.

Rabbit answered, looking for a shirt, "They're usually out playing or riding horses."

"With that weird Storyteller breed," Buddy added, staring at Rabbit. "He don't even have a name, just 'Storyteller' fer chrissake."

"Quit bitchin'," Rabbit said, pulling on a gray sweatshirt that said INTERNATIONAL INDIAN TREATY COUNCIL on it, flopping her breasts at Buddy playfully, then covering them up. "Let's go see if there's some leftovers from Christmas dinner, which you two rudely declined."

"Yeah!" Philbert exclaimed from the other room.

"The bull's awake," Rabbit said with a laugh.

Bonnie laughed and went in the other bedroom and kissed Philbert lightly on the cheek. Hanging over the bed was their Bundle. It was hanging from a string nailed to the ceiling. "Good morning."

"Mornin'."

"You want some eggs or something?"

"The fasting is over?"

"Well for now. I don't want you starving to death."

"Then I'd like about fourteen eggs and a loaf of toast."

"He's serious," Rabbit said in the doorway.

"He might get two or three eggs and one piece of toast," Bonnie decided. "I'm serious about your diet."

"Okay," Philbert agreed, embarrassed. "But first, how about a hug?"

"Oh, no you don't." Rabbit intervened, pulling Bonnie away. "We'll be here another three days."

"By the time you've showered and dressed," Bonnie shouted as Rabbit pulled her away down the hall, "we'll have some breakfast on."

"That's music to my ears."

Two other people squeezed into the bathroom just ahead of Philbert, so he rummaged around for his cleanest dirty socks and undertrou in the pile of clothes and junk thrown in a corner of the room on the floor. There wasn't anything resembling a chest of drawers. It was a pretty sorry excuse for a house, if you want to know the truth. But you can blame that on the Bureau of Indian Affairs, goddammit. They created this mess.

He peered out a very tiny window that was very dirty

and saw that a bright blue sky over a bright green and brown world promised another bright and beautiful day on Grandmother Earth. Philbert touched the Sacred Bundle hanging over the Sacred Bed and prayed, "Piva Maheo, thank the Mahuts and Maiyuneo for this great gift, and your good and powerful blessings. Take care of all the living things, and thank you for my new family and friends."

"There's some clean clothes for ya, Partner." Rabbit spoke suddenly in the doorway. "Oh, uh, so there you are," she grinned, looking at his nakedness. "Jesus, I never seen such big shorts, Phil. They're as big as a pup tent."

He looked at his clean clothes she put on the bed, and tried to cover up. "Gee, uh . . ."

"Don't be embarrassed. I seen plenty of men before."

He watched her walk out and stood there dumbly. He looked at his clean shorts, socks, jeans, and a black T-shirt with a Mimbres flute player on it in white. "Gee, thanks," he shouted, and quickly slipped on his shorts. Nobody had ever washed clean clothes for him before, not once in his whole life. It made him sniffle a little bit.

He slipped into the bathroom between two people coming out and three others trying to get in; he didn't know any of them.

In the other part of the house *Star Trek* was playing on a color TV (the colors were all screwed up so that Mr. Spock's skin was purple, but everybody watching thought it was some weird deathray from some aliens), and it held center attention in the living room.

The kitchen was piled up halfway to the ceiling with dirty dishes and huge buckets full of some kind of soup (or maybe it was dishwater), piles of potatoes, boxes of commodity-issued powdered milk, a Panasonic Electronic Typewriter RX-210, boxes of files and newspaper clippings, some half-finished pottery, and large elk bones drying on a rack. The tiny refrigerator was stuffed with huge boxes of dried fruit and assorted herbs, a pitcher full of something that looked like buttermilk, a couple of rotten tomatoes, some more elk and deer bones and the jaw of a coyote, a bucket of brown eggs, some leftover yams and corn on the cob, a side of venison, and an empty wine bottle months old.

Bonnie gagged. "It reeks."

"No, that's normal," Rabbit agreed. "I'll bet this kitchen ain't been cleaned in a year. I been too afraid to come in here alone."

Bonnie began clearing yesterday's plates out of the brown sink and turned on the hot water.

"YEEEOOOOWWWW" Philbert roared from the back of the house. "WHAT HAPPENED TO THE HOT WATER?!"

"Sorry," she apologized quietly, and turned off the faucet.

"Maybe if we can scour through to the stove, we can git to frying that venison the boys poached yesterday."

"Okay."

"And there's some eggs the kids scrounged up from some chickens somewhere."

"I don't see bread or a toaster."

"Here's some," a quiet Indian lady offered, coming in from the living room. "I baked it in the outside oven this morning."

"All right!" Rabbit exclaimed, accepting the two aromatic loaves from the short, round, brown little lady. "Thanks."

"You bet," the lady replied. "You can toast it in the oven and I'll go get some fresh butter I churned and some plum preserves."

"Great." Bonnie smiled. "My name's Bonnie."

"I know. I'm Violetta."

"Hi."

"I found the stove," Rabbit said, scrubbing away at grease splatters. There was also a plywood board where someone had been silversmithing turquoise rings. "Look at this beautiful turquoise."

"Yeah."

The gems gleamed like the sky inside the cluttered little room. Violetta left, with a short sideways glance at the women.

Bonnie asked Rabbit, "How'd she know my name? I never met her before."

"You kiddin'? You're famous. You're all over the TV and newspapers."

"I'm done with my shower," Philbert shouted from down

the hall, sticking his wet black head (soaked in long hair) out the door.

"Okay." Rabbit started to run the water in the sink, using some Tide soap.

"Gulp," Bonnie muttered, stopping her activity. "I managed to forget about all that for a while."

"Yeah, well, we're gonna have to do something, make a getaway or something pretty soon."

"Yeah. So . . . you washed Philbert's clothes?"

"Yeah. One of the ladies over across the compound has one of them ringer-type deals."

"Thanks."

"Sure."

A couple more Indian ladies rejoined them, along with Violetta, and they tore into that kitchen like beavers working over a mountain creek. It made Bonnie feel better to be busy, but she couldn't help notice a sinking feeling coming over her slowly but surely. They blazed on the dishes. They cooked up a feast. They scrubbed down the fridge. They kept Bonnie cheered up with one joke after another, but her spirit began to sag and sag with every passing minute of realization and awareness of her predicament. She was in a lot of trouble. She had broken out of jail! She knew from long experience that cops have practically no sense of humor about such things, and judges are even less lighthearted about such breaches of propriety.

The women got in each other's way making the coffee, setting the table, and rounding up the troops for breakfast.

"Come and get it!" Violetta bellowed, in a voice so great that it seemed impossible it came from a woman so small.

A rumble like stampeding buffalo rattled the walls as Philbert and Buddy pretended to be disputing precedence as they came down the hall, shoving each other playfully against the walls and making various animal sounds that sounded like hungry buffalo. Several elderly men exaggerated the situation and pretended to jump out of their way, in fear, remarking that they were very sorry to be around such impolite behavior.

"Gangway!" one of them declared.

Acting like slavering beasts, they fell into their chairs and knocked pictures off the walls. Children barely escaped with their lives from being crushed to death underneath the stampede. Hash brown potatoes were seen flying out the windows and buckets of coffee sloshed through the starving redskins, sounding just like toilets being flushed.

I came in just about then, with Sky and Jane and Jennifer, and stepped back a foot in horror and astonishment at the savage scene. "Am I in the right house?"

"Step right up," Bonnie shouted happily over the tumult. "There's only a few dozen eggs left. You better move fast before Philbert gets 'em."

Phil waved a deer bone in greeting, a full pound of food in his cavernous mouth. He felt bad that he had backslid a little on his diet though.

The kids ran bravely into the melee and snatched a plate of chow from a kindly elderly lady, battling away in the midst of it all, and Phil found time to rumple Sky's hair, pinch Jane's cheek, and give Jennifer a big buffalo hug. They brushed off the annoying displays of affection and stuffed jam in their mouths.

Three or four dogs made a bold attack through the door the kids had left open, and the riot entered new proportions as animals screamed, barked, and other animals leapt at the table. The humans repelled the four-leggeds, the four-leggeds regrouped for a counteroffensive, but a regiment of women with brooms drove them off amidst a clamor of yelps, whelps, and men spluttering out their food in wild hilarity at the chaotic drama. About seventeen people and five dogs were all moving and expressing themselves at once in a room about the size of an average tipi, so you can imagine it was a pretty disorganized scene for a few minutes.

Finally the dogs were driven back outside (with a few shreds of meat hanging from their dripping jowls that the merciful men had thrown to them, further irritating the women) and the uproar started to wind down. Daffy Duck cartoons on TV reinstated a more civilized calm, taking over where *Star Trek* had left off, and Philbert was working quietly on his seventh cup of coffee, enjoying the soothing effects of the animated cartoon. Sky came over and sat, on his lap, and Bonnie smiled at them as she filled the fourth bucket of coffee in an old blue-and-white speckled urn on the stove.

"I'll do the dishes," Philbert offered. "You sit down and digest."

Buddy gave him a startled look from where he sat on the floor, watching Daffy knock hell out of Elmer Fudd, and mopping up the last of his yellow egg yolks with a piece of bread.

"No, that's okay," Bonnie replied politely.

"Sky boy," Philbert instructed, "go tell your mama to do what I told her."

"Mom—" the boy said, not taking his eye off Elmer Fudd, with whom he sympathized.

"Okay, you talked me into it." She dried her hands on her pants and came over and sat on big Phil's lap too.

"Ooooo," he grunted.

"I'm not heavy, am I?"

"No, but I am," he groaned. "Get up. I gotta go to the can and finish breakfast."

"Gross," Rabbit grimaced.

He limped off down the hall, while I leaned on the fridge with a cup of coffee. "The kids came up with a plan for you all to make your getaway. Jane?"

The cartoon was over, and Jane cut away from the Barbie Doll commercials. "Yeah. We've been monitoring the news, and the pigs have roadblocks up everywhere for us. I mean, it looks like they got every cop in the world out there looking for us."

"Really?" Bonnie questioned.

"Thicker'n flies on shit," Buddy explained.

"Especially you, Mama," Jane continued. "They flashed Uncle Buddy's picture, too, and Rabbit's. We're surrounded. So what some of the kids were saying yesterday is that we could circle around Taos on horses and maybe make it to Colorado before—"

"Horses?" Buddy asked. "That's crazy, it's winter out there. Me and another boy been fixing up that red-and-white van out there and—"

"You won't get half a mile," an Elder said.

Buddy took umbrage at that. "And you'll freeze in half an hour on a horse. We're in the mountains here."

"I know, Uncle," Jane retorted.

A gigantic fart echoed up from out of the bathroom like a cannon going off.

"Hey, Phil!" Buddy called laughing. "You all right?"

As the Storyteller, I insisted my way back into the fun; it's always better participating in an adventure than sitting back and telling about it. "I think a cross-country escape is your only hope. Sure it's cold, but I can go with you and show you the way, and Violetta here and Old Codger and Old Girl and some of the other elderlies know every rock and bush. There's a few cow cabins and sheepherder trailers where we can hole up and get warm, too, on the way."

"It'll be fun," Sky added.

"No it won't," Buddy disagreed. "That's too hard for kids. And where do we get horses?"

"I got 'em," old Codger argued. He was the same liar with long braids who had been telling ghost stories around the campfire. He was sitting on the floor.

"What?"

"Three mares and a colt."

"How old are they?"

"Younger'n me," Old Codger snarled.

"Oh, c'mon, Bud," Rabbit said. "It sounds okay."

Philbert came out of the can and rejoined them, looking considerably more at ease.

"Whadda ya think, Chief?" Jane asked him. "You been listening?"

"I ain't no chief," he replied. "I don't even know who my daddy was."

"So?"

"Well, so." Phil shrugged. "Buddy's right. It's too cold and dangerous for kids."

"Yeah." Buddy nodded.

"Maybe I should just give myself up," Bonnie said quietly. That made everyone stop for a minute, and watch a *Superman* movie come on TV.

"No," Philbert said, even more quietly.

No one knew what to say for a minute or so.

"How about this," Rabbit suggested, and everyone was glad to hear someone say something, anything. "The pigs maybe don't know Phil and the kids. Well, they probably know Sky and Jane from the juvenile hall, but . . . well . . . They could take the van while me and Bonnie and Bud'll light out across the woods and rendezvous with ya somewhere. Us three have been the only ones really identified on TV, is that right, Jane?"

"Yes," Jennifer answered.

"She asked me," Jane scolded the other girl.

"So?"

"So yourself."

Sky said, "I haven't seen me on TV."

"So yeah," Jane answered Rabbit's question.

"You're too bossy," Jennifer said to Jane.

"Where do we get food?" Bud asked.

"I don't know if I want us to split up," Phil said.

"Mom, Jane is always trying to be the boss of me."

"You kids quit fighting."

"But—"

"Shut up."

"I haven't been on a horse in years," Bonnie complained. "Not since I was a girl. I don't know if I can ride."

"And we don't have warm clothes."

"I'll get ya some," the other Elder said. His name was Grampa Jimmy. "God, you're bellyaching like some white people, ya softies."

"Oh yeah?" Buddy bristled.

"Yeah," Grampa retorted. "In the Old Days you wouldn't a lasted a hour."

"They didn't have helicopters and infrared spotlights in the good ol' days."

"I don't think we have any choice," Rabbit allowed. "Surrender is completely stupid. I ain't against goin' horseback."

"The Elders can show us the way," I repeated, helping the story along, looking at Philbert. "We won't get lost. You can load up on food and supplies in Taos and take Grampa here to hook up with us again at the old Arroyo Seco north of town. You know where that is, don't ya?"

"Of course I do," Grampa snapped. "We should all go," he added, looking at Violetta and Old Codger and Old Girl. They all nodded agreement. "An Elder's Council kind of deal."

"So there ya are."

"The only other problem is," Jane said, pulling out a wad

of money in her pocket, "we're down to two thousand one hundred dollars, and if you gotta save two grand to give back to the tribe for the bulls you stole from—"

"I didn't steal 'em," Buddy interrupted irritably. "I just haven't paid for them yet. And where does a kid get off—"

"—and so as you said, Chief, that cuts us pretty close to the bone," Jane finished.

"—handling all that money?"

Philbert disagreed. "I said I ain't a—"

"And the hell with the Tribal Council anyway," Buddy concluded.

"Well now I don't know," Rabbit wondered.

"You may need a cinch for one of the saddles," Grampa suggested, "and the stock'll need some oats."

"Oh yeah, right," Buddy snorted. "I'll bet them mares're older'n you are."

"Well, if you don't want my help, ya disrespectful young—"

"No, no, now come on, you two."

"Well if he—"

"But how're we gonna—"

"I don't see where—"

Bonnie felt a pre-menstrual cramp squeeze the shit out of her suddenly. Oh great, she thought, this is just what I need. And she wondered about her IUD, too, which should have been replaced six months ago. If it wasn't one thing, it was another.

"We'll need more'n a hundred dollars to get all the way to Montana."

"I said to hell with the Tribal Council, didn't I?"

"Maybe we should go roundabout to Utah."

"Or Kansas? That's ridiculous."

"Who's ridiculous?"

"I didn't say—"

"We can't go all the way on horseback."

"Why not?"

"It's stupid, that's why not, Grampa. Whadda ya think this is, some kind of movie?"

"Why not?"

"Why not what?"

"Who's saying—"

Then two young Picuris men burst into the room and addressed Buddy. "BIA cops are coming in, Bud."

Buddy immediately jumped to action. "How many and where?"

They ran out the door, followed by two other men who had joined them for breakfast. Violetta and Grampa Jimmy hurried toward the door, too, hastily talking. "Let's get the Elders assembled around here, too, to join the warriors—"

"Hey," Philbert asked, "what's going on?"

Violetta stopped and looked at him and Bonnie. "The warriors will set up a perimeter around us, and we've had scouts out ever since Storyteller brought you in here. Now the Elders will set up another circle around you, inside the warriors."

"Huh?"

She spoke to Bonnie. "Arantzazu and the other *cacique* chief-women want to talk to you about your Sacred Bundle. When we get back."

"You stay here," Grampa instructed Philbert.

They hurried out the door, as did most of the other people who had been in the house all morning, leaving only Philbert, Sky, Jane, Jennifer, Bonnie, Rabbit, and me in the house, which was suddenly very quiet. We stood in the living room and looked out the big picture window. The Plaza outside seemed empty, and gray storm clouds were blowing in.

I explained. "Buddy's been working with El Cuartalejo and the other old AIM warriors he's known since you got here. Shall we get on the dishes?"

"Dishes?" Philbert asked, totally befuddled. "I should go join the warriors, shouldn't I?"

I smiled and put my hand on Philbert's shoulder. "No, not you. We are the clowns and we have to stay put."

Bonnie sat at the kitchen table and stirred some sugar into her cup of coffee, watching the men and Sky attack the dishes. She lit her fourth Winston of the morning. She stirred the coffee absentmindedly but didn't take a drink. Rabbit sat in the living room and watched. The girls watched *Superman* on TV. They could hear nothing outside except the rising wind.

Then they saw two BIA police cars pull into the police

station across the graveled plaza, with PICURIS TRIBAL PO-
LICE written on the big supercharged Dodges, and some
elaborate shield decorating the sides of the cars. Two big
Indian policemen got out of each car and looked around,
then went inside the adobe building. Dirt and trash blew
across the concrete sidewalk in front of the building, and
swirled up around the American flag on a big pole, waving
against the gray sky along with the yellow New Mexico flag
and a Tribal flag.

Superman flew off to his Fortress of Solitude in the
North Pole and consulted his elders from other worlds.

Only a few minutes went by when the cops came back
outside, stood looking around for a minute beside their cars,
and then got back in and drove off to the south, where the
only paved road into the Pueblo went back out into the American wasteland beyond. The Pueblo was in a deep, wide river
valley surrounded by big, beautiful mountains and forests, far
away from the modern world, on the borders.

As Philbert washed the plates and Sky dried, the Elders
walked in the front door. No one in the house saw where
they came from. I put away the dishes and went to say
hello to them, and introduce them to Bonnie, to whom they
directed all their attention. Philbert and Sky kept working
in the kitchen.

Grampa Jimmy and Violetta came in first, then Old Codger and Old Girl, followed by a very small and very skinny
and very, very old, old woman. She spoke in a strange language and Grampa translated for them, speaking primarily
to Bonnie. "Arantzazu says she is very glad to meet you."

Bonnie stood and shook the woman's hand. "I'm glad to
meet you."

More oldtimers streamed through the door. They were
introduced as Rosila Petago, Perfealio Zepato, Beditchcheeglechee, Tonita Veneno, Candanaria Elote, and several
other incomprehensible names. They spoke the Picuris and
Apache languages, which is Southern Athabascan for you
linguists out there, and Bonnie looked slightly dazed to be
the center of attention of these men and women. Rabbit
helped me get them all some coffee, and Grampa turned
off the TV.

When they were all settled in chairs and on the lumpy

old couch, with coffee and sugar and milk, Grampa said, "Arantzazu is the *sawish cacique* of Picuris. Some who do not know us say she practices *hechiceria,* sorcery, and has the *mal ojo,* evil eye."

"But that is Christian bullshit," Arantzazu said suddenly in perfect English.

The elderlies all broke out into wild laughter and drank their coffee, thoroughly enjoying themselves.

Philbert peeked around the corner, and several of them pointed at him and said something to each other in Picuris, pointed at him, and laughed. One old man with two teeth asked Grampa something, and he spoke to Bonnie. "Jusepe Zaldivar says the Spirits have told us you are a Sacred Woman."

Bonnie's eyes grew wide as the Elders all grew silent and solemn very suddenly, and stared at her. "Me?"

"Jusepe is our *curanderia* from the *cienaga—*"

"Your what?"

"Uh, healer, wise man. He is the son of the Querecho Chief Hiamovi, but we let him live around here anyway."

The Elders all laughed again. Jusepe said in English, "This Vaquero wishes he could be half the Cocoyes of the Querecho Teyas!"

Grampa smiled, and then addressed Bonnie again. "You should do a ceremony before you carry your Bundle. Arantzazu wants you to go with her to the *kiva* right now."

"I have a *ma-caiyoyo* for you," Arantzazu said to Bonnie.

"A what?"

"Crystal from Monster Slayer."

"Oh."

I squatted next to Bonnie and said, "When I brought you here I didn't know exactly what I was doing. All I knew was that I was telling the story of your rescue without being fully in the picture. Now you have come here, to the Picuris Nation, because it was and is the most hostile of all the border Pueblos to christian civilization. Taos, Picuris, Pecos, Acoma, and Jemez were always the strongest holdouts against—"

Jusepe interrupted. "We never christianized like San Juan Pueblo and San Ildefonso and those others on the Rio Grande."

"We were often at war against those farmers," Grampa added, "even before the damn Spaniards and Anglos came."

"We are Querechos and Teyas, Mountain Apaches and Cocoyes!" Arantzazu declared proudly. The others all nodded and made words of agreement in their most ancient and most authentic tongue.

"Then Popeé came," I continued, "and—"

"Who?" Philbert dared ask, fascinated by it all.

"Popeé," Jusepe repeated. "A great *ololiuhqui arbulario*."

"Don't ask." I grinned. "We'll be here all week if I have to explain just the basics of this culture. But Popeé was like a medicine man and a chief from San Juan Pueblo three hundred years ago. The Catholics almost whipped him to death on a whipping post one time, accusing him of being a witch in league with the Devil and all their sick lying . . . Well, don't get me started on the Catholic assholes and the millions of people they murdered. Popeé realized these were evil spirits from across the salt sea and they would have to be destroyed before they destroyed everyone and everything else first. In 1680 he led the so-called Pueblo Revolt here and drove the Conquistadores completely out of New Mexico. It was a stunning victory for the Indians, even greater than Sitting Bull's and Crazy Horse's on the Little Big Horn."

"Yes!" Grampa whooped proudly.

"And no one ever hears about him," I added.

"Popeé kept the whole Revolt a complete secret," Grampa explained. "The Spanish were caught completely with their pants down. The whole area up and down the Rio Grande struck at once on the same morning, and no one—"

"It—"

"He did it," Jusepe explained, "because he traveled from one village to another, hundreds of miles apart, on a whirlwind."

Silence went through the room as the Picuris and Apache Elders looked at the Cheyennes.

Philbert asked, almost whispering, "On a whirlwind?"

"*Sí.* Hundreds of Spanish soldiers were killed before they could lift one gun or sword."

"We kicked the shit out of them!" Grampa added.

Arantzazu said something in Picuris, and everyone looked at Philbert with new interest. I told him, "She says your Indian name means Whirlwind."

Philbert's eyes grew wide with wonder, confirming the observation without saying a word.

Buddy and El Cuartalejo came in the room. "The cops are gone. It was great! They couldn't figure out what the hell was going on. They were sure we were here, but then something distracted them it seemed like, and they just drove off. It was crazy. I never saw cops act like that."

"That's good news, Buddy," I said. "Come in and sit down. We were talking about Popeé."

"Oh, all right! He's always been one of my heroes."

"But after twelve years of peace and intelligence the Spanish marched back in," Old Girl complained. "Just came right back with their army and screwed everything up again."

"Yeah," El Cuartalejo sneered. He was a big, strong, dark man, with a huge barrel chest. "De Vargas, the big hero of the Hispanos."

"Puta pendejo!" Violetta cursed.

Philbert cleared his throat, and they all looked at him. "What? I didn't say anything."

"You wanted to." Arantzazu smiled. "Go ahead."

"I . . . uh . . . well I was just wondering about what you said before about what the Spirits said about—"

"About the Sacred Woman?" Jusepe completed his sentence.

"Uh . . . yeah . . . uh . . ."

Arantzazu stood up, and so did Violetta and Rosila and Beditchcheeglechee and Tonita—all the women. The men remained seated. "We must go make the ceremony. You are coming into your moon, Bonnie, and the bad *brujerias* will kill you if we don't do this now."

"Can I go too?" Rabbit asked.

Violetta smiled. "Sure."

Arantzazu led Bonnie out the door, as Rabbit asked Violetta, "What's the *brujer—*"

"Witches."

Bonnie cast a quick frightened glance back at the men at that word, but then she was out the front door and gone.

Philbert looked nervously after her. Grampa laughed. "Don't worry, Fat Boy, they're not bad witches, not like the goddamn christians mean."

"Yeah," El Cuartalejo grinned, pouring himself some coffee.

The men shifted in their chairs. They all seemed totally relaxed. Sky and Jane and Jennifer looked bored. Philbert leaned against the wall and felt dizzy.

Buddy looked puzzled. "What did they mean? Bonnie is a Sacred Woman?"

3

HOW THE PEOPLE
WENT TO TOWN
AND SAW SOME MAGIC
PICTOGRAPHS.

I WON'T GO INTO THE SACRED CEREMONIES OF THE INDIANS too much because we really don't trust the sneaks out there who might try to use this information against us. I know most of you readers are pretty good folks and wouldn't harm a fly, but there are a few really sneaky chiselers out there who would love to get hold of some of our special spiritual power and make a few bucks on it, so I just ain't gonna reveal the secrets. Sorry. When you get your house cleaned up we'll take you into the real *kivas* and make the hair stand on your back; but until then I'm afraid you're just gonna have to settle for a glimpse or two around the edges of all the wonders of Nature Indians remember. I know this will give my enemies in the schools a field day, and they'll say, "Ah, this guy is a phony." True enough, and fair enough.

Suffice it to say that Bonnie got the bejesus zapped out of her by Arantzazu and the Girls in the Women's *kiva*, and came out of there with her hair a little frizzled around the

split ends. I mean to tell ya, she looked like she had just
been electrocuted. You wanna talk about shock therapy,
well, you ain't seen nothing until you've seen what true
sorcerors can do. They'll put the Whammy on you. And
Rabbit? All she could do was stare straight ahead of her
like she'd seen a ghost (which she had: but that's all I'll tell
ya).

The women wandered back over to the house they were
letting me stay in, poured themselves some coffee, and sat
back down as if nothing had happened. Bonnie drifted in
as if she'd just returned from being held prisoner by Martians and went silently to the bedroom. She came back with
the Bundle, or at least she had something wrapped in an
animal skin of some sort, and Rabbit and Violetta helped
her with some other things: they had some plants and
leaves they laid on the skin in the middle of the living room
floor, some owl feathers, and a kind of rattle. The Indians
watched them silently. Buddy was obviously dying to ask
a thousand questions, but he knew better. Philbert was in
awe.

When the preparations were done, and the Bundle was
wrapped in a large coyote skin and resting on Bonnie's
lap—as she puffed on another cigarette—Jane couldn't hold
herself back any longer. She asked, "What's that, Mommy?"

"I'll explain later, Jane."

"Why didn't you let me go with you to the . . . thing, or
whatever it is?"

"I'm sorry, Honey. You should have asked."

The girls stood up and looked at the Bundle on Bonnie's
lap, and touched it. Jennifer stepped back, as if her hand
had been burned. "It's hot."

"Yes." Bonnie replied strangely. "Philbert, could you
come here a minute?"

"Yeah." He loped right over and knelt on one knee beside her.

"We have to leave right away," she said. It was almost
like an order.

"Okay. Where?"

Grampa Jimmy said, as if he knew everything that was
going on, "We'll show you when we get there."

El Cuartalejo turned to Buddy. "I'll take Philbert and the kids into Taos in the van, and you guys go horseback."

"Rendezvous at Arroyo Seco," Jusepe added.

"What about the warriors?" Buddy asked, unsure who was in charge or what the hell was going on.

Grampa snapped irritably, "Warriors are out on the flanks with the scouts, Elders' Circle inside them, and the Sacred Bundle in the center."

"What about the money?" Jane asked.

"We'll need it," Violetta said.

Jane sighed. "The Chief got the money, he busted Mama out of jail, it was his car—"

"Who?" Jusepe asked.

Sky pointed to Philbert.

"The Chief should decide about the money," Jane decided, giving Violetta a dirty look.

"Yeah!" Sky and Jennifer agreed together, seconding the nomination.

"The kids are right," I added. "Somebody's gotta be in charge. Bonnie can't carry that responsibility too."

"I would like Philbert to be the Chief too," Bonnie said quietly.

"Chief?" Buddy frowned.

Grampa stood up in front of Buddy. "Yeah, you ever heard of it?"

"Now look, Grampa, I don't want to go up against you—"

"Listen to me, you young—"

"Grampa!" Violetta and Arantzazu both commanded.

He looked around at them. "All right, all right. But I just wanna say that the men have some say in all this too. I wanna say that if we had a Chief, just one Chief we'd elect, we could get rid of that damn Tribal Council and throw the bureaucrats over the cliff! That's all I wanna say. A Chief in the traditional way wouldn't hoard his wealth like that, that's all. People are hungry here, dirt poor, a *real* Chief wouldn't stash away a wad like that for himself. He wouldn't. That's all I gotta say. If you wanna throw me out with the dishwater, then go ahead, ya modern soft young pups! Flush me down the toilet, I don't care!"

"No one's saying we want to flush you down—"

41

"I prefer an old outhouse hole anyway! Then you're out in the air, free and easy, a part of nature. A part of nature. These new indoor holes, you can't feel the wind and air blowing on ya. The hell with ya!"

"You're right," Violetta said quietly.

"Philbert?" Bonnie asked imploringly.

He was alarmed to see the care and responsibility in her face. She was worried. "I'm not a Chief, Bonnie."

"You don't have to be. Just . . ."

"I agree," Jusepe said.

Buddy looked at him. "Agree with what?"

Arantzazu spoke in Picuris for a long time. When she was done, Violetta summarized. "Whirlwind got the money, Arantzazu said, calling you by your secret name. For now you should decide about it. And Red Bird wants you too."

"That's good enough for me," Jusepe said. The other Elders all spoke their assent.

Philbert saw they wanted him to say something. He had never been so embarrassed. "If the Elders want it, then . . . I was always taught by my Uncle Fred to do what the Elders want."

"That's right, we're the government," Grampa reiterated.

Buddy snorted. "All right, Philbert, what do we do?"

Philbert looked at him. "What you said before."

"What?"

Rabbit spoke. "Bonnie and me and you go on horseback around Taos and meet the others in the van."

Grampa said, "Yeah. We'll ride too and get some more horses and cut down all the fences on the way too! And I think we should round up the bootleggers first and throw them off the cliff as well!"

"Okay okay, Dad," Violetta counseled, trying to calm him down. "One thing at a time."

"We'll set up the warriors around you, Buddy," El Cuartalejo said. "All around out there in the hills."

"Warriors," Grampa snorted. "We'll see how tough you are."

"Can I ride a horse too?" Sky asked.

"No, Honey," Bonnie decided. "It's too cold. You go in the van with Philbert."

Jusepe said, "I'll go with you. We can get the other horses ready and—"

"Hanh!" Grampa laughed and smacked his hands together. "This is gonna be fun!"

"And then we'll have a wedding tonight," Philbert said suddenly, still kneeling beside Bonnie. "Me 'n' Bonnie in the traditional way."

Everyone froze.

"Huh?" Bonnie gasped.

He tried to smile at her, but mostly he looked like he was going to be sick. "Okay?"

She stared at him. "I . . ." she tried to say, but only moronic noises came out of her. It was all just too much to handle.

"Without you," he croaked, amazed at the words coming involuntarily out of him, "I can't decide anything, or do anything. I'm not a leader or anything. I wasn't even a human being without you. I love you so much."

Everyone sniffled, even Buddy. Rabbit wiped a tear off her nose. Sky hugged Philbert's leg.

A kind of light music floated up and over the lost and forgotten little village in the New Mexico mountains, the Sangre de Cristo as the Hispanos called them, and high up in the clouds, higher even than the living air of the world the music tingled through the enchanted Spirit World and it played on the celestial R3 Road-rated receiver and CB radio of a gleaming new Buick listening to the song coming from a warrior's heart. "He *is* a Chief," the mystical pony heard the Powers declare, "and she is sacred too." Philbert felt the odd music tingling through him, and he shuddered.

He hugged Bonnie, and he saw a Vision flash for an instant across his mind (did it come from the Bundle on her lap? Or did it go into the Bundle at that moment?), and the Vision was like a protective guardian angel who would never let him or his people come to any harm. Bonnie felt the tingle, too, but she thought it was only a strong emotion, or a shiver.

Arantzazu stood up and touched Philbert and Bonnie, one gnarled old hand on top of each of their heads. "It is not time for such a decision as this, My Children. We will have the cleansings of six moons before the solstice."

Philbert looked at Bonnie. "But . . . do you want to? Will you marry me?"

"Oh yes," she whispered. "I think so."

"Oh boy," he breathed again.

Arantzazu smiled. "It is meant to be."

She went to the doorway, and the Elders all stood. It was time to go.

The stormclouds had all blown by of course, now that the ceremonies had been performed. It was a perfect afternoon for an escape. Everyone avoided the central plaza of the poor adobe pueblo village, where the watchful eyes of the Tribal Government could watch everybody and everything happening, and the U.S. Government could watch them. What with the corrupt politicians in Washington and the corrupt politicians in every Tribal Council on every Indian reservation in the country, almost every single man, woman, and child effectively got screwed. So, like most Americans, these ragtag folks snuck around to the back door and made their plans to live, and escape, hoping to avoid discovery by their Enemy—the Government. They paid their taxes, and they hated it, and they knew it was wrong, but they also knew they'd get the shit kicked out of them if they didn't pay, and pretend to go along with the patriotic program, and be nice about it besides. Yep, ol' Popeé saw it all coming.

Everyone gathered on a side road of gravel, away from the relentless surveillance and scrutiny of the central plaza, and said their goodbyes.

Philbert instructed Jane to go around and give each of the Elders and Warriors there fifty dollars, for all their help. The money was quickly accepted and eagerly appreciated. About half the village turned out just about then, curious to see if the rumors of Great Achievements were true, and when Jane laid a cool fifty on each one of the heads of the families—after Grampa Jimmy screened each one of them, tossing out a couple of winos who had weaseled themselves in between all the respectable citizens—they quickly became devoted believers and loyal followers of the new Chief.

Adamantly denying his great new station and exalted status, Philbert declined to make a speech or foist himself off as anything more than he was. I would have liked to make a big, elaborate pageant out of this dramatic event, but practical considerations made stealth and a quick getaway higher on the list of priorities. Dozens of horses were reined up and led off into the steppes, and a dozen old vans and cars sputtered to life.

Bonnie was helped up onto a sleek black stallion someone had loaned her, and she carried the Bundle on her back, tied with wide rawhide ropes across her shoulders.

Philbert stared at her forlornly. "I don't know if we should be splitting up like this," he said, holding her hand.

"We have to," she whispered sadly, feeling weaker and weaker with every passing moment. "The cops know Buddy and Rabbit and me."

"Yeah, but . . ."

"The Elders and Warriors are fanning out all around us for miles," I interjected, getting on a strong roan mare. "The people are all helping, Philbert. And I'll stay with Bonnie every second too."

"Good."

"There's a sheepherder trailer five miles up that way." Grampa rode up on a randy buckskin gelding. "You know where it is, Storyteller?"

"We'll meet you there for a rest and a warmup."

"Okay."

"See you later tonight, Whirlwind!" he yelled, and rode off at a trot after the other Elders, who were already riding into the trees.

Philbert waved at them. To Bonnie he asked, "Got your thermos of coffee and sandwiches?"

"Yes, Honey."

"I love you."

"I love you too."

"Oh, come on." Rabbit smirked impatiently. "This is getting repulsive."

Buddy shook Philbert's hand from his saddle, smiling at his friend. "See ya in a few hours, Philbert."

"Buddy Red Bird."

The four people and five horses—one of the mares had her colt following along—pulled slowly away. They were the center of the war party, and maybe even a New Nation, Philbert thought as he watched them. Sky and Jane and

Jennifer stood beside him and hugged him, and watched too. The Chief watched sadly as they went down a dry slope of sagebrush and dormant yellow grass, across a rocky little draw down below the pueblo, and then disappeared up into a juniper grove off to the north-northwest. The pale yellow sun heated up the high-altitude plateau to a comfortable forty-five degrees, and there was no wind. Only a few patches of snow on the shady northern slopes of the hills betrayed that this was in the first days of winter and the last days of December. A few crows circled out to the west, and a chipmunk ran along a telephone wire over on the south side of the village next to New Mexico State Road 76. Sky touched Philbert's hand. "I wanna go with them."

"Me too."

But they went and got in the back of the van, squeezing in next to Jusepe Zaldivar and Violetta and about fourteen other Indians crammed into the old heap. The other five or six cars were idling and waiting to follow the van in convoy. That way, they figured the cops at the roadblocks wouldn't be able to pick out Phil and Sky and Jane and Jennifer in the jumble of red faces. Maybe. Everybody was a little nervous about it, though, as these Cheyenne visitors (and the one white girl, Jennifer) had really shot up Santa Fe and destroyed about half the town, if you were to believe the television news. The cops were really pissed about it.

Philbert spoke to Violetta. "I'm confused."

"Welcome to the club."

"How far was our wreck from here?"

"Just a mile or so," she replied, pointing over the hill to the south. "We heard the explosion, what was it, three nights ago? And then all the lights went out."

Jusepe giggled. "You Cheyennes knocked out the power for a hundred miles around here. It was great."

Philbert tried to smile. "Yeah. All I remember was walking up the road with Bonnie and the others. But then what?"

Violetta gave him a mysterious look. "Storyteller was waiting for you, and brought you in here."

"Who is he?"

El Cuartalejo jumped in the driver's seat. "You guys ready?"

46

"Ten minutes ago," Jusepe complained, shivering.

The big square-faced Picuris man grinned and slammed the door. He turned the key and nothing happened. The engine didn't make a sound. He tried it again. Nothing. He kept trying but nothing kept happening. He kicked the floor. He banged the steering wheel. He cursed up a storm (Vietnam Vets had a bad habit like that, of cussing, which they all learn in the U.S. military services, which are hot-beds of richly expressive vernacular).

Half a dozen people piled out and opened up the little hood in the front of the van. They looked at the engine.

"You got gas?"

"Yeah."

A couple more guys came over from the other cars. They poked around at things in the engine, and gave it a deep, profound scrutiny.

"Is your battery okay?"

"Yes, goddammit!"

"Might be your distributor cap."

"Maybe the spark plug wires."

"Could be some frost got in the gas line."

"Or the fuel filter."

"I might have half a can of STP over in my trunk. Let's try that."

"Let's all just get in the other cars for now."

"No. Hell, I gotta get this fixed in town."

"But you can't even get to town."

"Have you looked at your battery cables? Maybe they're loose."

"You might just have some bad gas."

"Let's try pushing it."

The elderlies remained stoic in the back of the van, sitting on some old starters and a greasy transmission case piled up in a corner. The men all jumped back in the van, and El Cuartalejo got back in the driver's seat—still expressing himself with some of the finer phrases learned in the Service of his Country—and tensely waited for a car to bump into the rear of the van. It started rolling slowly down a slight slope toward the paved road. Philbert was playing Crazy 8s with about six kids. The rig began rolling faster while two or three guys outside were shouting instructions to each other. The driver popped the clutch, and it jerked, tires squealed (bald tires have that tendency), the engine reluctantly grumbled to life and started to die. The driver gunned it frantically, and it roared wildly, a cloud of white smoke pouring out of the back.

"All right!"

A few more people jumped in and closed the doors, at a run, laughing, making several felicitous remarks about the high quality of American manufacturing, and that baby swung out south on the road and they were on their way!

When the sublime 1973 Dodge van took a right turn to the west on the highway, Sky looked out a tiny window on the side of the stagecoach and said, "That's where we went off the cliff."

"Where?" Philbert asked, struggling to get up and look out.

"There."

They sailed past the Site of the Accident just a few hundred yards over the hills and through the woods from the pueblo, but you couldn't see much—just a dry sandy slope and a gully. You couldn't see the bottom of the gully from inside the van, or through the gray cloud of smoke emanating from the broken exhaust pipe of the van.

"I heard they hauled that wreck to town," Old Girl remarked. She was sitting placidly on a greasy piece of machinery that might have been part of some engine once.

"Oh yeah?"

"Taos."

"Ohyeah?" Philbert repeated. "I wouldn't mind stopping by and seeing it if we have time."

Violetta had a question for him. "How come you ran off the road and blew up everything?"

It was a reasonable question, and Philbert was about to attempt a reasonable answer, when El Cuartalejo interrupted. "We got us a roadblock up here!" he shouted. "You guys from Montana better scrunch down."

It didn't seem all that likely—for you purists of plot construction out there—that there'd be roadblocks four or five days later on this back road, or that every detective in the world wouldn't have figured out in five minutes that the Indians who had shot up the State Capital of New Mexico would have hightailed it to the nearest Indian hideout just up the road from that suspicious car wreck, but if you've ever had any dealings on the wrong side of American Law (like some authors I could name, who have been in several kinds of jails in a number of states), then you know them law enforcement guys are a pretty disorganized bunch. It takes them about a year just to get around to some routine paperwork, let alone figuring out the unpredictable movements of desperate criminals. They're not the brightest fellas you'll ever meet, and some of 'em are downright morons. So you'll have to excuse this little scene if it looks a bit like Broderick Crawford setting up a roadblock like in the movies. You gotta feel a little sorry for them poor cops. They don't know any better.

"Can I see your driver's license and registration?" one of them demanded of El Cuartalejo (who was profoundly annoyed) in his best voice of authority, when the van lurched to an uneasy stop in the middle of the road. The Voice of Authority looked real tough in his aviator sunglasses and his crisp starched uniform, but you knew he was just a regular guy around his house, in a T-shirt and holey socks. His wife probably yelled at him to fix the back porch just like millions of other slobs.

A couple more Dagwood Bumsteads circled around the van, getting out of several more ominous-looking State Patrol cruisers, checking out the license plates, peering in the windows at the wall-to-wall Indians inside, acting like they were John Wayne or somebody. It would have been funny if they didn't also have great big pistols strapped high on their waists, and a couple more of 'em watched a few feet away with big shotguns held loosely in their arms.

"Could everybody please step out of the van for a moment?"

Everybody stepped out, and it would have been almost like an old Buster Keaton movie with an endless stream of midgets and clowns emptying impossibly onto the road—except that in the old days the Keystone Kops were funny, but today they were all serious and respectable like the Hill Street Blues. It's too bad that comedy has gone downhill like that.

Indians piled out of the seven or eight other wrecks behind the van, and the State Troopers began to look a little nervous as about fifty irritable Indians began milling around. The drivers all had their licenses and registrations in order. The Sergeant in charge wanted to test them for alcohol. A few dozen kids charged off to play down one of the rocky slopes, and the Sarge tried to order them back into the lineup, but even he felt foolish about it. The kids stood around looking at him when he yelled at them but, hell, they were just kids. A big piñon tree was calling out to several of them to climb it, and the tree won out over the Sarge. He had a mess of younguns, too, and he knew there wasn't any realistic prospect of getting them down out of those delectable branches any time soon, so he wisely gave up on it. Two more carloads of Indians pulled up behind the traffic jam—why is it there never seems to be any less than five Indians in any one car?—and it was rapidly getting out of control. The Troopers couldn't find the suspects in this crowd, anyway, as they looked from the three photographs to the fifty or sixty faces that kept shifting around in circles and coming back around again in the lineup, so he waved the first van through and then all the rest. It was hopeless.

So you see, them Savages sneaked on through the clutches of Democracy and Jesus like they always had, confounding law and order with lawlessness and disorder. It was too bad that we couldn't have had a good ol' rip-roaring shoot-'em-up like in the old Little Rascals flicks, but the Kops had lost their sense of humor, I guess. What a waste.

So Philbert and his Gang cruised on down the highway to Taos just a-singing and a-laughing without any more concern or drama than you or I might experience on a Sunday drive to the shopping mall. If they were all a little bit disappointed that they hadn't seen a little more action or excitement, then they didn't show it. Sometimes it's okay to have a nice, peaceful day, even if it is a little boring.

Philbert leaned up and asked El Cuartalejo, "So my friend, how many warriors did you and Buddy have out in the hills?"

"Three," the Picuris said with a straight face. He looked at Philbert and they both laughed. Oh it was good that there are such fine revolutionary guerrilla armies out there in the mountains!

The first thing they did on the outskirts of Rancho de Taos was pull into the first cheap self-service gas station and quick food stop, since all nine or ten vehicles (somehow the word had gotten out to more Indians in some kind of miraculous way that a war party was going into town, *and* somebody had gas money) were running below empty, and about half the kids were running on full. As the men pumped regular and unleaded into the old heaps, none of them newer than ten years old, with monetary assurances from Jane and Philbert that, for once, they wouldn't have to sneak out without paying, the kids ran for the toilets and the candy bar racks. The women sat in the vehicles and changed diapers, rearranged the cramped quarters, and cussed the men. But they were all mostly pretty glad to be out in the bright sunshine of late afternoon and on the move, laughing, joking, and swigging a few root beers and diet Dr. Peppers. Jane passed out a few more fifties to a few more Elders with appropriate credentials and letters of reference, and a few more cars full of Taos Hispano brothers joined them, and even a few Navaho Apaches thrown in here and there. Philbert decided he was hungry, and a dozen kids suggested they get pizzas over at the mall.

So off they went, growing substantially with a few Utes and Hopis joining in, and it really did begin to look a little like a revolutionary guerrilla army invading the mall, and swarming into the pizza joint. A few responsible mothers and fathers in Procurement and Supply had gone over to the Safeway to load up on provisions for the upcoming Campaigns and Bivouacs, but they would try to rejoin the main force as soon as they could.

Reconnoitering the pizza joint, Philbert stepped boldly up to the counter and gave general orders. "We better start with about twenty deluxe combinations." He knew that he was drooling, and that this was a serious backsliding on his diet, but a commander has greater responsibility to his troops. "And a mess of garlic bread and a few dozen extra-large Pepsis."

Two or three shocked little white high school boys and

girls behind the counter took the brunt of this surprise skirmish and suffered heavy casualties, frantically rolling out dough and sloshing sauce. Jane slapped down a cool $200 worth of heavy artillery. Indians passing by dropped in to say hello to a few of their relatives, and have a bite to eat, and pretty soon there were about a hundred of 'em spilling out into the corridors, dismaying the usually calm and placid white folks (fulfilling *their* own cultural customs by buying a pile of goods in the shops). Completely routed by the brilliant flanking maneuver, the Veho honkies made quick detours around the noisy laughing Native Offensive. After satiating their appetites and in complete possession of the battlefield, Philbert asked the kids if they might like to go check out the movies and see what was playing.

"*YEAH!*"

Jusepe suggested, "I been wanting to see *The Son of King Kong.*"

"*YEAH!*" fifteen kids roared in unison. "LET'S SEE THE SON OF KING KONG!!"

"Okay." Philbert smiled simply. All great generals since Napoleon have recognized the effectiveness of the simplest battle plans.

Battalions of kids fanned out at a dead run in every direction, yelling, "WE'RE GONNA SEE THE SON OF KING KONG! C'MON, EVERYBODY!"

Somehow they found the multi-cinema that is in every single shopping mall in every single American town larger than a thousand population, and somehow the movie they wanted to see was actually playing there, and it was actually going to start in ten minutes. Sometimes, when Destiny rides with a Chosen People, the gods and goddesses are on the side of Right. It was thus with our Freedom Fighters, and the attack on the multi-cinema would be studied later at West Point and Sandhurst. It was a brilliant maneuver, pure genius to launch a further offensive when the field had already been taken and the day won. Generalissimo Philbert risked his whole expeditionary force with the bold twilight assault on the vastly superior body of the enemy's stronghold. This was a heavily entrenched bastion where the Imperial Commodore and General of the Armies Ronald Reagan held total sway. No one had ever attacked The Hollywood Legions!

But, O Divine Fate of Fates, there it was, playing right next to *The Son of King Kong—Powwow Highway!!!*

With magnificent insouciance, Philbert's Legions paid scant attention to the dramatization of their lives. That was mostly because the film had received a very limited release from the Studio Army and it was being ignored to death, as usual, buried. It was a familiar tactic. Strategizing by splitting his army into a dual flanking maneuver, Philbert Buonoparte ignored the ignorant and they all went into *Kong* instead. Every security rent-a-cop for miles around formed nervously around the perimeter of this unruly mob, but since they weren't actually doing anything illegal, and they had bought out at least one business, the Pizza Joint, which had to close for lack of any more inventory, there wasn't much they could do. The mob poured into the quiet, clean little cinema complex and they all pointed to Philbert—who had two kids riding on his shoulders and two or three others crawling on him—when the terrified boy in the polyester red uniform asked for their tickets. Jane fired a deafening salvo by slapping down a cool $300 for the tickets, and another $250 or so so that everybody could have a few candy bars and of course popcorn and pop. The concession stand became seriously depleted of supplies as the army foraged the countryside and stripped it, and one of the brave girls who worked there was carried from the field by medics and was crying hysterically in the back room. A dozen other customers found themselves under siege inside the little theatre as wild Comanches jumped back and forth over the seats and their parents, like good NCOs, yanked their arms out of their sockets, and barked like Drill Sergeants, "BEHAVE!"

"SHUSH! PRIVATE DOGFACE!"

The previews started, and everybody cheered wildly as the slick trailer for *Powwow Highway* breezed by. It was of great satisfaction to them to know that an international strategy was at work upon The Ignorant Enemy. The feature presentation came on and everybody clapped. Morale was high. Four kids sat on Philbert's lap (including Sky, who, as an indispensable adjutant, never left his commander-in-chief's side), as the candy boxes and empty 7-Up cups piled up several feet on the floor all around him. After a while nobody could move their legs because of all the trash, but still, they didn't seem to mind. Popcorn and Milk Duds and Junior Mints kept flying as the Supply Corps was extremely well organized and kept a steady and reliable flow of refreshments coming up from the rear lines. The front-line combatants hid their eyes and screamed at the scary parts of the movie, as all combat troops have faced the terror and horror of war, but there were many instances of bravery and courage beyond the call of duty. Jusepe had his feet up on the seats in front of him, licking a huge sucker. Old Codger and Old Girl gobbled chili dogs, stared wide-eyed at the monster gorilla on the giant screen, and never once flinching.

But at last, alas, Peace comes to all Warriors, the shrieking climax arrives, and the movie is over. The lights came up and everybody filed out with the discipline of veterans, grinning, triumphant, their butts a little sore, their stomachs a little queasy, but happy. A soldier is never so much alive as when he faces Death. Moving slowly, satisfied, they all ended up out in the huge parking lot and lingered around the Motor Pool. Civilians once again, the ennui of peacetime boredom and the ingratitude of their countrymen settled over the evening like cigar smoke stinking up the American Legion Hall. What do we do now? What can compare to the life-and-death truth of the struggle for democracy and glory and victory? Huh! What Price Complacency?! It was dark now, and everybody was trying to enjoy the quiet night, leaning on their old rattletrap Chevies and Fords.

"We're busted," Jane informed a group of them around Phil.

"Really?"

"Flat broke, not one sawbuck left."

Nobody seemed to care much, including Paymaster Philbert. I mean, what's money? It leaves Traditionals cold. It's nothing. They had full gas tanks, full stomachs, good friends and family all around, great war memories, who needs those green frogskins of the whitemen? If it might have made an American a little sick to his stomach to have blown two grand on handouts to strangers, and gas and pizza and movies, it didn't bother genuine oldtime Indians. Generosity was one of the great virtues of the oldtimers, along with endurance and wisdom. They felt good. They weren't worried. Something would turn up. They could always re-enlist.

"You know," Jusepe wondered aloud, "I been wanting to try an idea I had for years. Maybe this is the occasion I been waiting to come along."

"What's that?"

"Well, this here is Indian land."

"Yep," they agreed. A few more people drifted over to the van and leaned on it, looking out across the silhouette of the mountains. They all knew Jusepe, and most of them liked him.

"These white people ain't got any real right to be here."

"You bet."

"I mean, we welcomed them like visitors but they don't care. They spit on us, killed everything in sight. They don't know *how* to tell the truth."

"Yep."

"So I been thinking," the skinny old guy said, rolling a cigarette. "Who's to say we don't have the right to charge 'em a toll for passing through our land? Just set up a road-block like they do and charge a buck a car for them to pass through. A buck a car. Like they was paying for a passport or a visa to go through a foreign country. Set up a immigration checkpoint, like up at that road to the ski area. Charge 'em admission to come through our land. We need the greenbacks for now, like it or not, so who's to say we can't do that, right now?"

"What about the cops?" somebody asked. "They'll roust us right out and to the joint."

"Not if we stick together," Jusepe added enthusiastically.

"It ain't illegal," Old Codger agreed. "This *is* our land."

"It'll hold up in court," Old Girl added. "'The Treaties—"

"There's enough of us right here."

"We could do it right now."

Just about then Grampa Jimmy came riding down the main road on his horse with about four other guys, trotting along. They saw the insurgents in the parking lot and clomp-clomped right over. "Howdy!" he greeted cheerfully.

"Where you been?" Violetta asked.

"I found that roan gelding that run off last week. He was way to hell over at Morton Lombaugh's place—"

"Dad," Violetta asked, "Where's Bonnie and . . . them? You were supposed to be—"

"Ahh they're alright. I saw 'em resting at the sheepherder trailer, so we went to find that roan. Then we saw you all crowding around here, on our way to the Dairy Queen."

"We're thinking about going up to that ski area and chargin' em a toll for passing through our land," Jusepe said. "Wanna come?"

"Damn right!" Grampa exclaimed. "That's been needin' to be done for a long time."

"I dunno," someone hesitated. "We got women and children—"

"Leave 'em right here for now, or they could go home."

"Maybe we should take them with us. That way the cops might not—"

"Well—"

"I dunno. If—"

"Whadda ya say, Chief?" Jane asked Philbert, who was trying to hang as far back in the background as he could.

Everyone turned to look at him, as he had, after all, sprung for the feast and war party. He gulped and shrugged. "I'm just a visitor here."

Grampa persisted. "You're more'n that."

"Me?"

"So what do you think?" Jane also persisted.

Philbert saw they were all determined to put him on the spot, so he tried to think. It was difficult. "Well, uh . . . I . . . was always taught to listen to my elders."

That's all he said. Everybody paused for a moment, looked warily at each other in the semi-darkness, and then burst out laughing.

"What the hell!"

A woman shouted, "I ain't gonna be left behind! Let's set up our toll road on that ski road! I bet a thousand cars come down there, just about now!"

"Yeah!"

It may sound preposterous to white people, steeped like you are in your rational fears of law and order, but have you ever heard of the Little Big Horn? Do you remember when about five hundred Indians took a stand against the entire United States way of life back in 1973 at a place called Wounded Knee? All that was was a bunch of Elders standing around, too, saying, "We gotta do something." Those old elderlies, I'll tell ya, they're hardcore. Nobody is more radical, red or white, than most elderlies I know. Most of 'em don't have no truck with polite petitions or politicians or much else to do with The System. They know better. And Indians, well, their folks and granddaddies were at Sand Creek, and they ain't no restless young malcontents who are bored and got nothing else to do with their time except get drunk and go squaw-jumping all the time, or playing Indian. Nope. A lot of 'em seek visions all the time. I know guys like Jusepe. I'll bet if you pressed your grandparents, no matter how well off they may be, they'd say the same thing: they're disgusted with the course of human events. They hate to see cuts in Medicaid and bailouts of billions of dollars for the savings and loan banks. They're real people. They say things like Jusepe and Grampa are saying all the time, and a lot more radical than this, too, all the time. Indians especially don't believe one goddamn word the Americans say anymore. Not one. You Indians out there know I'm telling the truth. A lot of black people know it too, and brown people. Rich Americans are lizards with forked tongues who'd screw their own kind, particularly if they're poor. I ain't got a whole hell of a lot against most poor folks of any color; it's the rich ones. They should all go back to Europe where they belong. Hell, they're all so goldang fired up about being Irish and Italian and all, why don't they just go back to Ireland and Italy where they belong, if that's what they're so proud of? It doesn't make sense that they hang around here.

And that's how that famous caravan of fifteen vehicles and four horses cruised through Taos and set up their own roadblock on the main thoroughfare to the Ski Area that famous night at the end of the year. And of course, as usually happens with these kinds of things, it quickly escalated into a much bigger deal than had originally been intended. Anytime Indians do anything to stand up for their rights, the Americans immediately go crazy and start screaming hysterically to "Circle the wagon trains!" or something equally ridiculous. It's pathetic.

The caravan pulled to the side of the road going up to Taos Ski Area, and it was innocent enough. They just parked along the side of the road and got out. Lots of people do it every day. Nobody thought anything about a string of old 1969 Pontiacs and 1962 Ford pickups and 1973 Dodge vans pulled over to the side of the road. It's a free country. The night was cool and still, Taos Mountain (sacred to a lot of Skins) just to the east of them loomed dark, and 1988 Jeeps and 1989 Volvos and 1990 Cadillacs with ski racks on their streamlined roofs zipped on by like it was just another ordinary evening in America.

Before anybody could stop him, Grampa stepped off his horse and right out in the road in front of the next 1991 Mercedes XL 450 coming down the mountain, and calmly waved his arms at it. The Michelin Tiger Paws squealed wildly and the silver-gray cruiser with Head Masters and Solomon step-in bindings on the French ski rack did a wheelie and came to a safe stop sideways one foot away from Grampa. The 1992 Citroëns and BMWs and Ferraris that were right behind it squealed and screeched and slithered sideways all over their Posi-Tractions and dual disc brakes, and the entire flow and progress of civilization grinded to an abrupt and startling halt, and dozens of halogen headlights and fog spotlights shone unnaturally out all over the snowy sagebrush hills. Horns honked in an exotic international disharmony. Angry voices shouted. Doors were opened and slammed.

Grampa walked calmly around to the driver's door of the first vehicle, still holding the reins on his nervous horse, and tapped on the window. It rolled down, humming electronically. "Hello," he said pleasantly.

"What's the matter?!" a frantic voice asked from the shadows. A pungent aroma of warmth and luxury wafted from the open window.

"Toll road. One dollar per car."

"Huh?" the white shadow asked, and looked out the window closer. "Has there been a wreck?"

"No."

"Hey, what's going on?!" another white shadow (in a skin-tight lavender jumpsuit) angrily demanded as it rushed over. "Has there been a wreck?"

"What's the delay here?" another shadow (female this time, in a cute chartreuse outfit) shouted.

"HEY!" a multitude of other voices shouted far up the rapidly lengthening line of cars, a congestion of traffic building in harmony to the horns honking and blatting out across the previously peaceful night.

Half a dozen phantoms in baby blue ski pants and chinchilla parkas rushed at the lone old man and the horse standing defiantly in the amber waves of car lights, but he stood his ground.

"What's going on?"

"HEY!"

"What's happening?"

"Let's—"

These people, who thought nothing of slapping down thousands of dollars for metal and wood slats to slide down a mountain, wearing plastic boots like leg irons that cost hundreds of dollars, paying ten and twenty and fifty dollars every time they took a few steps around the Warming House at "The Area," in the chic restaurants and boutiques and saloons, these same people grew livid when they found out an old Indian was charging them one dollar for a toll on the public road up to that extravagant gyp-joint and rapacious place of sport and play. These same people with their golden cocaine spoons around their necks who thought nothing of the slaughter of thousands of trees and the maiming of entire mountains so that they could fly in from L.A. and D.C. and have a wonderful vacation from their vacuous but well-paying jobs sliding and schussbooming down those raped slopes grew outraged when their super-highway was blocked by eccentric Locals. It was illegal! Their taxes paid for this! How dare they! These same people experienced genuine shock! They were offended! They were confused!

"Get out of the way," one man instructed calmly. He was used to authority. "You have no—"

"You get out of the way," Grampa re-directed.

"What is this?" someone else snarled from the back of the gathering confusion. "Give him a bottle so we can be on our way."

"HEY!" somebody else shouted.

It came from behind the old man, and everyone looked. Four very dark and dangerous-looking men came walking into the car lights. They weren't wearing peach-colored jumpsuits and mauve ski caps. They didn't have blow-dry haircuts and designer mittens.

"Now what?" a ski bunny whispered.

"You don't talk to our Elder like that," a deep voice like a black bear rumbled. It was El Cuartalejo.

"Huh?"

"What?"

"Pay the toll and count yourselves lucky," he commanded.

A lawyer in a sensible navy blue parka argued, "You have no legal right to—"

"Shut up."

It was an odd moment. On one side of the standoff one group of people hadn't the slightest understanding what was going on. This wasn't happening. It wasn't possible. Authors make up these things. It was a movie. On the other side, the other people understood all too well what was happening, and it was just the same old story.

"What do they want?" someone on the ignorant side asked.

"I dunno."

"Are they Indians, Daddy?"

"I think so. Yes, I think so."

"*Real* Indians?"

"I don't know. Yes, I guess so. I don't know."

A sensible woman finally said, "They want a dollar, give it to them. This *is* their land. Let's just go."

An Indian said, "You don't talk about our Elder that way."

"Okay, okay."

"Let's just pay the dollar and—"

"HEY! This is our land! You're trespassing!"

"Now look, fella, I don't know what century you're living in but—"

"No. You look!"

"This is—"

Would the cops have shown up about now? Probably not. Like I said before, they're a bunch of pretty disorganized guys, and if traffic on the ski road was now backed up almost a mile, they wouldn't have noticed, probably. They were probably too busy rousting speeders out on the highway or hassling high school kids at the McDonald's for throwing their french fries or something. So it was left up to the doctors and lawyers and bankers to deal with the Pueblos and Apaches and Cheyennes as best as they could, at least until the boys with the guns and the sirens showed up to clean up the mess the doctors and lawyers and bankers made.

And then twenty five more Indians got up enough courage, finally, and came into the light out of the night, and the fun-loving crowd saw that this was not just the antic of a lone malcontent or two. They backed off a few feet.

"Uh-oh."

"What's going on?"

Someone on the knowledgeable side said, "You people think you can just keep on going the way you are forever?"

"You think this is a free ride?"

"You're the ones breaking the law, not us."

"The Law of Nature."

"Now get back in your fancy cars," Jusepe ordered, "and get out your fancy money and we'll let you on through, so you can go have a fancy dinner in a fancy restaurant and sleep in your fancy condom."

Violetta giggled. "That's, uh, condominium, Viejo."

"Yeah," Jusepe agreed. "Which is more than you ever gave us."

And the sheep backed off from the wolves once again. The ski bunnies cowered in the presence of the hawks, and they went meekly back to their sheep-wagons and rabbit-cars. They shrank inside with their guilt and resentment all over again, and hid from it all over again, and they obediently paid their tribute to the angry predatory forces of the night, and they weaseled on down the road in their Jaguars and their Cougars and their Cherokees. They knew they had been in the presence of a kind of glory, briefly, and that the anger of the night was the madness of the denial

61

of their history, and it was in the deep voices and the dark eyes of those men and women back there on the road. The episode had terrified the sheep and the bunnies, but it had thrilled their lambs and kids. Why had Daddy acted so funny? Why did Mommy get mad? What were the Indians talking about?

The first cop car, with his red-white-and-blue lights flashing, passed the flocks going down the hill, and everybody going both ways kind of wished there wasn't going to be the kind of trouble that there was going to be.

The Highway Patrol cruiser pulled past the last car parked on the side of the road facing up to the ski area and slowed down. It looked ominous. He passed a few more of the old Chevys and Oldsmobiles and radioed for backup units. Dark and dirty figures loomed. Saabs and Peugeots rolled down the other way at long intervals. The superhighway was clogged with confusion.

Officer Esai Sandoval got up to the actual roadblock and hopped out. "What's going on here?"

"Nothing."

Red-white-and-blue lights circled the empty fields across from the jammed road, on both sides. "Let's get this traffic moving."

No one moved.

"This is illegal interference with—"

"Hi," a little girl greeted.

"Huh?"

"Can I play with your handcuffs?"

"What? No. Now who's in charge here—"

Other kids circled around him, like the well-trained veteran squad they were. "Is that a real gun?"

"You children get . . . where are your parents?"

"Over there."

"Can I hold your gun?"

"No." The officer stepped up to the crowd of people stopping each car. "What's going on here?"

"Oh hello. Hey, is that you, Esai?"

"Yeah. Uh, who are you?"

"Oh c'mon Esai, Tommy Cuartalejo. We went to Taos High together."

"Oh yeah, Tommy, how ya doing? What's going on here?"

"Remember when you caught that touchdown pass I threw against Velarde?"

Just as Esai was about to grin with the memory, a boy unsnapped his holster, and Officer Sandoval wheeled around wildly, slipped on the icy pavement, lost his balance, and hit his head hard on the fender of a 1973 Dodge van. He went out immediately, coldcocked, and rolled sideways onto the snowy cover over the *rojo* dirt at the side of the road. He was out like a light.

"Jesus!"

The group of kids looked around for a squad leader. "Whadda we do?"

"I dunno."

PFC Sky took his gun out of the holster, just because he liked guns, and it discharged accidentally, into the air, just as another cruiser came blasting up the road and right into the middle of the scene. It was bad timing, that's all. Everyone dove for cover, and hearing the gunshot, Officer Escobar in the second cruiser mistook the whole situation and swerved wildly to his left—sure that Cuban infiltrators had come in from the Mexican border as they had been warned about in last week's Security Briefing. He smashed into the rear fender of a Mercedes-Benz, which had been trying to sneak by without paying the toll, it spun around twice and slid into the borrow ditch on the other side of the road. A woman screamed maniacally somewhere (as she got the gun safely away from Sky), but Officer Escobar, who was a rookie on the force, leapt out of his damaged vehicle (its radiator had ruptured on the Mercedes and was squirting hot greenish-yellow anti-freeze five feet into the air), and began blasting away indiscriminately with his .357 Magnum at the Cuban Commies coming from every direction. Pontiacs peeled off across the fields, bouncing over fences, and a 1941 DeSoto crashed gleefully into a $50,000 Custom El Dorado.

A third cruiser screamed up from town, swerved to miss a group of fleeing women, and slammed irresponsibly into that same hapless Mercedes that lay sticking up out of the borrow ditch at an unfortunate angle. The front bumper of the third cruiser, with Tito Dotayo at the wheel, lost its connection with reality and flew forty feet through the air and exploded into the rear window of Esai Sandoval's idling supercharged Dodge, and it exploded like a bomb. Fortunately, Esai himself was not in the vehicle at the moment—you may remember that he was out cold as the head of the roadblock—so he was not injured further. The concussion of the blast threw Officer Escobar head over heels two hundred feet out into the cow pasture, but his landing was mercifully cushioned by several gigantic cow pies, and he slid to relative safety, with only cuts and bruises over ninety percent of his body. Meanwhile, Tito had lost control of his cruiser and rolled eight times across the field on the other side; but of course he had on his seat belt, so he was okay. The Mercedes, by the way, was spinning around and around like a top from where Tito had clipped it. It was totaled.

It's hard to say exactly what happened next. Hundreds of people of various denominations ran crazily out across the fields like refugees being strafed in a World War II movie. The night sky lit up as several other cars exploded from the flames licking from Esai's former cruiser. Devout Catholics knelt and were sure that Armageddon had erupted. They said later from their sanctuarios that they could see the blasts as far away as Colorado. Somehow, a running war had begun inside the tranquil borders of the World's Greatest Democracy, and there were even a few people who said it was none too soon. It was long overdue, they said.

4

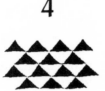

HOW THE FUN CONTINUED
ON INTO THE EVENING, AND
OF A METAMORPHOSIS
OR TWO.

WE FOUR OUTLAWS ON HORSEBACK HEARD THE EXPLOSIONS ten miles away, but we were on the western slope of a wooded hill so we didn't see the fireballs shooting up into the sky over Taos off to the east.

"What was that?" Bonnie asked out loud.

"Probly a sonic boom," Buddy replied nonchalantly.

Rabbit wished she had a joint right about then, as she let her old mare take the rein down the slope. They had been listening to me telling lies about the mythologies of this area, and it had been more than a coincidence, I claimed, that no cops had seen us, or that we had no trouble at all with anyone on the way.

"Yet," Rabbit commented skeptically.

"It's the moonlight," I insisted. "There's a protective shield in the world on nights like this."

"Road apples."

Buddy grinned. "You just making this up as you go along?"

I smiled, brushing my long ponytail out of my eyes. "Don't you know I'm what your European ancestors would call a 'wizard,' Rabbit?"

"No, I didn't know that."

"A wizard?" Bonnie gulped.

"Yes. I can make our trip a safe and peaceful one, or dangerous, tragic, funny, anything, with a wave of my imagination."

"A joint would sure make this conversation go down a lot easier," Rabbit muttered.

"My pen is a magic wand. Don't you think it's just a little odd that we've been riding horses on an idyllic night in an enchanted land and it seems a little like we're not really in control of all this, you and I?"

"I think," Buddy said, "that there's a lot of superstition around here. Most Americans would say *they* are the Great Power, not us, not magic."

"Who cares what they say?" Rabbit contended. "I saw some shit in that *kiva* this afternoon that . . . I don't know what."

"I could make a joint appear for you, right now, Rabbit. I can make you disappear, Buddy. Anything, anything at all. Don't you know that about our world? This isn't the real world we're in right now, right here. This is the Creator's Dream. Look at your moon shadow on the ground. That's real, not this. I've debated about whether I should reintroduce marijuana into this story, or even the *ololiuhqui datura* hallucinogen the Skins say Popeé took to turn himself into a whirlwind."

"Oh, it was a drug?" Rabbit asked.

"Ah, now you're interested, eh?"

"Well, at least it's a physical explanation."

"I wonder." I sighed. "The Eleusinian Mysteries of the Greeks, and Tlaloc, the mushroom-god of the Masatecs in Oaxaca, Mexico, the lightning-engendered visions of *Amanita muscaria*. I've known people who've taken all the drugs, and they talk about the most incredible things. They really seem to have a lot of belief in the most extraordinary, supernatural phenomena, the existence of extraterrestrial spaceships and auras and channels."

"All that New Age crap," Buddy sneered.

"I took a lot of drugs," Bonnie said quietly.

I asked, "Do you feel any better for it?"

"What do you mean?"

"Has it helped you? Was there . . . knowledge that—"

Bonnie thought about it. "I don't know. I don't feel too good most of the time."

"We did a hell of a lot of acid," Rabbit explained, almost apologizing. "It's a recreational thing mostly, I think. Most druggies I've known are screwed up."

"There were a lot of visions," Bonnie continued. "There really was a . . . uh . . . a kind of . . . uh . . ."

"'A transcendent vision, you could say," Rabbit suggested.

"Yeah! That's the word I was trying to think of. Transcendent."

"Did you ever do the *Amanita muscaria* mushrooms?" I asked. "Not silly-cybin, but the real stuff."

"No, I don't think so," Bonnie thought.

"I've heard of that stuff," Rabbit said. "It's like poison, isn't it, if you take too much?"

"Yeah."

"Like henbane or—"

"Yeah," I said. "The Indians around here use *calabazilla* to ward off evil; it's like a wild gourd. The *gente de chusma* are flying demons and they sprinkle mustard seed on the doorsill to keep them away, and other malign spirits. *Espigas de maiz* is deemed a useful weapon against bewitchment."

"What about that *datura* you mentioned," Rabbit inquired. "I've heard of that."

"Yeah, even the Aztecs mentioned *datura*, called *ololiuhqui*, which the Spanish have corrupted to *toloache*. It's a powerful narcotic that, depending on your dosage, causes everything from dizziness to terrifying hallucinations. I personally wonder about the use of such words as 'hallucination.' What is that?"

"Isn't it like peyote?"

"I guess. I've never taken them," I replied. "I'd have to trust a really expert person with the most powerful plants, because I think if you take the absolute maximum you can, you really could . . . well, I won't say fly or even defy death, because you can do those things without drugs, if you're a sorceror."

"Yeah!"

"But . . . I didn't mean to get off on this."

"If it applied to Popeé," Buddy said, "and I've heard that, too, then wow, what we could do to change the world for the better with that kind of power. Yeah. And Sweet Medicine, what about him? There are sacred roots associated with his Bundle, the Mahuts of Maheo, and all."

"That's right."

Bonnie shook her head. "I'm lost. It's just too much for one day. When are we going to be there, Storyteller?"

I smiled at her. "Soon. Look at the moon. She will relax you. She is the inspiration of poets, the Muse, and that's what I was trying to explain earlier. Your ancestral heroines of nature, like White Buffalo Woman, as well as Isis from Africa, all over the world, are your milk, Love. Maybe she doesn't want me to introduce elements like plants into this story, unless I know what I'm talking about. The indigenous way on this hemisphere knows which of our worlds is real and which isn't, which of ourselves is real and which isn't. I am only the shadow of the creator, you see. I am his ghost, but I can manipulate him, too, as your dreams manipulate you, Bonnie. Dream on these things. Should I pause here and look at the moon?"

It was a beautiful moonlit night, the sky a dark blue and the clouds a pale gray as the satellite waxed—a new sliver. It had been the dark of the moon, the time of sorceresses, when she was in bed with Philbert and the Sacred Bundle bound them together. Groves of aspen, beech, pine, and cottonwood stood like wise sentinels listening to the earth's shadow as it waned—the reverse of her sister, always—after the Winter Solstice, and the groves were sacred to poets for their seasonal magic, the days growing longer and the growing season returning, the fertility of sacred chiefs offering new seeds of life for the queen deep in the soil, deep in the lairs of bears, deep in the graveyards where their ancestors dwelled.

"Stand on the moon," Storyteller whispered, in a voice that, in the perfectly still night, sounded otherworldly, magical. "Cast your sacred twin into that Other World, where everything is the opposite of this one, upside down and backward, and you will discover your True Self. You will see your Dreaming Body. You will see yourself on the earth, from the moon."

The others all rode, and looked at the new crescent, and listened to the eerie silence. Not even the wind was blowing. A few black clouds scudded across the moon suddenly, and an owl hooted. A dog growled viciously somewhere far away.

"Far out," Rabbit muttered.

Bonnie shivered; sudden terror swept through her, and just as suddenly it was past.

Buddy looked at his horse's head as the night was getting darker. The new moon was almost down over the southwestern horizon. He said, "Indians have a saying: we could almost excuse the whiteman for bringing us whisky because he also brought us the horse. He used to roam these lands thousands of years ago, in the time of the Giants, but he died off. He is a sacred animal, with a lot of the thunder power of the west."

Rabbit loved the elegiac poetry of this moment, and she felt love for Buddy Red Bird too. "Far out."

"It's almost like a movie." I smiled.

"Yeah."

"Look!" Buddy said suddenly, and the horses stopped at his command.

They had come around to the northern slope of the hill, and a tall red-and-white television antenna loomed directly in front of them on top of the hill, and in the background shot was the town. Several small black mushroom clouds puffed up over the far northern perimeter of the sprawling tourist town of Taos, and a boom echoed up suddenly from the east toward the high snowy mountains. Then another boom.

"What's goin' on?"

"That ain't no sonic boom, Chief," Rabbit said.

Buddy said, "That looks like a TV station. Let's go check it out."

"Buddy"—Bonnie hesitated—"I don't want to. Let's just get to wherever we're going."

"I just want to find out what's goin' on. C'mon, Sis." He trotted over to the small building underneath the antenna tower.

The rest of us trotted after him.

At the front door, beside a graveled parking lot where two mobile television vans were parked, the four riders dismounted. "I'll hold the horses," I offered.

"Good," Buddy decided, and walked in the building. It was cold outside. Rabbit and Bonnie reluctantly followed him inside.

Inside, the modern receptionist's area, with pretty Formica furniture and functional pictures of Taos (with burros standing in front of picturesque adobe haciendas) on the walls, and soft orange carpeting on the floor and glossy magazines on the table, was empty. Nobody was there. A big color TV was high up on a swivel platform in a corner of the wall, suspended over a desk with a silent electric typewriter on it. The three visitors looked at the TV, which was broadcasting the popular show *Miami Vice*. Solemn synthesizer music was humming behind handsome policemen shooting it out with sleazy Cuban drug dealers. Then the program was brutally interrupted by a sign: NBC NEWS SPECIAL REPORT. A local newsman in a blow-dry haircut over his anonymous good looks stared glumly at the camera.

"We interrupt our regular programming for a news bulletin," he said. "We will resume *Miami Vice* exactly where we interrupted it. Hi. I'm Jim Turner for KTAO-TV Eyewitness News. Several explosions and apparently a gunfight with State Police erupted just minutes ago on the Taos Ski Road just northeast of town. It's not known exactly what the cause for this is, but there have been preliminary reports that unknown terrorists may have instigated an attack on passing motorists. I repeat, this is only a preliminary report, and we hope to have Jan Griswold on the scene momentarily on our KTAO Instant Eyewitness News Mobile Unit for more complete information."

"Terrorists?" Rabbit eyed Buddy.

"There have been reports of some injuries to several law enforcement officers, but this is unconfirmed. We have tried repeatedly to contact the Sheriff's office, but no one has answered the phone. Oh, here's Jan now."

Jan came on camera and she was a cute young thing. Behind her, in the night, police sirens and flashing red-white-and-blue lights were going off in an apparent pande-

70

monium. A mob of people were standing around in the background as Jan held the microphone closely to her and kept looking nervously around her. Her voice was trembling.

"Jim, I'm at the intersection of the Taos Ski Road, and this is a very wild scene here. As far as I can make out from what I hear on the police radio, a group of disgruntled local Indians have set up a roadblock about a mile up the road from here and . . . I can't seem to find out what else is going on."

"What were those explosions, Jan?"

"Well, Jim, as far as I can make out they were police cars blowing up. This is almost a panic scene here and—"

"Police cars . . . Has anyone been killed?"

"I don't know. We're just not getting any information here yet."

"You say that Indians are involved in this?"

"As far as I can tell, yes, Jim."

"What about the reports of terrorists that we've been getting?"

"Well, I don't know. Where have you been receiving those reports?"

"Yeah," Buddy snarled.

"I don't know, Jan. It was on the AP wire teletype."

"I don't know anything about that, Jim. I do have a lady here, Mrs. Pamela DePew from Philadelphia, Pennsylvania, who came through the roadblock, she says, just minutes before the gunfire apparently broke out. Mrs. DePew, can you tell us what happened?"

"Well," Mrs. DePew gasped, drinking a cup of coffee (she was wearing a gaudy ermine parka over a fuchsia polka-dotted jumpsuit). "I don't know what happened. All these people in the dark stopped our cars and demanded we give them a dollar for a toll, or something."

"What did they say, Mrs. DePew? What did they look like."

"They wanted a dollar for each car." She shrugged. "They said they were Indians and it was their land. So I gave them a dollar."

"WHOOO!" Buddy yelped. He was very excited.

"Jan," Jim asked (looking briefly, and oddly, around the

studio as he heard some strange yell), "can you ask Mrs. DePew if they had guns, or if they've taken any hostages?"

"Oh, you asshole!" Rabbit snarled.

"Mrs. DePew, did they threaten you in any way?"

"No, I guess not. No, they were very nice."

Just then some kind of flare or skyrocket or something went flying crazily just behind the two women and exploded off camera. Jan screamed and ran out of view, pulling Pamela with her, spilling her coffee all over her ermine. For one insane half minute no one was talking to the camera as it held steadily on the chaotic scene at the intersection.

Bonnie gasped, "There's Philbert!"

Sure enough, Philbert walked into the picture and grinned inanely at the camera, and then Sky and Jane and Jennifer walked in, too, holding his hands, and waved at the camera.

"Hi, Mommy," Jennifer said.

"Whaaaa?" Rabbit stared.

They made funny faces at the camera like they were making home movies. In a few seconds the camera jerked wildly, and the picture went blank. It was surreal. It was spooky. It was primetime television.

Jim came back on the picture in the studio, and he looked pretty confused himself. "We seem to have lost the picture momentarily. We'll return after these messages."

A woman in an efficient herringbone suit hurried into the receptionist's lobby at just that precise moment. "Can I help you?" she asked the three visitors.

"Yes, Ma'am," Buddy said, immediately turning on the charm. "I'm Buddy Red Bird, and I'm here to give you an exclusive interview right now about the fast-breaking news events you have been covering so well."

"You're who?"

"The one who broke his sister out of the Santa Fe jail a few days ago and every cop in the State has been looking for. Check your own files. I can tell you more about what's going on at the Ski Area, but I want a live interview right now."

"On the air?"

"Live," Buddy smiled, admiring her figure. "You'll scoop everybody. Probly get a writeup in *Newsweek*."

She looked him over too. "Follow me, Mr.—"

"Red Bird. Buddy Red Bird." He smiled at Rabbit and

Bonnie, and went around a corridor with the business-woman.

The two women stared at each other in amazement. Rabbit said, "I ain't missin' this."

She hurried around the corner behind them, and Bonnie was left alone in the lobby. She stared at the commercials on TV. A pickup truck leapt heroically off a cliff. A woman cleaned a toilet bowl in delirious happiness. AT&T told her how good they were. The First Bank of Taos explained all the good things they were doing for their customers, who always come first. Jim came back on, and Buddy was sitting at the news desk next to him!

"We have more to report on the further developments on the crisis at the Ski Area," Jim said, with his most sincere look of concern. "Sitting with me is Buddy Red Bird, whom authorities have identified as a fugitive connected with the jailbreak in Santa Fe a few days ago. Mr. Red Bird, why have you chosen to come here this evening?"

"Jim," Buddy said, giving the camera his most experienced look, staring sternly and sincerely at his television audience as he had learned to do over years of experience as an "activist," "I am indeed a fugitive from American law, as you said. But I don't feel that I have broken any laws. My sister, Bonnie Red Bird, was illegally incarcerated in Santa Fe, and if your viewing audience could hear the circumstances around her arrest and the conspiracy to frame her up, and the conspiracy against American Indians in this country, you would agree with me."

"But, Mr. Red Bird, you tore down an entire wall of the Santa Fe city jail. That—"

"Yes we did."

"And stole a hundred thousand dollars from the city safe!"

"No, it was only twenty-two thousand. And I'll tell ya, Jim, all that money was illegally stolen from the people of New Mexico, in the form of traffic tickets and parking fines. I feel confident that if parking fines and traffic tickets were tested for their constitutionality, the Supreme Court would reverse—"

"Mr. Red Bird, can you tell us anything about this violence being reported from the Ski Area?"

"Yes. It is part of our battle plan to retake our land, which was illegally stolen from us."

"What?"

"Even the courts, Jim, have upheld the inviolable legality of the Indian Treaties. Technically, Taos still belongs to the Taos and Picuris people. And I want the good law-abiding citizens of New Mexico to know that Bonnie didn't do anything wrong. She got involved with some bad elements in our society, drug dealers, but I can provide documented evidence of FBI and CIA complicity in the international drug traffic coming up here from Panama and Colombia that—"

"You said something about a battle plan?" Jim asked, sweating profusely. The producer woman was signaling something frantically at him, but he couldn't understand what she meant. And a strange woman was beside her, too, arguing about something. "What did you mean?"

"I mean," Buddy said, using his deepest voice and his most angry stare (Bonnie thought he looked extremely handsome), "there is a war going on in this country. A war between the third world peoples living right here within the borders of the United States of America and the rich—"

The producer woman made a sign like cutting her throat, and then shouted angrily, "We cut to a commercial. We're not going to have this kind of cheap rhetoric on the air, Mister."

Rabbit angrily stayed right with her as they approached the news desk in front of the cameras. "Oh you're not, eh?"

"Right on." One of the cameramen grinned.

The producer shot him a hateful dart. "That's enough, Garcia! Red Bird, the cops are probably here right now."

"What, you called the pigs!" Buddy jumped up angrily. "They are not pigs, they are human beings!"

"Unlike you, Babycakes!" Rabbit screamed, and punched the woman in the face with her fist. She flew up over the news desk with her legs wide open.

At just that moment the director yelled, "We're back on the air!"

Bonnie watched in amazement as the producer threw a beaver shot right into the screen. She fell backward over the desk, and papers went flying. Jim fell off his chair and disappeared underneath the producer, who wrapped her legs around his head, and they disappeared behind the desk, his head hidden under her dress. Rabbit and Buddy laughed wildly, and so did Garcia and a few others in the studio, who enjoyed seeing that bitch get her due.

But, as always, there are a few suckasses around, and one of them tackled Buddy on top of the desk and they slid across the picture. Something broke somewhere and everyone started shouting. Jim's distinctive voice was heard shouting through the melee, "They're taking over the Station: Run for your lives!"

Rabbit zoomed in for an extreme close-up and ordered somebody off screen, "Keep it rolling, Peckerhead!"

Buddy jumped back into the frame, and his shirt was torn off. He stood on the desk and declared triumphantly, "The Indians are Uprising! All Chicanos and Hispanos, join us! HAU HO WHOOOOOO!"

Outside, I couldn't help but hear the commotion and peeked inside, still holding the reins of the four horses (the colt stuck close to his mother). "What's goin' on?" I asked Bonnie.

She gave me a crazy look and ran outside, and swung up onto her horse. "I don't know." She grabbed the reins and spun around and galloped out of sight into the dark trees.

"HEY! BONNIE!"

But before I could mount and chase after her, the horses all broke loose and ran off in three different directions. And before I could exclaim about this unfortunate turn of events, Buddy came running outside half naked.

"No cops here yet?!"

"Cops? No. Bonnie's run off and—"

"She'll be all right! DAMN!" Buddy exulted, as he watched the producer slam into Rabbit in the lobby, and the women wrestled across the orange rug, hair and brassieres and knuckles flying. "Look at that broad fight."

I couldn't help but look for a minute, as it was a pretty licentious sight. "Yeah."

Rabbit got up and gave the bitch a good kick and ran out the door. "Let's get the hell outa here! Where's the horses?!"

"They ran off."

Buddy was already moving to one of the mobile vans. "Let's see if the keys are in there."

Rabbit swore. "Where's Bonnie?!"

I was already running in the direction she had gone, across country to the west, away from town. "This way!"

Rabbit stood there in the doorway and watched the men running around. "FUCK!!"

The van roared to life, and Buddy screamed like a maniac again. Rabbit saw several burly-looking men rumbling toward the door, and the producer bitch was back on her feet with a look of murder in her eyes. Rabbit saw a handy piece of two-by-four wood laying on the ground, and she slid it in between the handles of the glass door. It held tight. The bitch hit the door running and bounced backward hard, against the burly men. Rabbit howled and shot her the finger. "Eat shit and die, MOTHERFUCKERS!"

Buddy screamed up in the van with the passenger door wide open, and yelled, "Jump in!"

"I'm way ahead of ya!" Rabbit screamed in the wonderful fury of the moment.

She piled in as he gunned it full throttle, gravel flying and wind roaring all around them. He screamed out the driveway and onto the side road as she pulled her door shut. They were both screaming at once, "You magnificent motherfucker! I want to suck your cock! You're a pretty great warrior piece of ass yourself!"

She unzipped his pants, licking his bare chest, as they roared down the road and toward town, toward the war and all the action, into the bright lights of the big city.

Utterly forgetting, in the heat of the night, all about Bonnie.

Bonnie rode through the pitch darkness on her black horse, unsure of everything. She didn't know if she'd ride into an overhanging tree branch and be brained, she didn't know if she was in control of the horse or if it was running free and wild, she didn't know if she was going up or down, north or south, east or west. The moon had set and the night was totally black. She couldn't see a thing. But all the sounds she heard terrified her: wind rushing past her head, owls and crows hooting and cawing, strange rustling movements behind the trees of unseen animals, dark, dark shapes in her mind in the world.

She tried to think of Philbert, and how she needed to be filled with his madness. He needed to bring her back to reality with his body, or take her further away from it. "I can't take this pain," she muttered.

Then, suddenly, some huge shape charged directly across her path and made her horse rear up in terror. She fell backward (pulled, she thought later, by the heavy Bundle still tied to her back) and hit the ground roughly. The wind was knocked out of her, and she couldn't breathe. "OH! UNH! AHH!" It was agony. She thought she was going to die.

She heard her horse running away, and she lay there on the cold, hard, snowy ground and gasped back to life. She heard something else running in the dark. Was it the Thing that had scared her horse? What was it? "Where are you!" she screamed madly.

She heard the heavy four-legged Beast stop and turn around, and start toward the sound of her voice. Oh no, she realized, I gave away my position.

The Thing paused, and then an even stranger sound came from its direction. It sounded like a person now, breathing hard, panting. Yes, it was definitely a smaller, lighter creature now, a two-legged.

Bonnie froze. She was getting her breath back now, but now she tried not to breathe at all, so that she couldn't be heard. She didn't move a muscle. She tried to disappear into the soil.

Steps were definitely coming toward her. They walked with careful stealth, as if they were used to sneaking up on people. Pure horror filled the poor girl's soul. It was the most terrible moment of her life when she heard the Thing stop directly over her, and stare at her, still totally invisible. She heard It breathe.

She felt Its foul breath directly in her face, and It spoke, in a voice like ice cracking in a river. "Are you dead yet?"

Bonnie sobbed. She whimpered in utter insane terror.

"Come die with me, Little Girl. You will be dead inside!" It declared, and at that moment she felt something sharp pierce her forehead. It was a wrenching, paralyzing projection, but, strangely, she didn't feel any blood oozing over her face. She didn't feel life slipping away from her as consciousness slips away into sleep.

Then a strong male's voice boomed suddenly, "Hey, what the hell's going on there?!"

The creature cursed in some foreign language and pulled away from Bonnie's face. She heard the man chasing it, then he was kneeling beside her. She asked him, in a strange faraway voice, "Am I dead, Storyteller?"

"Oh, Goddess, no," I cried, and cradled her in my arms. "Oh, what have I done? What have I done?"

5

HOW PHILBERT SAID
GOODBYE TO AN OLD FRIEND,
AND HOW A NUMBER OF
PEOPLE SCATTERED OUT
ACROSS THE COUNTRYSIDE.

AFTER PHILBERT'S GANG GAZED INANELY AT THE EMPTY camera, and made clown faces at it, in that surreal moment which the Red Bird Gang witnessed at the TV station, they watched the reporter lady diving for cover from a passing skyrocket, her hair smoking where it was singed by the fire, screaming her guts out, so they casually moved over closer to another Instant Eyewitness News Mobile Unit to watch the monitor. They eyewitnessed Buddy discussing the relative merits of American Justice as it applied to Bonnie's case, and their efforts—not unlike Robin Hood and his Merry Men of yore—to redistribute parking meter money. It also held their complete attention when they saw Rabbit coldcock the producer-bitch and All-star Wrestling erupt starring Buddy and Jim Turner, the KTAO anchorman.

"Wow," Sky exulted. He loved Wrestlemania. Zeus was his favorite.

They enjoyed the show. It had a lot of action, sex, and violence. It would probably get high ratings. More TV stations around the country would, at tomorrow morning's meetings about their ratings, seriously consider adding some kind of live confrontation segment to their programming.

But all Philbert could really think of, throughout the sublime two-way television hookup, was where Bonnie was; just as at the same time Bonnie herself was watching Big Phil on the tube, she was worrying about him and the kids. In this way, the Storyteller's Thesis of one movie watching another movie—or to put it in more literary terms, there was a Lewis Carrollesque dichotomy-conceit (ha ha! Let the goddamn college professors try to figure out that one!)— was proven. Just where is the earth in relation to the moon during its full phase, eh?

It all made Philbert realize that it was time for him to go find her. Grampa Jimmy and Jusepe Zaldivar wandered over next to him at just about that same opportune moment, so they all agreed it was probably time to get the hell out of there before the National Guard showed up. El Cuartalejo pulled up in the van right about then, too, as, as is well known, Indians are psychic when it comes to these kinds of telepathic emergencies. They were about to hop in the getaway van, when Violetta and a carload of women peeled up.

"Hey," Violetta challenged, "where's Bonnie!"

"We're gonna go meet 'em now," Grampa Jimmy explained confidently, as two more cop cars raced by, going somewhere.

"Where?"

"No Tongue's hideout," Jusepe whispered conspiratorially, leaning in her window.

"Oh yeah. You mean down over on the Big River there?"

"Yeah, they're heading there."

They exchanged a few more pleasantries and then screeched off in several different directions. There were also a few more war ponies charging around here and there, to confuse the cops. It was a time-honored Indian tactic. Nobody knew quite where the hell they were going, but that was good. They all had the same vague general idea about where they'd end up, so it was okay.

Another Eyewitness News Mobile Unit screeched up just a few seconds after the terrorists left, and Buddy and Rabbit hopped out to investigate the status of the other News Units sitting there. The two troublemakers had a fresh gleam of satisfaction in their eyes, probably from some recent coup or scalp they had taken from some enemy.

Although cop cars and fire engines were screaming and racing around helter-skelter back and forth, Buddy asked, "Where is everybody?"

"I dunno. Oh, there's that Girly Doll," Rabbit said, pointing to Jan Griswold, who was climbing out of a ditch.

"Oh, hey," Buddy yelled, going over to her. He grabbed her arm. "Come with us and we'll give you the scoop of your life."

But for some reason, Jan screamed hysterically and fought to get away from him. "NOOO!!"

"Oh, c'mon, I'm not gonna bite—"

"HELP!!" All she saw was a half-naked Savage trying to drag her into the bushes. Poor Jan. She was from New Jersey and had only moved out here a year ago, after repeated assurances from everybody that the West was no longer as Wild as she had always thought. She ached with all her heart to go home to Daddy and work in his cockroach extermination business again.

Rabbit was also persuading the cameraman, whose name was Chuck, to join them. He didn't seem to mind. So they all managed to pile into the Mobile Unit and drive away in a civil manner, as Buddy explained in his most charming manner (as charming as a Savage can be with no shirt on and his pants half unzipped) that "With you folks along, we can say we're all on assignment, and the van isn't stolen."

Meanwhile, El Cuartalejo's old van bounced along in another direction, still belching various clouds of white and gray smoke, while Grampa Jimmy happily counted his take for the evening. "Seventy-four bucks," he concluded. "Not bad for a couple minutes of work."

Everyone acknowledged that it had been an agreeable effort and that they should do it again real soon.

"Shoulda been more," he complained. "If the cops hadn't a come along and spoiled it all—"

"Aw, you're never satisfied," Old Girl chortled beside him.

They shared a few more jokes as the van humped on

through the downtown Plaza and squealed around a corner (around a loose clump of drunks loitering on the pretty little Plaza) and down a back street. Jusepe and Old Codger kept an eye out the back window for the cavalry. Jane sat in the passenger seat up next to the driver, and Philbert squatted on the floor between them, watching anxiously out the front window with Sky and Jennifer.

Philbert was hopelessly lost. It was an unbelievably dark night in a strange city, and all the dark streets looked equally mysterious to him. He desperately missed Bonnie; so he gazed out the window, a wistful look on his face that all lovers seem to have. It's pathetic. They bounced up one street and jostled down another. They went past an old junkyard, and he glanced sideways at the heaps and wrecks piled along the road and spilling out into the chamisa and cactus fields.

Something caught his eye and he screamed, "Stop!"

El Cuartalejo freaked, and the van jolted sideways and came to rest up next to an abandoned old taco stand. "What the hell?!"

"Why'd you yell like that?!"

Philbert crawled over to the sliding panel door on the side. "I saw Protector."

"Huh?"

He got out. "I'll just be a minute."

"What?"

Jane explained, sighing deeply. "It's his stupid old car that went off the cliff."

Sky hurried after him, where he was already hoofing it over to the little junkyard of wrecked autos. The others made irritable remarks, but bided their time. What else could they do?

We don't want to intrude too much on a man who has stopped to pay his last respects to an old friend because these are private moments of sorrow, so all I'll say is that, sure enough, there was Protector, laying in a line of other graves between all the other fallen comrades of miserable mankind. Phil and Sky stood solemnly and silently, their heads bowed, praying each in their own way beside the bones and rusting flesh of Their Dearly Beloved. The shit-brown paint job was still recognizable under the burned black flesh, and a tear rolled down their eyes as they remembered the sacred pony who gave his life so that others may live. Oh, they had had so many adventures together! They had had a lot of fun. The time they shot up Sheridan, Wyoming, and the capture of a Dragon, and the valiant eve when Protector tore down the jail walls to liberate the Princess. Philbert sobbed at just the name of Protector! Oh! How could life be snuffed out so quickly and eternally? Why must radiator hoses and ball bearings stop throbbing and cranking so suddenly, so permanently? Death was a cruel mystery! It was too much to bear, and he walked away slowly, the boy comforting him by holding his hand. O thou hideous fates! How can a man turn his back on his brother and just leave his dented bumpers and bent steering wheel to lay there all alone in the dark cold ground forever? O Protector, Protector, thy name will live forever, as long as men sing songs of glorious heroes! No matter that thy body is a twisted mess of broken glass and a crushed engine block, thy spirit is clean and whole somewhere, shining and good and glorious!

No one said anything as Phil and Sky got back in the van and they rolled away. A graveyard is a solemn place and most men have respect for it. They could see Phil was in mourning and they admired his privacy. They were sensitive people. Sky kissed his cheek lightly. It is one of the great tragedies of life that there is nothing more to be said about the grief of mankind at such moments as these.

"We got a pig on our tail," El Cuartalejo announced rudely.

They all looked around in unison, as if one neck had been ordered to swivel and one head had become alert to the ever-present dangers of life, and sure enough, there was that old red-white-and-blue anthem singing on the road behind them. The driver gunned it, and everyone slid sideways as he hit a corner going sixty miles per hour.

"What the hell?!"

"They recognize the van!" the warrior screamed.

"Damn!"

"Pigs just hassle us for nothin'!!"

It was Kit Carson screaming after Geronimo all over again. They went up a side street and down a dirt road.

Dogs jumped frantically out of the way and a jackrabbit
darted in front of them and they startled each other—its
eyes were glowing in the dark like a sorceror's. Things flew
up on the road all around them, and it looked like curtains
as the big supercharged cop car was almost right on the tail
of the clattering old van, and they could feel the hot breath
of the pursuer snorting fire from his nostrils.

"Where's Arroyo Seco?!"

"Turn up here!"

"Where?!"

"What?!"

Just when it looked like the cavalry had 'em cold they
went through an intersection on a deserted country road
and saw another Defender of Freedom madly chasing another Reject of Society and everyone slammed brakes,
swerved recklessly, because, as they could all see, there was
no way the two chases were going to miss each other.

"Watch out!"

You know how it always seems like a big truck coming
the other way always seems to get at a little narrow bridge
at exactly the same time you get there? No matter how
desolate the highway has been for hours, on one of those
endless roads in the west, and you're sure you're gonna die
as the fucking semi-trailer misses you by two inches and
blows you sideways as it roars by at about 190 miles per
hour? Well, that's how things seemed at this particular junction of our story. Zip! Zip! Zip! And the other old clunker
(full of Chicanos shooting the finger out the windows?)
zipped just in front of the van, the van zipped perpendicu-
larly just in front of the other cop car, it zipped just in
front of the final cop car chasing the van (all of this a
beautiful maneuver worthy of the U.S. Air Force Thunderbirds showing off at an Air Show), but, darnit, the last cop
caught the last corner of the rear bumper of the second-
to-last cop and, I swear to God, the two cars went flying in
formation up and over the road like two airplanes soaring
off into The Wild Blue Yonder.

"YA HA HA HOOOOOOOOOOOOOOOOOOOOOOOOOOOO
OOOOOOOOO!!!!!"

On occasions like this I'm reminded of Goofy in the old
cartoons when he screams as he goes flying off a cliff or

something. Remember? That's what them cops sounded like as they did a few loop-de-loops and barrel-rolls; and they might have even tried for a cloverleaf in the sky if they had had a little more loft on their takeoff.

"YOW WOW WOW WWOOOOOOOOOOOOOOOOOOOOO OOOOOOOOOOOOOOOOOWW!!!!!"

But they finally had to quit clowning around and come back down to earth. Miraculously, both cars landed on their wheels right in front of each other, a hundred yards away in a cow pasture, bounced violently about a dozen times, and then stopped cold. They sat stone silent in the dark, and only a little steam was coming up out of the enraged bowels of the vehicles and a little cloud of dust around them. Luckily, the teeth of one Officer had flown up to the ceiling and his neck had stretched about two inches, but otherwise he was okay. The other Officer was not so lucky, as they had to perform surgery later to remove his seat belt where it had become embedded into his skin. But everyone who observed the condition of the vehicles later, and heard the story of the Miracle, admitted that the Creator must have been in a very forgiving frame of mind that evening. He might have had a soft spot in His heart for pigs, as He knew they were only the stooges of the Exploiters and other Rich Bad Guys.

The two other (unscathed) barnstormers stopped and watched the spectacular stunt. They applauded. It was really very impressive. Very professional. Then they drove off in their opposite directions, and the quiet night was left to its own resources again. A few magpies went over to investigate the accident, but otherwise the two immobile cavalry detachments were just another footnote in history sitting lost and forgotten in just another empty pasture.

Grampa said, a few miles down the road, "We better get out up here."

"Huh?"

"We should hightail it by foot."

"Yeah," Jusepe agreed. He leaned up to El Cuartalejo and explained. "We'll hole up over at No Tongue's. You know where that is, don't ya?"

"Yeah," the big warrior nodded. "I'll go over to Taos Pueblo and hook up with the troops there."

"And tell 'em where we are," Old Codger added. "We'll have to get scouts and messengers going back and forth."

"Yeah."

"Cops'll be everywhere."

They pulled over and chewed over a few more details, and agreed it was wisest to light out across country. Philbert couldn't believe they were going to have to walk. No one had very heavy coats on or anything; just some crummy old things they'd scrounged up at Picuris which had been scrounged up at secondhand stores around. But he and Sky and Jane and Jennifer and Jusepe and Grampa Jimmy and Old Codger and Old Girl all hitched up their socks and buttoned down their collars and thanked the driver for all his help. He thanked them, too, and then disappeared off into the great uncertainty of civilization again. They stood out in the cold black expanse in the middle of somewhere and shivered. It was cold. It was spooky. It was lonely.

"I feel better already," Old Girl declared.

They didn't have a damn thing to their names. They didn't have a pot to piss in. Grampa had even given his seventy-four big ones to El Cuartalejo. They started tromping across the road and went northwest.

Philbert had a lot of questions. "But what about the others?"

"Like I told ya," Grampa explained in the dark, "that was the intersection back there where we was supposed to meet 'em."

"You didn't tell me that."

"Well, I meant to. I forgot, in all the excitement."

Philbert stopped walking. "I can't leave Bonnie behind."

"She wasn't there."

"And besides," Old Codger added, "them cops are there now. Ambulances and god knows what all else will be there by now."

"If their radios are still workin'," Old Girl allowed.

"It'll be okay," Jusepe said, stopped beside Philbert and the kids. "She's with Storyteller, and he has a lot of power."

"And Violetta and the other women were gonna hook up with them," Old Girl said kindly. "They know where to go."

"They'll find us."

"Out here? How?"

"Hau," Grampa answered, acknowledging the Indian greeting in the affirmative.

The Elders all acted like that settled it and they kept on walking quickly like they knew where they were going. Philbert carried Jane on his shoulder for a while, then switched over to Sky for a while, reluctantly following the oldtimers out across the barren sagebrush. Little patches of snow muddied up the passage, and he often stumbled in the dark, but the great genius of Philbert Bono (whose Indian name was Whirlwind) was his great trust in the Old Ways. He didn't know where in the hell he was and he didn't see how his darling Bonnie could ever find them now, but she was with that Storyteller fella, who seemed to be holding some aces up his sleeve (although he often acted like he wasn't playing with a full deck either), and the others, and the Elders seemed absolutely confident that everything would be okay, too, so he bided his time. What else could he do?

Over hill and under dale they trudged in the dark. They went up rocky slopes. They stumbled down through cactus patches. Cockleburrs clung to their pants by the dozens and thorn bushes grabbed at their sleeves.

"How far is it?" Phil asked after an hour. The kids weighed heavily on his back now, very heavily, as Jennifer was taking her turn.

"Oh, 'bout only another four or five miles," Old Girl answered cheerfully. She was a short, round, plump old gal in a faded ugly dress and tennis shoes on her dark brown legs, a long old Salvation Army overcoat hanging down to her knees.

Phil tried not to groan, as he couldn't let an old woman outwalk him. He was supposed to be a young buck, after all. If his big heart was working overtime and his lungs pounded like drums, that was his fault for being so fat and out of shape. Hell, he'd never been *in* shape, probably not even when he was a baby. He regretted all those combination pizzas now, and all those Milk Duds and Jujubes he'd eaten; Bonnie would kill him for backsliding on his diet like that. He let Sky and Jane and Jennifer walk for a while, as his back was shrieking to be put out of its misery, but the selfish children clamored to be carried again, shameless about their poor physical conditions and bad city upbringing. Grampa gallantly hoisted Jane up on his shoulders like she only weighed about a pound, Jusepe hoisted Sky, and Old Codger hoisted Jennifer. The kids then actually slept in the cold darkness. Oh, it was beautiful too. It was icy. It could kill you and not think once about it.

They went down a very, very steep slope and rocks rolled all around them as they half-slid/half-ran down the dangerous thing. The kids didn't even wake up. Phil took over carrying Sky, to prove how tough he was, and the boy weighed about three hundred pounds. He hung limply like a huge lump of extra fat on top of Phil, but down they went, down, down, like they were descending into the Inferno. It was an impossible decline in his mind, too, and panic swept through him suddenly as he felt a shiver of terror run through him: maybe these foreigners were evil and were going to kill him or torture him! He began to really doubt these old people. Who were they anyway? He didn't know them. Maybe they were crazy. They didn't know where they were going. If they were so all-fired smart, why were the Indians all screwed up and going down the toilet for the last hundred years? They would get them all killed, if Phil didn't break his neck first. He could see it now—he would be paralyzed for the rest of his life, a vegetable in some foul Indian Health Services hospital, drooling his Jell-O off onto his starched hospital nightgown and blubbering some unintelligible nonsense to some indifferent nurse. That's if he didn't die right out here on this crazy plateau or whatever it was right now, first. He could see himself launching off a cliff like one of those divers down in Acapulco and splattering on the rocks below. Where were they? He wanted to cry. But no, down they went, down they kept going, rocks and stickers jabbing at him, sliding on his fat butt, a mountain as indifferent to his intense discomfort as that nurse in the IHS hospital.

He heard a funny noise, like wind rushing through trees.

"There it is," Grampa said, down below him.

"What?" Philbert dared gasp aloud. He couldn't see a goddamn thing.

They stumbled and slid and slithered a few more hundred yards (it seemed like hundreds of miles), and then it leveled off and the funny rushing of wind grew louder. He saw an ancient man waving at them from the doorway of what looked like a sod house, but it could just as well have been a mound of mud or a big rock for all the difference it made in this weird landscape. There were no lights or moon anywhere, but somehow something was reflecting some kind of illumination that he could see, sort of. Then he realized that they were next to a river and it was glowing from some internal source.

"What's that?"

Grampa chortled in the dark. "The Rio Grande. We're safe now."

6

HOW THE TERRORISTS
MANIPULATED THE RUNNING
DOGS IN THE MEDIA,
AND OF A GENERAL ALARM
FOR OUTSIDE AGITATORS.

BUDDY RED BIRD SMILED AT THE TELEVISION CAMERAS AS they prepared for the press conference at eight o'clock sharp the next morning, oozing his characteristic charm. He was wearing a beautiful costume of traditional Taos serapes and squashblossoms and a lot of other really cool stuff. The females in the Press Corps were especially turned on by the handsome son of a bitch, who could have been a soap opera star if he had wanted to. He had summoned them here at the central council chamber in the picturesque Taos Pueblo and, boy, were they getting some great background shots to insert later. Buddy sat at a table with a number of handsome Indian Elders in gorgeous costumes, and they all looked appropriately concerned and solemn. When everything was set and everybody was ready, Buddy began:

"I'd like to read a prepared statement, and then you can ask questions. Five hundred years ago this continent was invaded by criminals and buccaneers frcm Europe. You were welcomed on these shores by Arawak and Carib Indians, whom your Spanish and Dutch and English ancestors promptly butchered or carried off in slavery back to London and Lisbon, to entertain your queens and kings. You were starving to death in New England and New France, and when Hurons and Squantos fed you, you turned around in gratitude and burned whole villages alive, and then gave Thanksgiving for it. For almost five hundred years we have seen the paradise that was this land systematically turned into a running sewer by your ancestors. We have seen tens of millions of Mexican Indians and Pawnees and Mandans and California Indians murdered in the name of Jesus Christ and John D. Rockefeller. You've had your bloody half a millennium, but it's over. The party's over, America. The rent is due. We, the hundreds of indigenous sovereign nations on this hemisphere, from the Arctic to the Antarctic, declare guerrilla warfare against you. Go home, Yankees. Before you kill every last living thing on this beautiful, beautiful planet of ours!"

Everyone in the room was crying. Then Buddy asked, "Any questions?"

"That's a very lopsided version of history," one whiteman in the Corps said, unimpressed and angered.

"So is yours," Buddy clipped.

"You say you are going to war?" the man insisted. "Does that mean you will persist in more acts of violence such as we have seen in New Mexico over the last week since you got here, Mr. Red Bird?"

"We can't hope to fight you with guns," Buddy replied calmly. "If great Warriors and Chiefs like Popeé and Sitting Bull and Tecumseh and Leonard Peltier and Tupu Amaru couldn't defeat you, when you had many fewer and inferior weapons, we can't possibly go up against your B-1B Bombers and Minuteman ICBMs and laser death-rays. No, we will shoot you with these television cameras, with electric guitars, with printing presses. We will beat you this time, because, for the first time, we have the technological means at our disposal to get the truth out. Yes, the Truth. That is our nuclear arsenal, Sir, and it is infinitely more powerful than all your hundreds of billions of dollars you spend every year for the Pentagon and the Propaganda Ministry

91

and the Secret Police. We will make documentaries about the sterilization of Indian women, just as the Nazis did in their own death camps, only in this country the death camps are called Reservations, and Barrios, and Harlem, Watts, South Chicago. We will sing songs for your children about the drug deals the CIA is making with fascist dictators around the world. We will get on television, we will plug into the personal home computers, we will infiltrate the very airwaves and brainwaves of the human race, and there isn't anything you can do about it."

"Buddy," one woman asked quietly, tears in her eyes, "can't you see that there are many people in this country who sympathize with your Cause? And that—"

"Yes, we do. But you are also patronizing us. Is it your 'Cause' when you have to go out and get a job and feed your children? I'm asking you a question."

"Well . . . I don't understand what you mean."

"This is our lives, not our 'Cause.' We don't want to fight you. We just want to live in peace, like you. But every time one of you liberals chooses to sit at home and complain, instead of going out there in the street and put your rear end on the line, then we lose a little more faith in you. We're tired of talk. We're tired of writing to our congressmen. The politicians are all a pack of crooks, as far as we can see. Your whole program is a failure, and we just can't afford to let you destroy the water and air anymore. It's a matter of courage, Ma'am. Yes, we are all, the good people of the world, up against a few really rotten bastards out there. But the bastards are winning because the good guys are cowards. It's easier to talk about saving the environment and going to meetings and circulating petitions, but what Indians have always known is that until individual courage is put on the line, evil will have its way. You may die, you may lose your job if you speak out against your boss who is dumping garbage in the Ohio River, but you'll die anyway if you don't, sooner or later."

One of the Taos Elders spoke up. "We want to get rid of the Tribal Council governments, which are killing us. We want to go back to our old Elders' Councils, which kept us alive for many hundreds of years. We lived in balance with nature. We listened to the plants and animals, and they told us what to do. Now, most of the plants are gone and we have nothing to teach us what to do next. All that is left are a few animals and the moon."

"But you can't just . . . go to war," the whiteman argued again. "It's absurd."

"Yes, it is," Buddy replied. "I know your wisemen in New York and Washington won't take us seriously out here. You're too full of the inevitability of your industrial progress, and the lies about democracy and reason which you have built up all around you for hundreds of years, like those buttresses on the cathedrals of Notre Dame and Cologne. I've been to Europe. Like Red Cloud and Geronimo I was taken to your great cities and I saw the hopelessness of opposing your wealth and power too. I went to Yale and studied political science. I went to Vietnam and studied about what the economics of capitalism and communism are all about. I saw your culture in the bloody fields of An Luac and Bien Hoa. I was at the Wounded Knee Siege in South Dakota. I've visited the battlefields of Antietam; I know how ruthless you are in the defense of your delusions."

The press conference was a flop. Neither side managed to persuade the other, or to really understand the other. Hundreds of years of ignorance cannot be overcome by a few impassioned words on the local and national news. Buddy would probably become famous, but only, in the mind's eyes of most Americans, as a successor to other rabblerousers like Malcolm X and Dennis Banks. If a few iconoclastic pundits might have compared him favorably to Uncle Sam Adams or Eugene V. Debs, then it would have been a caustic comparison, and, if you had dug beneath the surface, you would probably discover the pundits preferred the calmer John to the crazier Sam of the semi-divine Adams clan.

Be that as it may, the police (both local and federal, if you want to know the truth of the situation) were much more active in pursuit of Buddy Red Bird's truths than the media were. The guy had broken laws, regardless of his reasons for them, and this is, as all the millions of citizens in American prisons and jails know full well, a Nation of Laws. The boys at the J. Edgar Hoover building in D.C.

assured the boys in the Justice Department and National
Security Administration (and half a dozen other bogus
fronts) that the Indians had close links to Libya and Cuba
and Nicaragua. This was exactly the kind of thing their
provocateurs and informants in the American Indian Movement had assured them could never happen. Not that the
boys who ran the country were worried. Oh no! They
laughed over their brandy and cigars that evening. A few
raggedy Indians weren't going to be able to touch them.
Maybe they'd have to allow a slight trickle of funds to go
out to the endowments and foundations to fund a few worthy Indian organizations, to show their good faith and the
inherent efficacy of the USA, and Peter Jennings would be
glad to do a few features full of his confidence in his inevitability as a whiteman. Lo, the poor conditions on the reservations and the miserable health standards of the Indian
Health Services and the Bureau of Indian Affairs—harrumph! harrumph! Something appropriate along those
lines.

Buddy knew he had his work cut out for him. He knew
it would be an uphill battle against the entrenched ideas of
America: such as the fine subtleties of ideas like Democracy
and Jesus that had been pounded into the masses for
centuries.

Rabbit watched him. She asked, when they finally got
alone in their room down one of the labyrinths of the
Pueblo, "It's not going to go to your head, is it?"

He gave her a long, slow look. "Ten years ago it would,
and certainly fifteen years ago it did. We screwed up a lot,
in AIM. We sold our people out a lot, just for our egos.
They waved huge amounts of money in our faces, and we
were just men. We were weak. We yielded to temptation.
Some of the leaders actually betrayed the People. I don't
know, Rabbit. I don't think so, this time. It's too late.
There's too much to lose."

She gave him a long, tight hug. She was alarmed to feel
his weakness, as if the strength was being sapped out of his
bones. She sighed and smiled bravely. "How about if we get
on the phone and call our friends? I knew Big Lester in
Texas might spring for a few grand, or ten, for gas money

to get your Warriors in Pine Ridge and Lame Deer down here. Whadda ya think?"

"Yeah, okay. We'll get on the phone."

"Good. There's a lot of Warriors out there."

"Yeah."

7

OF THE DESCENT
OF THE SACRED WOMAN INTO
THE UNDERWORLD, AND OF
HER ADVENTURES WITH THE
NECROMANCER.

PHILBERT WAS DREAMING. IF HE THOUGHT THAT HE SAW A blond woman saying something to him somewhere, on a mountain slope in Mexico maybe, then it was probably all just a part of his continuing fantasy about being a Warrior and a real Indian and everything. You and I know what a complete putz he is, right? Nobody this idiotic could be in the same league as the great Cheyenne Chiefs like Little Wolf and Morning Star and Roman Nose. So let the moron dream about beautiful blonds in the fantastical dream-world, and let them speak mysterious messages to him. We know it's a dream, even if he doesn't.

He woke up suddenly and bumped his head on a shelf hanging over him. "Ow." It was a collision with his re-awakening. It was the same morning that Buddy was off declaiming to the world, but Philbert was on a dirt floor in the corner of a tiny adobe shack under some wooden shelves and behind an old bed made out of deer and buf-falo hides. He ached from the tip of his little toe to the top of his big ears (from his long hike last night). He groaned feebly. He yawned and his jaw ached. He wondered about the half-remembered dream, which was already disappearing into the passing seconds of consciousness. He picked his nose. He scratched his balls. All the usual things we all go through every morning.

Then, with a pang of real pain, he remembered Bonnie. "Hey," he exclaimed, looking around for her. Where was Bonnie? He saw Old Girl over in a corner of the shack cutting up something on a crummy little handmade wooden table, and putting it in a big pot cooking on a wood-burning stove under a tiny window. She was humming some old Indian song. She was scratching her ass. She brushed her gray hair out of her eyes. She ignored Philbert.

Bright sunlight was streaming in the window. The white rays of Grandfather rested on another old wobbly wooden table and two rickety chairs. A mess of herbs and plants were piled on the table. A buffalo skull hung on the wall, and a lot of other sacred objects, like eagle feathers and tobacco pouches and a lance too. A lot of coyote bones and wolf skulls and a fox head with its eyeballs and fur still on it lay all over the place. An old photograph of Geronimo with another Indian was thumbtacked on a wooden wall next to shelves laden with jars full of red spices, beige seeds, beans, leaves, and grasses. A huge string of red peppers hung on the wall, and ears of multicolored maize, and a pile of squash. The place smelled of good piñon smoke and tobacco.

Philbert had to take an urgent pee so he crawled to his feet like a badger crawling out of his hole. He tossed the holey brown army blanket off him and pulled on his baggy jeans. His dick flopped out of the pup tent of his white boxer shorts and he quickly stuck it back in, hoping Old Girl hadn't seen it.

"Good afternoon," she said, not even turning to look at him.

"Oh . . . uh . . . good . . . is it . . ."

He really had to take a whizz so he hunkered outside, working the rusty door handle out of its slot and stepping into the sunshine.

Boy, was it a pretty day. He went around the corner of

97

the house to take his leak, only to stumble right on top of
Grampa and Jusepe and Old Codger and the ancient old
man he had seen last night (who, until now, he had not
been sure was also a player in some dream), sitting on the
ground and jawing.

"Well, good afternoon," Grampa said, attempting the
same old joke.

"Yeah, uh, oh . . . What time is it?"

"Time?" Jusepe asked, a little annoyed about it. "There
ain't no time out here."

They all looked at the sun. It was just coming around the
cliffs over the Rio, blazing on the beautiful piñon and juniper groves along the river bottom. It's still morning, Philbert realized. The old guys laughed. He grinned sheepishly.
There's nothing more shameful than a city dude dragging
ass out of bed hours after the country know-it-alls have
been up since the chickens cockle-doodle-dood. Farmers
love to kid late sleepers like that, as if they're superior because of it or something. Myself, I'm a night person and I
don't see anything wrong with it.

But Philbert's bladder was about to pop so he tiptoed
barefooted back around the front of the house, stepping
lightly like an elk over the cold, snowy ground, and went
around to the other side. There he found Sky and Jane
and Jennifer playing contentedly with some colored balls
made out of wood.

"Oh, you're up," they said.

"Hi."

Sky gave him a tight hug around the waist and he was
sure that would do it. Piss would burst out of him like a
water balloon and it would all be over. "Daddy, can you—"

"Daddy?"

"—take me over to the hot springs that No Tongue says
is over there?"

"Oh, uh, yeah, maybe later." Phil scurried frantically over
behind a pine tree and unzipped. The kids followed him
and watched. "Hey."

"And you know what?"

His teeth were floating as he whipped it out. Well, they'd
just have to learn that there was nothing wrong with taking
a leak. It was natural. "What?"

"Well, uh, you know what?"

"What?" Urine gushed out of him like a fire hose and sprayed a two-foot circumference five feet away. The children were impressed.

"Dad? Daddy?"

"Ahhhh . . . what?"

They watched the pee soak a big circle of snow down to the ground, revealing pine needles and yellow grass underneath. Phil groaned as he felt his stomach expand again as room was made for it, now that his bladder was easing off. His mind was coming back into focus too. Steam rose up from the spray. It kept gushing unbelievably, without a letup.

"Can we?" Sky asked.

"Who's . . . No Tongue? The old man?"

"Of course," Jane answered, fascinated with his big wiener.

"No Tongue, huh?"

"Yeah, can we?"

"What?"

"Go over to the hot springs!" the boy repeated in exasperation.

"Oh, there's a hot springs around here?"

"YES!" the three kids snarled irritably.

The current kept pouring undiminished out across the crisp air. Coherence was returning to Philbert's mind. "Is your Mommy here?"

"No, but you know what—"

"No?"

"—we found a—"

"Where is she?" he asked.

"I dunno."

The stream finally slowed down and Philbert could breathe again. He felt better. It trickled down to nothing and then he became aware again of how stiff he was all over. His bare feet were turning bright red in the snow and he was cold in his black-and-white Mimbres T-shirt. A light northerly breeze blew off the big deep river, which ran deep and green in this narrow gorge.

"Jane is looking at yer wiener," Jennifer tattletaled.

"Oh . . . sorry," was all he could think of to say, as he

99

absentmindedly put his wiener back in his shorts and zipped up.

The children giggled. "You're funny," Jane said.

"I am not," he joked.

"Yes you are," Jennifer insisted.

"Did you say your prayers this morning?" he asked.

They looked confused. "No."

"Just say 'Thank you, Powers, for another beautiful day, and take care of Bonnie.' "

They made faces at this stupid suggestion and went back to playing with their balls. Philbert sighed, and danced like one of those hippos in *Fantasia* in a ballet over the cold ground. He went back around to where the men were jawing and sat on a rock next to them. They ignored him. They were talking in some old language that he didn't understand. He looked at the river, and the seagulls zooming over it, and the sparrows chasing around in the trees. The air was a brilliant blue and it seemed a lot warmer down here than it had up on the cliffs. He looked around behind him at the cliffs. It seemed impossible that they had come down them. They were straight up and down. There didn't seem to be any path. He rubbed his cold and sore feet. And this little house was almost invisible, even as he leaned against it. It was the color of the ground. It looked like a rock. It looked like a tree. He let his aboriginal imagination flow like the river and wondered if he was even here. The words of the men could have been the wind. Their language in his ear could have been birds singing. The patches of snow on the ground could have been sunspots in front of his eyes. The cold ground was a dream. The sunlight on his face couldn't be real.

He wondered idly if everybody had already eaten breakfast. Could he have slept through it? Unheard of. Or was he still sleeping? Implausible. And, most unrealistic of all, for the first time in his life (except for those three days of fantasy in bed with Bonnie, which were the greatest fantasy of all), he didn't think about food. For some reason he wasn't hungry. It was impossible. He didn't want to eat. Pure fiction. Maybe his insane mind was even trying to tell him that he should sacrifice a little until Bonnie found them—hopefully. He wanted to sacrifice. He wanted to be as simple as this spot. He wanted to get up early and be thin and strong like these old traditional men. He glanced admiringly at them. The one the kids called No Tongue was very, very old, but he was also very, very spry. He made no sounds at all, but he smiled constantly with a full set of teeth, and nodded and listened attentively. It was clear that Grampa and Jusepe and Old Codger were communicating with him somehow—not counting the quick, incessant hand signs they were all using. No Tongue had an elkbone knife, and he was whittling a small figure of a girl on a piece of cottonwood. He flashed quick signs with his knife—as if whittling words out of the air—and the other men answered with their hands and their tongues. But no, there was some other means of communication that was going on between them, and it wasn't exactly in their hands or their mouths, or even in their eyes, or their frequent laughter. It was as if they were listening to other voices from the squirrels and the hawks circling around the cliffs on the other side of the river, and they were seeing things in the breeze as it blew through the prickly cones above them in the trees. Voices and visions of other worlds floated all around the morning and rested like the clear air on the shoulders of these men, and Philbert had no doubt that they were good voices of the Other World creatures, and that these were holy men. He felt that he had been given a great honor to be able to sit here with them. Love filled his wonderful heart and he looked up at the beautiful white sun. He squinted and tears came in his eyes.

Then he heard the men laugh, and they were looking at him. He picked out words like "Cheyenne" and "Bonnie" in their conversation, and they were all looking at him. Jusepe said in English, "No Tongue likes you. He knew you were coming."

"Oh, uh . . ."

"He says we will have to do a lot of curing ceremonies to the Hactcins and Cheetins to bring your Bonnie here and to save her, if you want."

"Me? Uh, oh yeah. What are hacteens and—"

"Spirits," Grampa said seriously. It was strange to see him so serious. It was unusual.

"Hactcins," Old Codger corrected the pronunciation.

101

"The Black Hactcin is the Trickster," Jusepe explained.

"Oh," Philbert realized, "like the *maiyun* of the Cheyennes?"

"Be careful!" Grampa said suddenly, almost fiercely. "Be careful, my friend. That's all I can tell you. We know you are a sacred clown, and that is a very dangerous thing."

"What?"

But the old men were already busy with a ceremony and didn't explain anything else for him. The ceremony was simple. No Tongue drew a big circle on the ground in front of them, where the snow had been cleared away, with the wooden doll he had just carved. The circle had about a two-foot radius. Then he drew six legs coming out of it and a little square head at the top with two eyes in the head.

"This is the tricky spiderman," Jusepe explained to him. The kids wandered over and looked at it, and Old Girl came outside too. "It is a magic love charm. This design will now tie your soul to the girl's soul, and you can't help finding each other, wherever either one of you goes, and falling in love."

"But beware," Grampa warned sternly. "Are you sure you want to fall in love with this woman?"

Philbert got a real stupid look on his face. "Yes. With all my heart."

No Tongue suddenly grabbed Philbert's arm, squeezing it until it hurt, and pointed at the spider drawing in the dirt. Grampa said to him, "And Soul!" No Tongue slapped the doll sharply into Philbert's hand. Then he pointed to Phil's shoulder: a large black spider was floating down on a web out of nowhere and it landed on his shoulder.

"Don't touch it," Old Codger warned.

"LOOK!" Jusepe commanded. They all looked up, and high overhead an eagle was circling the house. Shivers ran through Philbert. He watched the spider on his shoulder. It didn't move.

Grampa stood up casually and yawned, back to his old relaxed manner. "I'm hungry. She'll be here pretty soon."

"It's ready," Old Girl replied, indicating the kitchen.

Everyone went inside to eat, except Philbert. He stayed with the spider and the eagle outside. It was now of paramount importance to him that Bonnie appear. Nothing else mattered to him anymore. If falling in love with her meant that he would have to miss an occasional meal, well, it was worth it. He listened and looked. He wouldn't eat, as a little sacrifice. He said a few silent prayers in his Tsistsistas and Suhtaio tongues, and made up a little song:

> *Noteh'mey messa*
> *Wihio Mahuts maiyuneo*
> *Piva!* Bonnie Red Bird! *Piva!*

Even when the odors of fried potatoes wafted out of the house and tempted him to float along with them, and then Grampa came out and smacked his lips and gloated at him, not even then did Philbert waver from his appointed task. The others all sat around him and waited.

An hour later, he saw Storyteller standing on the top of the cliff where the eagle finally circled out of sight, and at the point where the spiderweb might have been coming from.

"HO!" Storyteller shouted.

Philbert looked at his shoulder. The spider was gone.

"HO!" Jusepe shouted back, and they all ran up the cliff, even Philbert. Well, he didn't exactly hurry, and it was a pretty steep haul. The others, including the children, reached the top way before he did. It kept him in quite a bit of suspense to find out what was going on, as the others all disappeared from sight above him. But finally he crawled and gasped over the edge, and saw a sight that made his blood run cold.

Bonnie lay motionless on a burro. She looked dead. The Elders were just lifting her off the tiny gray animal as I finished a long explanation. "—I didn't see who or what did it."

Old Girl looked at No Tongue. "La Llorona?" she asked, frightened.

No Tongue shrugged. He was more concerned about getting Bonnie off the burro. The men carried her toward the invisible path down the cliff.

Philbert was in a panic. Bonnie was white as death. "What's . . . what happened to her—"

103

"We don't know yet, Son," Jusepe explained. "It's bad, though."

"Maybe one of the witches that are out in these mountains," Old Girl whispered. She was plainly in shock, and very scared.

Grampa was organizing the descent to the cabin. "You kids stay up here until we're down with her, or you'll knock rocks all over us. Stay up here."

Jane was crying. "I wanna be with my mommy."

"What's the matter with her?" Sky asked.

"She's sick," Old Girl explained to the stricken boy, hugging him.

The children watched Grampa and Jusepe take Bonnie over the edge and out of sight. I took Philbert aside. "There's . . . I don't know how to explain this, Philbert. It's like there's a piece of glass in her forehead."

"What? How—"

"Something, or someone, stuck a sliver of something into her brain. That's all I can figure out. Jusepe said that's right."

Philbert felt his throat constricting. It wasn't possible. What were they talking about?

Old Girl looked across the barren sagebrush to the south, back toward the mountains of Taos. "Someone's coming."

They could see half a dozen figures approaching on horseback. They were running, and soon the sounds of hooves pounded the ground. Violetta pulled up on a brown horse with no saddle. Five other women were with her, including a few whom Philbert recognized from Picuris. Violetta asked Old Girl anxiously, "How is she?"

"Still alive, but just barely."

The pronouncement sent a convulsion through Philbert.

Violetta dismounted and gave orders to the other women. "Corral the horses over there and set up the *curanderia* circle! We have to hurry!" Then she turned to the others. "We found your horses, Storyteller," she told me.

"Oh, good. I found this old burro and carried her here on it."

"Good," Violetta breathed, watching the other women lead the horses to a fenced corral that Philbert had not seen before. It blended right into the landscape. "And another set of prints too. Of a mare, I think. We trailed her, and found Goost-cha-du panting in the trees where we had chased her."

"Oh no!" Old Girl sobbed, stricken with horror. "Are you sure? Goost-cha-du herself?"

"Yes," one of the other women answered as she walked over. It was Tonita Veneno from Picuris. "She's my sister."

Violetta interrogated me. "What did you see? It's important that you tell us exactly."

"I couldn't see much in the dark, but I'm sure there was a black horse, a night mare. And then the next thing . . . There's no other way to describe it except that . . . it was a woman all of a sudden. She was wearing a black shawl and black dress."

"Just like the little Christian ladies at Mass every morning," Tonita whispered angrily.

"Yes, that's her," Violetta said. "Now think: did she say anything?"

"Yes."

"What?"

"What did her voice sound like?"

"I don't know. It was like ice cracking under a river," I answered. "I couldn't hear the words. I was running through the trees as it was, and it's lucky I found Bonnie at all. I saw that . . . creature bending over her and I shouted. It ran away."

"Yeah," Violetta groaned, taking a huge deep breath. "We saw the horse run across the road. We almost hit it in my car. We were looking for you."

"I was afraid of something like this," Old Girl cried.

"Who is . . . what was her name?" I asked.

"Goost-cha-du," Violetta said, staring across the prairie.

"The most powerful sorceror in these mountains," Old Girl added.

"Why?" Philbert asked.

They all looked at him, then they looked at the children. Jane was crying too. Tonita tried to explain gently, "She was my sister, once. We grew up together at Isleta Pueblo, down by Albuquerque. She was always very smart, but strange. Standoffish. She became very religious and wanted to become a nun."

"As we all did, probably," another woman commented.
The horses were all corralled now.

"Yeah," Tonita agreed. She was a pretty lady of about
fifty, short and very very dark, almost black. "We went to
Mass every day and took Communion, everything. Confes-
sion of our sins, every day. Every little thing was a sin to
Felicia. That was her name. Every little thought, like about
sex or any kind of pleasure, even a little bit of happiness
like eating one of the delicious tortillas our mother made
for us, Felicia thought it was a sin. I don't know." She was
crying.

I looked down the cliff. "We can go down now. It's clear."

"Okay," Violetta commanded. She was clearly in charge
of the women. "We'll spread out and make a circle up here,
on both sides of the river."

Old Girl nodded understanding. She led the children
down the cliff, and the men followed. I stayed behind Philbert, who looked very upset. Sobered.

I spoke as we stumbled down the path. "Those women
are a curing society, Brother. They'll protect us now from
Goost-cha-du and her followers."

"There are others?"

"Yes."

Philbert wanted to scream out "WHY?! WHY?! WHY?!"
but he knew how Indians felt about witchcraft. He had
been around it all his life. White people dismissed it all
as superstition, but I can tell you, the Christians are the
superstitious ones, not us. We have always known there are
complex Other Worlds right beside this one, and an infinite
complex of other types of Beings on this world, of inorganic
as well as organic matter, but you brought all this suppres-
sion and disease about The Devil to our hemisphere. You
brought the sickness of guilt and sin with your missionaries.
We knew about the abuses of Power such as sorcerors have
always been prone to, and there are indeed many terrors
and dangers lying in wait on the edge of reality and normal
sanity, but God Damn It, you brought the profound disqui-
etude of Franciscan *maleficiadores* and their Inquisition, their
tortured fears of bewitchment that resulted in the black
magic that resulted in the Church's orgies of bloodletting
against so-called heretics and witches and were-animals.

106

You're the sick fucking savages, not us! I won't even go into the way the monks and friars ripped unborn babies out of the wombs of Indian women, just because some man lusted after her and she rejected him. You can read your own documented history. It's all there in black and white.

Don't tell me about Indians running naked on the prairies killing animals and eating them raw, or taking scalps.

I'm sorry, I can't find anything funny about this. Evil is one thing I respect, and there are no jokes available in my quiver. I love Bonnie with all my heart and soul, too, and I can feel Philbert's tears and horror as he saw her lying on No Tongue's bed in his shack. Can you imagine what it would be like to see the first and only human being who ever loved you lying there dying of five hundred years of Genocide? I am sobbing out on the dirt with Philbert too. I can't see or think through the veil of my grief. How could you do this to us? How could you let the pirates and Jimmy Swaggarts and Popes and Tammy Faye Bakkers run rampant over our beautiful forests and valleys? When are you going to sit on the railroad tracks and stop the missiles, like that great and brave Vietnam Vet did, even if it means the engineers of the Holocaust run over you and cut off your legs! That man should be elected your President.

Dozens of Indians arrived throughout the day to help Bonnie. Very elaborate curing societies exist in the American Southwest: how else could they have survived the deliberate attempt at annihilation that was the official policy of the Government of the United States of America? By all rights, all the Indians should have been dead by now. Most Americans wish we were. But somehow, we've got to be the toughest people who've ever lived. And if there are powerful women like Goost-cha-du who grew up to be evil, well, I don't blame that holy little girl whose name was once Felicia. I'm not saying that Indians are all good and righteous all the time; absolutely not. Nobody is more disgusted with the way Indians have screwed up than I am. Indians are just about the biggest fuckups I've ever seen. But at least they don't go around raping entire continents and annihilating whole species of plant and animal life, and then tell themselves what great and good fellers they are!

The curing societies did everything they could to protect

107

Bonnie, throughout the night, but it wasn't enough, and they knew it. The Elders talked long and hard about it all night, and into the next morning. Runners fanned out all over Indian Country to carry the news of the crisis.

It was Violetta who noticed Philbert. He was still lying prostrate out on the cold, wet ground, down by the river. He had been listening to the water rushing past, lapping at the sand and rocks and overhanging tree branches dancing along the surface of the water. He had been thinking about the star nations, while all the time trying to burrow into the dirt like a worm. He felt lower than the lowest bug. In his hunger, he tried to conjure up the spider's power again, but nothing came. He lay beside the spider drawing in the dirt No Tongue had drawn, but nothing happened. When Violetta sat down beside him, and stared at the river, he looked through sorrow-stained eyes at her. She shook her head in response to his silent question.

Old Girl came over and sat beside them. "We've burned sage to drive out the bad spirits, and sweetgrass to attract the good ones. Jusepe gave her horsemint tea and smart-weed as she lay in the thick buffalo robe. She sipped it weakly, and opened her eyes, her eyelids as thin as flower petals."

She is getting as thin and transparent as last night's wax-ing moon, Violetta thought.

Old Girl kept talking, as if it would help. "We purged her with red oak and the blossoms of prairie clover and gave her half a teaspoon of a melon emetic. We made her chew the purple lily and the muskrat food, sweetflag, for her fever."

"The foreign sliver has to come out," Violetta barely breathed. "It has to come out."

No Tongue came over and everyone else was following him. He roughly grabbed Philbert's wrist and looked inquir-ingly, angrily, at his empty hand.

Philbert didn't understand. Grampa almost snarled at him, "Where's the doll we gave you?!"

"I didn't . . ." he muttered. He couldn't remember what happened to it. He looked around foolishly in the dirt for it.

Grampa slapped him hard in the face. "Idiot! Fat pig! You've killed her!"

The women recoiled in horror at this cruelty, and Philbert howled wildly and his eyes rolled into the back of his head.

He felt himself falling into a black bottomless pit, howling like an animal. The pit glistened like the shiny silvery glass shard that he imagined was in Bonnie's brain. It was a hideous Night Mare. It didn't burn with devils like the hell of the Christians, but it was, nevertheless, a dank Underworld like the inner bowels of the earth, like the inside of a volcano at the end of a long tunnel, bloody with the pain and curse that comes with all sacred things. It was a river of blood that is inside all women, and at the end of it he imagined, or dreamed, that he saw Bonnie tumbling head over heels, screaming as she fell toward the mouth of a Necromancer, a dead body opening its mouth to swallow her whole and forever. He was like a cruel eagle, or some kind of predator that kills in the mysterious way of the universe.

He knew with absolute certainty that he was a Spirit named Whirlwind now, and that, if he could only keep breathing and reach out and grab her, if he could catch her in the mad headlong plummeting down toward the foul mouth of the Eagle waiting to devour them both, he could save her. And himself. He stretched with all his being, but she was still out of reach. He couldn't do it. Everything went black.

8

HOW THE WARRIORS PURGED
THE LAND OF EVIL.

BUDDY WAS SITTING IN THE MIDDLE OF A MEETING AT TAOS
Pueblo the next morning when the runner arrived from
No Tongue's place. The meeting was a total disaster. Everybody was arguing. Goddamn Indians, Buddy thought. Always this same damned selfishness and jealousy. Everyone
wanted to be the chief, everyone wanted it done their way.
One family had a vendetta against another, and you would
never get them to agree about anything, or work together,
even if it was a matter of life or death.

Buddy watched as the runner, a young kid of about sixteen who had obviously been running long and hard from
somewhere, passed on a message to one of El Cuartalejo's
lieutenants, the lieutenant whispered a message to his boss,
and Tommy leaned over and whispered something in Buddy's ear.

Buddy immediately jumped up and ran out of the meeting room. Some of the would-be chiefs in the room were

glad to see him go; others stopped arguing and wondered what was up.

In the office, Rabbit was sitting alone, staring at a notepad in front of the telephone, which she had been on for two days. Big Les was sending ten grand right away, and she was sending it on to the troops in South Dakota and Montana and Colorado who would soon be on their way. Despite all these developments, Rabbit was sitting there crying, for no reason, when Buddy ran in the room. She was just crying, for no reason.

When he saw the state she was in, he passed right on through without saying a word.

In five more minutes he was running outside with his boots on and a warm coat. He picked a fifteen-year-old gelding that was the leader of the herd of mares, which was unusual. He was a proud, plain-colored horse named Cimarron who loved to run. Buddy had been riding him around yesterday and they hit it off pretty well. One of the Taos Elders said he could use him if he wanted. He borrowed a saddle and was almost done with the cinch when El Cuartalejo and a dozen other men found him.

"You can't get out of here, Buddy!" El Cuartalejo explained, hurrying over to the tackle shed. "You know they've got the whole village cordoned off, waiting for us to—"

"I'm not asking anybody to go with me," Buddy muttered. It was plain he was determined about something, and very upset.

El Cuartalejo put his hand gently on his friend's arm. "I know how you feel, Brother. I have sisters too. But—"

Buddy swung up on the horse and galloped away without another word. The other warriors looked at each other, and then ran for all the spare bridles. There were some good mares perking up their ears in the corral. They knew that gelding and wanted to go with him.

Taos Pueblo was completely surrounded by cops and media. The cops hadn't gone in to arrest the known felons because some bleeding-heart Jew lawyers had them tied up in court somehow, over jurisdiction or something; and besides, the media were watching the cops almost as closely as the cops were watching the Indians. There was sure a lot of peek-a-boo going on in the Land of the Free.

Then a lone horseman burst out of the crumbling mud city behind some crummy old trees and jumped an irrigation ditch, took a sharp bolt to the right, and then the left, and was through the "cordon" before the Boys in Blue could put down their coffee cups. The rider tore off across an open field, in clear range of fifty rifle scopes. Did they pick him off, like in the movies? Did they drop him as they had often imagined at the Police Practice Range? Nope. There were too many bleeding-heart Eastern cameras around. The rider headed straight west, across the edge of Taos, and toward the Rio Grande, ten miles to the west.

But the cops didn't know where he was going, or who he was. They were still back at the cordon around the Pueblo, running around in circles. When another batch of lunatics dashed past the Jeeps and TV vans, it got downright comical, all over again.

I'll spare you the details of the farce, and relate only that Buddy crossed the main highway and threw the steady traffic of civilization into a tizzy. It wasn't often that the happy tourists saw a wild Indian dash across their path on a horse that looked like it was actually enjoying running at a reckless headlong pace over the hills and through the woods. And then before they could even get their Kodaks and Polaroids out, a dozen more lunatics charged past and completely disrupted the normal routine. Where were they all going? Are they *real* Indians, Daddy? Why are you getting so mad, Mommy?

Buddy heard a church bell clang somewhere off to his left, and it sent waves of cosmic reverberation through his cranium. He galloped down a side road and saw a big new Mormon Church sitting on a lovely hillside with landscaped gardens all around it. It was made of the finest red brick. It had a tall white wooden steeple rising three stories toward Heaven. A magnificent set of bells (from Germany, in case you're interested) rang out an inspiring chorus of "The Lord's Prayer" over loudspeakers for the whole Valley to hear.

For Thine Is The Kingdom
And the Power and the Glory
For-EVVVVVVVEEEEEEEEEEEEERR

It drove the Indian crazy (as it was meant to). Buddy took a short foray to his left, and charged the Bells! He hated them! He was going to . . . to . . . he didn't know what, but—

"Hello," he said, and reined his steed to a sudden stop, foam flecking madly from the beast. "What's this?"

It was a five-hundred-gallon gas tank the good Pastor used for his fleet of Church Cadillacs, which sat parked next to the beautiful rectory next to the beautiful House of God. There was no one around. There was a ten-gallon gas can next to the Pastor's Mansion. Without a thought, Buddy swung off his pony, filled the gas can from the pump, which was not locked, left the gas running all over the perennials in the garden next to the Pastor's Mansion, and strode over to the Bell Tower calling out its praises to its Creator, and the heathen splashed gasoline (from Saudi Arabia, in case you're interested) all over the thing. He flicked his Bic lighter, tossed it in the puddle of petroleum collecting at the base of the Tower of Babel, and it burst into flames.

"HOKA HEY LET'S POWWOW!" the heathen whooped. "HAU HO WHOOOOO!!"

He had another delightful thought and grabbed a burning bush next to the Tower and tossed it at the very large pool of Industrial Might back at the five-hundred-gallon repository, and it exploded with a fury that scared even our Red Devil from Hell. Unfortunately, the wind was blowing the wrong way, and the lake of fire blew over to the Pastor's humble abode and molested its sacrosanct chambers too. Oh, the Demon was having a Field Day today!

El Cuartalejo and his warriors caught up about just then, just in time to enjoy the conflagration cooking the Christmas Goose. They stopped for a full minute or two to appreciate the spectacle. Contrary to common knowledge, red brick can burn, and indeed, it *did* burn up this one particular Temple of Jesus Christ and His Latter-day Saints.

Buddy rode over and chuckled with his fellow Red Devils.
"Looks like the Church caught fire."

"Wonder how it happened?"

"Faulty wiring, probly."

"Coulda been a careless cigarette."

The passersby passed on by—as they had not completely
forgotten they had places to go and things to do, and there
were a few people who would probably have liked to inter-
vene in their progress.

A few good parishioners ran screaming out of the Temple, screaming holy terror, and missed seeing our heroes
disappear off into the sunset to the west, out across the
open fields. The concerned parishioners had a few other
things on their mind.

It was a good thing the other warriors caught up with
Buddy, because he didn't have the slightest idea where he
was going. But the other boys were familiar with the ter-
rain, having grown up here all their lives. They knew every
rock and piece of trash for miles around. They all rode in
silence at a trot, savoring the sweet silence, now that the
church bells had been replaced by fire sirens and various
other kinds of racket emanating from civilization. The
wind, as I mentioned before, was blowing unfavorably for
Jesus, from the west, so it wasn't long before the gallant
warriors heard nothing but birds singing their own hymns
to the sunset, and horse hooves stumbling over broken debris left over from various fatal attempts by developers to
build more suburbs out here in the desert. The patriotic
developers lamented the backward resistance of locals, and
the backward locals stumbled over the concrete and asphalt
of several aborted housing areas. Why, asked the developers earnestly, why are some people so opposed to *all*
Progress?

So onward they rode, anti-christian soldiers, out across
the open desert that was still somewhat pristine and free of
some of the worser debris of america. There were still jet
contrails crisscrossing in the scarlet clouds, and power lines
going all over hell from reservoirs and dams and other
profitable sources of benefit for mankind, and roads, and
railroad tracks, but mostly (and oh, a lot of fences, I forgot)
it was still clean and open and pristine. It was clean and

pure, and the warriors felt okay. At least there weren't any National Guard helicopters strafing them yet, or missiles coming out of nowhere to ruin their evening. (Just exactly *who* are the National Guard protecting us from? Chinese hordes sweeping down from Canada? Or Mexicans up into Texas? Maybe the Commies are gonna come slithering up out of the Oceans like salamanders and eat San Diego.)

Whatever, the Arsenal of Democracy failed to detect a dozen insects dismount in the dark at an invisible corral on a cliff overlooking the remote Rio Grande. There were, after all, hundreds of miles of cliffs out there, running around everywhere. We can't pinpoint every single inch of space, General.

To make a long story short, Buddy reached his sister's bedside as fast as he could. It was a solemn scene. It was terrible.

Philbert lay unconscious on a bed next to hers, and they were surrounded by dozens of grim Indian Elders. No one spoke. A single kerosene lantern cast eerie shadows on the room in No Tongue's cabin. Buddy knelt beside his dear friends, and, with a warrior's unerring instinct, he saw that something was missing. Without a thought, he put his sister's hand into his best friend's hand.

At that moment, with only the slightest gesture that only true geniuses can discover, Whirlwind found Red Bird in the vast darkness of the Deadly Thunderbird. Lightning exploded in the world as he grabbed her hand, as they fell through the spiral of total oblivion.

A Great Chief appeared suddenly, galloping on a pure white stallion the color of milk, and his breath was the thunder. Whirlwind saw him come up out of the river, and he spoke: "I am Sweet Medicine!" Red Bird heard him say, "I am Bear Butte!" She saw a beautiful Yellow-haired Woman standing on a Sacred Mountain, motioning for her to come. Red Bird stopped her breathless, dizzying fall and walked toward the woman.

Then she was gone. Whirlwind saw the Thunder Being ride toward the Sacred Woman on the Mountain, and She was Bonnie. Then she was gone.

Bonnie opened her eyes and saw the beautiful blue sky

115

etched by barren tree branches above her. Was it a dream? She felt herself breathing, and then she tried to think. To remember? Had she been cast under a spell by all those bad women in that *kiva* that day? Arantzazu was a witch, and so were all the others! She had been betrayed by the same people who pretended to be her friends!

Buddy looked at her. "Bonnie?"

"Huh?"

Philbert opened his eyes. "Where am I?"

He leaned up on his elbows and saw that he was lying on a buffalo robe next to the river. Bonnie was lying on a robe next to him. Her eyes were open. She was looking at him with the strangest expression he had ever seen in his life. Buddy knelt next to them, and dozens of strangers all around behind him.

Little Sky put the wooden doll in Philbert's hand. "I found this just now, where you dropped it in the snow."

The doll was a figurine with yellow hair now, made of corn tassels. It had strange, symbolic markings burned into it, like wood carvings or brands. Philbert looked at it in his hand, and his eyes couldn't even begin to describe what it meant.

Buddy touched his forehead. "We saw lightning come out of the river night before last, and No Tongue said we should move you out here."

"Bonnie?" was Philbert's first question.

"Red Bird," was all she could say, in correction.

"Red Bird," he repeated. "And I am Whirlwind."

"Yes," she agreed. Then she had a question. It overwhelmed her, although she didn't have the slightest comprehension why. "What is . . . where is Bear Butte? We . . . I have to go to Bear Butte. Where is that? Mexico?"

"Bear Butte?" Buddy repeated. "That Mountain we stopped at in South Dakota on our way here?"

"Yes."

Whirlwind looked at Red Bird.

9

OF FOLK WAYS AND CULTURE HEROES, AND OTHER THINGS OF WHICH ONLY ANTHROPOLOGISTS AND PSYCHOLOGISTS UNDERSTAND.

ARANTZAZU HELD A THREE-INCH SLIVER OF CRYSTAL IN HER hand. It was about an inch wide and so thin as to be almost transparent. "This came out of your forehead."

Bonnie looked at it in wonder. She couldn't say anything, or think about anything except that she felt an overwhelming relief to have finally, after almost a lifetime, heard the words the Yellow-haired Woman was speaking to her. She could listen to the Voice and not wilt in a despair of incomprehension. Relief—it was the only way to describe how she felt. More had been pulled out of her than that piece of glass rock; a weight had been lifted from her shoulders.

"You're still very sick," Violetta warned her. "You'll have to recuperate for weeks."

Bonnie frowned. "But I'll be okay?"

"Yes," Arantzazu replied. "I think so."

Bonnie felt herself looking at the women gathered around her bed under the trees. "You old witch." She was

117

amazed to hear herself say it, and also that she felt no fear of these women anymore.

They all laughed delightedly. Old Girl joked, "Look who's talking!"

The men looked curiously, and a little fearfully too, at the sliver of crystal. Jusepe commented wonderingly, "When the bolt of lightning burst out of the river, our sawish cacique pulled this out of your head. It is like the lightning."

"It is sacred," Arantzazu agreed. "We must completely remake your Sacred Bundle with this, and the fetish of Corn Woman."

"And," Bonnie added, resting on her elbows, "Whirlwind's medicine objects."

"Yes."

"There is a lot of work to do," Grampa added. Then he smiled at Whirlwind, who flinched under his gaze. "I'm sorry, My Friend, for slapping you. I had to do it. You are a *koshare* and you had to be jolted into action."

"I did?" Whirlwind asked (for he was no longer Philbert). "I am? What is a *ko*—"

"A *koshare* is a Pueblo Indian clown. Only you can dream of the Thunder and Lightning Beings."

"Only you," Jusepe added, "could go after the Woman in the Other World. You agreed to when you made the bond with—"

Whirlwind looked at the doll in his hand. Yes, he understood, without really knowing the facts of such things as these. Anthropologists and Psychologists can probably explain these folk customs to death, but ordinary folks simply trust themselves and their spirits. You can spend the rest of your life in museums and libraries studying up on all this stuff, but, well, I'll admit it. I'm prejudiced against academics and schoolteachers, so I'd better just shut my mouth. It was enough for Whirlwind to just go with it, and not think too much.

And Buddy? He was amazed and in awe, and all that stuff, as that sliver of rock really was kind of glowing with some kind of light, and he saw the lightning come out of the river with his own eyes, too, but, wow, he didn't know what to make of it. One minute he was up at Lame Deer drinking beer and pissed off at the world, and the next minute he gets a call from his sister in jail in New Mexico and Philbert cruises by in an old bomber of a Buick, and the next thing he knew he was shooting it out with the cops and burning churches. He's watching his sister being revered as some kind of holy woman, and listening to talk about Thunder Beings and *koshares* and witches and . . . He shook his head. Politics was easier than this shit. He listened to these crazy Apaches talk about taking Philbert and Bonnie (er, Whirlwind and Red Bird, as they were called now) to a cave in the rocks where Monster Slayer, their great culture hero, had emerged from Time Immemorial, to found their race. *Monster Slayer,* no less. It was starting to sound like a Saturday morning kids' show.

So, everybody (there musta been dozens of goddamn Indians crawling all over the place now) hoisted the two sick dreamers on litters, and hauled them up along the narrow gorge along the riverbanks a few hundred yards, on their way to "Monster Slayer's Cave."

"*Sipapuni,*" Jusepe explained to him as they strolled along ceremoniously, with several drum groups appearing out of nowhere and some other flute players and bell ringers improvising some old tunes. "The path from the navel, the place of man's Emergence from the Underworld."

"What I don't get"—Buddy struggled to formulate a question—"is why everybody is so concerned about Bonnie all of a sudden? You don't even know her. We're Cheyennes."

"She has had a great vision," Grampa replied, joining them as they strolled through the chokecherry bushes and willows. "Arantzazu saw her in a dream many years ago."

"Oh yeah?"

"We've been expecting her," Jusepe added matter-of-factly, as if it was the most common thing in the world.

"And"—Buddy frowned, more confused than ever (have you ever noticed that? The more questions you ask, the more questions you think of?)—"that's why you all have flocked in here—"

"You're famous too," El Cuartalejo remarked, walking behind them. "You Cheyennes have come down here to help us. We appreciate it."

Buddy couldn't, for the life of him, think how he had helped the Pueblos and Apaches around here. All they'd succeeded in doing was drawing cops from the four corners of the world, like flies to a piece of carrion. But there's no way to figure Indians.

Jusepe just continued his blithe dissertations, and the others pretended to understand what he was talking about. "This Cave was where Monster Slayer emerged to found our race, and brought us our laws."

"I heard the *sipapuni* was over in the mountains behind Taos," El Cuartalejo offered.

"Nope, right up here," Grampa said positively. "It is the *kivaove*, the visible part of the Underworld Kiva protruding above ground."

"Nobody knows for sure," Buddy heard Violetta mutter. He grinned at her, and she grinned back at him. "Take about seventy percent of what Grampa says with a grain of salt."

"You can say that again," Old Girl chimed in.

Grampa pretended to give them a dirty look. "What? I know what I'm talking about. I know what I'm talking about."

"You can say that again," Violetta joked.

"Oh yeah? Well I do! Anthros come from all over the world to sit at my feet and learn the wisdom of the ages."

"Ho ho ho!" Violetta guffawed right out loud. "You charge 'em big bucks and then tell them a pack of lies, nothing but one big lie after another."

"So?" Grampa asked rhetorically. "That's what they wanna hear. They don't want me to reveal the secrets of the ages, the mysterious—"

Old Girl explained to Buddy. "He's got museums all over the world thinking he's a *hechizero* and a *posi powaqa* and a *tuhika* and every other kind of medicine man and shaman imaginable. Nobody could be all those things at once."

"They don't know that," Grampa commented seriously, keeping a straight face.

No Tongue made a couple of derogatory gestures, and the elderlies all howled with laughter. Even Arantzazu grinned at Grampa and poked him in the ribs.

"I fulfill a vital function," Grampa told everyone. "If those white coyotes came snooping around for the *real* information we'd—"

"Yeah, it's a good thing you share those fees they pay, and honorariums," Violetta interrupted, "or Goost-cha-du would fry your skinny little ass for breakfast!"

After more general merriment, Bonnie asked, "What about her, what's-her-name?"

"Goost-cha-du," Arantzazu said. "She's the one who put the curse in you. I don't know where she is, but I'm sure she's hightailing it as fast as she can hundreds of miles away by now. You and your boyfriend brought in some big guns in the Thunder Nation."

I made a note of that. I was following along and trying to keep track of the dialogue, in case I needed it for a book or a movie someday.

"Here we are," Jusepe said. He had moved up to the head of the column of partyers, along with No Tongue, and they stopped in front of a thick clump of willows and red oak bushes growing vertically on a sheer rock wall of granite and rose crystal and limestone and shale.

Buddy couldn't see where they were. It looked like the same old desolate cliff they had been following for half an hour. The big, deep, green river flowed tightly behind them, right up against the cliff, almost. It was a lovely spot, sort of. But wild. Isolated. And there was the eerie sensation you get when you think somebody is watching you from behind. Buddy turned around to look, but there was only the Rio Grande, flowing swiftly and broadly over the loose gravel, shallow and broad. On the other side, equally steep brown, barren, and rocky cliffs rose to the flat sagebrush-desert stretching to Arizona.

Arantzazu and Jusepe and No Tongue helped Whirlwind and Red Bird off their royal litters and lifted them up into the clumps of brush. Everyone else, as if on some signal, sat down and rested and waited. They didn't seem to be concerned about anything. So Buddy squatted by the river and took a drink. It was cold and didn't taste too polluted. When he looked around, the five people who had gone into the bushes were gone. They had disappeared. Grampa motioned for him to take it easy.

I didn't go in the Cave, either, so I can only conjecture as to what happened in there, or what it was like. I'm much too irreverent to be allowed in such places. All I know is that Arantzazu was carrying Whirlwind's medicine bundle, as well as the Corn Woman fetish and the lightning-crystal and all the other stuff she'd given Red Bird back at the Picuris *kiva* a few days ago. Which seemed like years ago.

They were gone all day. We tried to catch some fish, and a few pretty nice bass and trout cooperated. A few fires were built, and someone had actually remembered to bring a few of those great big skillets, and some salt and pepper were produced, and a metate grinding stone helped some *piki* and pinole bread and cornmeal along. The Merrymakers boiled some pinole and *atole* gruel to go along with the fish; and, apparently, one of the guys there was a Hopi, and he had a bucket of some *knukwivi* he'd brought along. That's a stew of lamb and hominy. The Apaches counterattacked with some of their famous *kahzyith* beef stew, and Buddy and I fulfilled our jobs by eating it all up with relish. After a variety of multicultural desserts were consumed, out of courtesy, we eased back on the natural chaises longues of rocks and bushes that were scattered with abundant plentitude out there on the patio, and smoked. The fragrant aroma of tobacco from their *baka* pipes wafted up the *barranca* (that's a canyon, for you illiterate Anglos out there), which was warm and dry in the late afternoon. The sun was already behind our obstructed horizon, but we didn't care. It was comfortable. We were cozy.

Talk just naturally rises to the surface at after-dinner intervals like these. I asked no one in particular, "What's the Indian word for cave? *Puesivi?*"

Grampa nodded. "You know our language pretty well."

"I was just trying to impress you," I responded with my characteristic modesty.

You could tell that was irritating to Grampa, but he tried not to show it. "Do you know about the *puesivi jacal* at the *kisonvi ngakuyi?*"

"Yeah," I lied. "Ask me something hard."

"Don't kid a kidder," Grampa snorted. "We are at the entrance of the home of the spirit beings, who rise out of the medicine-water at the center of the nation."

I shrugged and yawned. "I knew that."

Since I don't want to bore you with all this mythological rigamarole, I suppose I should relate that, right about here,

Whirlwind drifted out of the cave hidden in the bushes. He smelled all the food, is why, I think. You may have noticed that our boy, for all his profound spiritual insights and improvisational genius, is possessed of an inherent fondness for all things edible. He tore into that fish soup, and lamb stew, and corn bread, like a man who hasn't eaten in days (which he hadn't). After about an hour, in which we all enjoyed watching him, and watching the sunset, he slowed down a little and answered a few of Buddy's questions.

"What have you been doing in there? What's going on? How's Bonnie? Where's—"

"What?" Whirlwind replied, and shrugged. "Nothin'."

Buddy was understandably exasperated, a little. "C'mon, Philbert! What—"

"Whirlwind," he corrected, a mouthful of *piki* melting in his mouth, "I prefer Whirlwind."

"Yeah, whatever."

"They're"—he explained, coming reluctantly to his final gulp. It was poetry to hear him—"laying out the medicine things and saying a lot of prayers. I didn't have to do anything. You got any matches to light this pipe?"

Buddy lit his pipe. Whirlwind puffed it to life, and lay back on the soft sand. Buddy waited a little more. "And?"

Whirlwind came awake again. "And ... uh ... what?"

"What ... I mean ..."

Whirlwind looked at his best friend with renewed interest. "Buddy, how ya doin'?"

"Huh? Me?"

"Yeah. I ain't seen you in a long time. I saw you on TV. You were great. What's happenin'?"

"Oh, nothin' much, just a whole damn revolution you and my sister have started. Why?"

"A revolution? Really?"

"Oh, I don't know," Buddy sighed. But he was still a little pleased that there were more than a few people there who were interested in whatever news he might have to report on events in the outside world. "You know you guys really started something when you pulled those antics up at that ski road?"

Grampa giggled with the recollection. "I was hoping we would."

123

"You did. It was a pretty wild thing to do."

"So you just naturally had to follow through on it and take over a TV station and steal a News Van and hold a worldwide press conference," I added. The others looked from him and back to Buddy, and then back to me.

"Yeah." Buddy frowned, puzzled. "I just naturally had to . . . say what's—"

Whirlwind was fascinated. "Buddy, you did all those things?"

"And burned a Mormon Church and—"

Buddy stared at me. "How did you know that?"

Whirlwind stared at me, too, but I wouldn't answer. I just whistled and looked at the stars coming out. They twinkled and twinkled.

Jusepe and No Tongue appeared suddenly beside us. They dug into the *kahzyith* without saying a word. They were starving.

Everyone waited for Red Bird and Arantzazu to appear out of the invisible *puesivi*, but they never showed. All night. Once, Violetta took the robes into them, and came back out after a few minutes without the robes. She didn't say a word to anybody. The others all walked back up the *barranca* to No Tongue's camp and sacked out.

Weeks passed. The women gathered at the *puesivi* of Monster Slayer, and took food in and out of the cave, and Red Bird appeared a few times. She went bathing in the hot springs nearby. Color was returning to her face. Her menstrual cramps passed. The women sang songs and kept apart from the men.

The men, well, they tried to manage without the women, which was pretty comical. The older guys tried to teach the younger guys how to hunt and live simply in nature, and how to keep hidden from the searching white men everywhere. Stealth was always a famous ability of the Apaches and Vaqueros and Querechos and Teyas around there. They tried to cook and do man-things, but I'll tell ya, we were getting pretty anxious to have the females return, for a number of reasons.

Whirlwind rested. And fasted. And slept. No Tongue made him a lot of tea out of all his weird herbs and plants.

124

I can't begin to tell you what they all were. I've never been much of a vegetarian, if you want to know the truth. I'd like to know more about the natural medicines of the earth and all, I respect the hell out of herbal doctors of course, as I respect everything. But I can't really tell the difference between soapweed yucca and plain old yucca, I really can't.

Buddy got antsy as hell and rode over to Dulce on the Jicarilla Apache reservation with El Cuartalejo and his warrior society, after a few days. Warriors have always been antsy that way, pretending to ride off on hunts and war and to do all kinds of things, when really they just like to blow with the wind and see what's over the next hill. Men are completely irresponsible that way; I know, millions of women have told me so. Dulce is off to the northwest of the Rio Grande, and I guess Buddy raised some more hell, and Rabbit was raising some more money and running up a helluva phone bill everywhere she went, but they had some press conferences too. I wrote them up some press releases on my portable Panasonic electronic battery-powered typewriter, which I had with me. It only weighs a few pounds and fits in my pack. Those Japanese, I'll tell ya, we couldn't have had the Revolution without their technology. Them Japs made everything a lot easier for us. Buddy absconded with one of their new broadcast-quality video cameras and was exposing the Tribal Council and the Bureau of Indian Affairs all over the reservation. New Mexico was up in arms, it really was. The warriors were having a lot of fun.

Back at No Tongue's rancheria, you might have thought we were just laying around all day, looking lazy, but we weren't. We were working hard; it just didn't look like it. I was especially working my ass off, as I always do. Ask anybody what a hard worker I am, they'll tell ya. I baby-sat a lot, for one thing. About a dozen dirty little ragamuffins had appeared out of nowhere to keep Sky and Jane and Jennifer company, and after a few days of exploring around out there in various other little caves and holes and trees, you couldn't tell those human children from pure naked animals straight from the wilderness. They could have been bear cubs for all they cared about keeping clean or minding their manners. You never saw such a pack of

filthy little creatures, happier'n piglets in slop. I did the best
I could to keep their fingernails trimmed and their ears
scrubbed, and they enjoyed splashing in the hot springs,
and didn't mind it when I brushed the bigger cockleburrs
out of their matted hair, but mostly all they were concerned
about was finding gold and bird's nests and looking at a
dead coyote skeleton under a rock across the river. They
found a sandy spot on the beach, and all fifteen of them
were busy one whole afternoon making sand castles.

No Tongue showed Whirlwind some old lodgepole pines
he had out back of his shack. Whirlwind understood that
No Tongue was giving the tipi poles to him for a lodge, if
he wanted them. Whirlwind thanked him and accepted the
fine gift. He was sort of learning how to understand the
old guy. Those poles must have been ten years old, but it
was miles over to the mountains to the east to cut fresh
ones, so he worked with them. The Elders were very, very
skittery about us showing ourselves at all to the world on
the surface above the cliffs: they were watching all the time
for the Enemy. We weren't allowed to build big smoky fires
at all, just little embers were allowed for cooking and heat-
ing; that's why we couldn't have no sweat lodges, which
needed big bonfires to heat the rocks. Anyway, those poles
were dry and cracked, laying under stickers and snow, with
a pile of hard old deer hides and skins piled in a crumpled
wad next to them. It didn't look very promising.

The biggest improvement in this development was that
the women finally rejoined us then. Bonnie came over and
went right to work helping with the hides. The Elders
showed us what to do; well, they mostly supervised because,
as Old Girl explained it, "You kids should raise your own
lodge. It's yours." We all joined in to help Red Bird and
Whirlwind, though, because they were really working their
asses off. And, surprisingly, the more Whirlwind cleared
the ground up by Monster Slayer's *puesivi* and shaved the
poles with a few rusty old tools from somewhere, and the
more Red Bird laid out the hides and cleaned the mildew
off, the better they felt, the stronger they got, the closer
they grew to each other. Even Sky and Jane seemed to
enjoy the work of fixing stone needles and sorting sinew
for threads so that Red Bird could sew the old hides to-

gether for the covering of the lodge. Old Girl was especially adept in showing her how to soak the hides in boiling cedar broth to make them soft and fragrant. Jusepe showed Whirlwind the correct rituals to fix the doorway so it faced a notch in the cliff to the east. Grampa patiently taught the kids to sharpen big pine stakes to nail down the hides in the ground. Violetta helped with the inner cloth and ground cloth for insulation. It went slowly, but the weather was very mild this winter, so no one seemed to mind. They weren't in any hurry.

They raised the tipi in midwinter, shortly before the new moon, when things are always a little rough. It looked all right. It was small, and dirty. Movie people would probably sneer at it, but more than one Elder cried to see a sacred lodge raise its circle back up to the sky at this holy spot, on Indian Land, again. Maybe we were poor and didn't have beautiful buffalo hide lodges and robes with all those artificial things Hollywood movies always have, which are always shooting all over the West in "authentic" Indian dramas, but we were the real Indians. We weren't just playing Indian.

Grampa was blubbering. "You make us proud." He began singing an old, old tune and, for some reason, tears just gushed out of him. There's no way to figure it.

Violetta took Red Bird off to one side, and I overheard her say, "Dad never thought he'd see our young people return to the good ways."

I forgot to mention that those elderlies liked to sing and play their drums every night, making a racket into the wee hours. Every night. Other people would try to sleep, but there they were, every night, those oldtimers howling at the moon and talking about getting the songs right and remembering this and remembering that. Then they'd invariably start blubbering about nothing, getting sentimental and melodramatic and who knows what all else.

The snows fell. No Tongue and Jane liked to fish, and they struck up a good friendship. She kept him laughing as she constantly described her knowledge of worms and economics and boys' wieners. He rolled on the banks of the Rio Grande in silent hilarity as she went on and on. They became great pals.

127

The men went hunting. No Tongue showed me and
Whirlwind how to make and use bows and arrows, but not
without a number of mishaps first, which aggravated and
delighted the Elders. Whirlwind shot a stone arrowhead
through the right nostril of his nose, and Grampa nearly
choked to death laughing. He made a fool of himself. It
was a pretty funny sight all right, but Red Bird got mad at
us as she nursed his nose, which bled pretty badly. He had
a bandage on it for a week. He and I took off with Jusepe
and Old Codger one time, scouting for game. We had all
taken turns climbing the cliff every day to take the horses
out to find grass and pilfered hay from nearby farms, and
tree bark to eat, being careful not to let any humans see
us. We went horseback to the forests off to the north and
south, and I was especially getting to be an excellent rider.
I only got bucked off Mandy a few times and jammed my
thumb once. There seemed to be more and more Indians
showing up from everywhere, so our camp was growing
considerably, and we had to range farther and farther out
for forage.

It was pretty romantic all right, in our furs and skins with
bows and arrows, and I don't care if you believe me or not.
One old Navaho guy gave me a real nice army bow he stole
from a Kmart in Farmington, and I got real toughened up
pulling that baby back. You have to be strong to shoot a
bow and arrow. But we did it and we knew it could be
done. New Mexico is still a very spacious place, despite the
damn power lines and trucks crisscrossing the roads everywhere. There's still a lot of porcupines and rabbits and red
pheasants out there in the countryside. I made a nice, warm
furry rabbit cap out of a couple little cute bunnies I massacred. Whirlwind and I were piss-poor shots and even worse
scouts, but Old Codger could usually sneak up on a critter
or two. He was recognized as the best hunter around. As
often as not we would return with at least a little something
for the dinner pot, and if we didn't, No Tongue and Jane
would probably have a few fish, and if they didn't, Red
Bird and Old Girl and Violetta would have some wild tur-
nips and carrots boiling away and Sky and Grampa would
have the table set. Occasionally, a few raggedy Indians
would float down the river on a boat and bring us some

tacos or tamales from Chama or Alamosa. Sometimes somebody would sneak into the grocery store somewhere and bring us back a few sacks of Doritos and a case of Dr. Pepper and fixings for Velveeta cheese sandwiches and Hostess Ho-Hos. We were roughing it.

After a few more weeks of this naturalism Whirlwind and I got so we'd go out alone and we could actually tell a deer track from a cow pie, we could get downwind of a wild turkey, and our crowning achievement was the day Whirlwind actually got an arrow in the hind leg of a buck antelope. I chased him on my old mare, Mandy, and got another in his neck. If Whirlwind's ornery mare, Perdita, stepped in a snake hole and he went flying head over heels into a mud puddle, and if I sort of slipped off my expensive fifty-dollar saddle (because, as some Elders said, I didn't know how to hitch the cinch up tight enough) in the excitement, and got kicked a little bit in the teeth, then that doesn't detract one bit from our kill. We both crawled in triumph back to our feet, blood dripping from the hole in my lip, Whirlwind smarting from an eight-inch scrape on his arm, and his eyes still a little cockeyed, and we looked at the dead prairie goat in the sagebrush. We whooped and hugged each other, even if our worthless horses had run away. It felt great. I just don't care if you don't believe one word of it. Whirlwind slung that buck with three tiny horns over his shoulder and we walked home, cold and dirty and bloody, and it was the third best time I've ever had in my life. The wintry afternoon blew gray and glorious in our faces and, I'll tell ya, there ain't *nothin'* like hunting, to a man. There's something real basic about it. I don't care what you say. We got back and skinned and butchered that Royal Stag, and said a prayer to his chiefly spirit, thanking him for giving us his life. Jennifer ate the raw liver, which almost made Sky gag. We had a real sociable evening around that feast.

Oh, I felt good out there, I admit it. One morning I strolled way up north along the river, alone, to watch the sunrise. I had sorta built myself a little lean-to of bushes and twigs on the opposite side of the river, being a contrary like that all my life. Everybody else was sleeping on the warmer east side of the river. I had a down sleeping bag

I'd brought in my pack, which was good to forty below, and I had some thermal longjohns, too, so I wasn't being deprived. Normally, as a city boy, I'd always hated getting up early, but those crazy Elders kept yapping about how they "get up with nature, at three or four in the morning, or else you'll be tired all day," and more nonsense along those lines, and I allowed how they might be right. So I'd taken to getting up before dawn too. As far as not being tired all day, I'll tell ya, I started dragging by midafternoon. I may have had the disadvantage of a college education, but I could see those Elders taking naps after lunch every day. Who'd they think they were kidding? I've had a lot of handicaps in my life, like being a Shakespearean actor and a big-city journalist and a lot of other worthless crap, too, but I could count how many hours there are in a day. I think you're nuts if you claim to only need four or five hours of sleep. Even if I only know how to rant and rave about Othello and Homer and Queen Maud, I know for a fact that it's good for me to get my eight hours of sleep.

I found a cozy niche on some warm logs and waited for the sun to rise across to the east. The morning was still gray, but starting to turn pink on a few higher clouds. There was a little notch in the cliff on the other side where the sun could pop up, like a bubble on a carpenter's level. Then I saw something that was probably the most beautiful sight in my entire life. Bonnie Red Bird stepped naked out of the hot springs. She stood right there in the dawn's early light, and it was like a goddess appearing before me. I know how you Americans hate poetry so I won't bother you with any more details of my fantasy. I know you think this is just one big wet daydream anyway.

She put on a white loose shift which dropped down around to the middle of her legs, and waved her long black hair in the air to dry it. She was humming some pretty little tune to herself, walking in my general direction. There were several hot springs all up and down the river, and she had found this one on my side of the river, a little pool between some green mossy rocks and a few pale iris bushes. She looked up and saw me. "Oh."

I smiled, unable to speak.

She didn't seem to be afraid. "How long have you been there?"

My first impulse was to make some smart-aleck remark like "All my life," but instead I could only look at her and see the future laid out before us.

She looked puzzled and walked closer. "You look good outside. I like your rabbit cap and leather coat."

I said, "I'm waiting for the sunrise."

"Oh, good," she replied, and sat down next to me, looking at the notch in the cliffs to the east. The sky was getting bright scarlet. She brushed her fingers through her wet hair. Her wet feet and ankles were only inches away from my moccasins. She turned her knees around and rested them against my legs. She was very close. "I'm cold."

I put my arm around her and snuggled closely.

She sighed, "I feel like I've known you all my life. Are you really a wizard?"

"Yes."

She smiled and looked at me.

I could tell that she wanted me to kiss her, and I could probably have made love to her right then, if I was a cad.

She asked, "What's going to happen to us?"

"We'll go to Bear Butte," I replied, whispering to her as if my words were a kiss in her ear, "and you and Whirlwind will live happily ever after."

She sat back and looked at me. "Really?"

I nodded toward the rising sun. I could have sworn that I heard a sweet melody out of Mozart floating in the air. The world was perfect and pure at that moment. The sun rose as gently as the song the Yellow-haired Woman was singing to Sweet Medicine on the Sacred Mountain, and we both heard it as if it were in a dream. Red Bird and I rested our heads against each other, as if we had known each other all our lives and had always been in love.

10

HOW THE
GARDEN OF EDEN MYTH
IS DEBUNKED, AND OF OTHER
ADVANCED ETHNOGRAPHICAL
NARRATIVES.

AFTER THE USUAL MIDWINTER THAW, THE SERIOUS SNOWS
and frosts followed. Drifts piled up against the central Ceremonial Tipi, and icicles formed on the less impressive nylon
pup tents and canvas jobs purchased from Army surplus.
Tiny wisps of smoke floated from the lodges so as to be
almost imperceptible to passing Comsats and Counter-
terrorism Surveillance Units searching high and low for the
missing core of Terrorists. Press conferences and emergency meetings too numerous to chronicle occurred almost
daily across Indian Country, from the bingo parlors of Quebec to the strip mines of Oregon. Indians were shooting
their mouths off from the Yukon to Uruguay, all of them
claiming to be chiefs and official spokespersons for their
oppressed peoples. White people didn't know who to believe. Obscured by all the hoo-ray our true genuine goddamn Indians hunkered down and tried to survive another
rough year.

In the middle of the nation sat our one rotten old tipi,

next to a forgotten cave in a forgotten cliff of Nueva Mexico. In the middle of Red Bird's Lodge sat the matriarch herself, shivering in a bear robe which someone gave her as a gift. She couldn't understand why they had to have such a puny fire, when there was plenty of wood around. But her family and elderly advisers crowded in on her anyway, each demanding more and more of her time. They expected her to be perfect. She'd even been forced to quit smoking cigarettes, as no one ever thought to bring her a pack of Winstons from town.

Over her head, where she slept with Whirlwind and Jane and Sky, hung the Sacred Bundle. It had been meticulously prepared and was now wrapped in various furs and robes, with a Zuni blanket wrapped around the outside. It was beautiful, she had to admit. She was proud of it. She had gone through enough ceremonies to last a lifetime, though. It was like one long Solemn High Mass that lasted for a week, for crying out loud. But . . . It did indeed have some kind of awesome, incomprehensible Power, which Red Bird could feel in her bones. It was wonderful and strange.

One evening, after dinner, everyone was lounging around her living room, bored. The tipi must have had a dozen people squeezed in there on the robes and rugs. Red Bird tried to distract herself from the endless monotony by beading a necklace for Whirlwind. She hated beading. How anyone could stand to string one tiny little bead after another on an invisible fishing line, for hours and hours at a time, was beyond her. You'd have to be a complete moron with absolutely nothing in your brain to waste your time like that.

Sky was pleading with me, for the umpteenth time, to tell a story. "Tell a story, tell a story," the kid kept yammering.

"Oh, okay," I shrugged. "If you have absolutely nothing better to do, I guess I could."

"Yeah, yeah!"

It was, you have to understand, the ultimate hardship for kids these days to even contemplate going one hour without television, or radios or tape decks even. I know this episode of our yarn will be totally unbelievable to today's American Child, let alone to go without any kind of electronic tube at all for weeks and months! Ah! A true nightmare! So you can see why I took mercy on them and agreed to concoct a few lies to help them through their impending madness. (I was, after all, known as Storyteller.) "What story?"

They looked blank. "I dunno," they all chimed in as if one chorus. Kids these days, I repeat, are in danger of completely losing their imagination.

"How about the story of Monster Slayer?" I suggested, as if I just thought of it.

"Oh, yeah!"

"Uh . . . what monsters?" (Kids love monsters, for some reason.)

I assumed my spookiest face and scariest voice. Even the elders scooched in a little to hear. "There are real monsters in the world, you know. Dragons."

A little four-year-old white boy named Sage gulped. "Monsters?"

"Yep. Big horrible dragons that are like Thunderbirds who would like to kill you in horrible ways."

"What ways?" Sky asked.

"Oh, I don't know. Like Freddy in *Nightmare on Elm Street*, to come into your dreams and make them real—"

"Oh, I like Freddy!"

"I saw Part Four where—"

"I liked Part Two when—"

Sage jumped up and acted like he was fighting some invisible foe. "I'll punch those monsters! I'm Freddy! I'll—"

The kids had been stirred into enacting their own stories and carrying on their own conversation, entirely separate from the story at hand. I said, in my deepest voice of adult authority, "You guys want to tell the story, or me?"

"You!" Jane declared forcefully.

"Yes," Red Bird seconded, "I don't want them going to R movies like that."

"Aw, why not, Mom? All the other kids—"

"Because," I explained, to the appreciation of the elders, "sick minds make those movies. I don't like them either. Blood and gore and devils, it's all done by bad spirits. There *are* monsters in the world."

The kids looked solemn at that. They stopped jabbering and listened to the wind make scary noises outside. The little fire cast eerie flickers on the walls of the tent.

"Monster Slayer," I began, "was a great Warrior and a Chief who fought those bad spirits. He was the greatest man who ever lived. He was very brave. It takes a lot of courage to face the dark dreams, alone, in the middle of the night. To face death. We are all going to have to die someday, and we will do it alone. We must face the Monster too."

I had everyone's complete attention now. I know, as the purveyors of slash-and-burn movies like *The Exorcist* and *Halloween* know, that there is a lot of Unknown Power in the universe. It turns evil when it turns away from knowledge and truth; when it just makes up things as it goes along, about demons and witches and heathen Apache savages. Yes, there are many examples of atrocities committed by Indians throughout American history, but the real atrocities are the lies which are perpetrated in the name of greed and self-importance and are passed off as history and art. When sacred words like "Goddess" are twisted into lies about Witches and the original sin of the Womb; when priests murder priestesses because they want the natural power of the world; and, perhaps most imperative of all, when our most sacred achievement and gift of all—Language—perverts itself and creates false words like God and Hell and The Bible until they, too, are evil twisted lies that have come to mean nothing. Man takes good ideas such as "Love Thy Neighbor" and makes it Hate. He creates doubletalk which calls nuclear missiles "Peacekeepers" and CIA political executions "Elimination with Extreme Prejudice." This perversion of our speech is the most insidious development of all in a world of insidious racism and pollution and genocide.

"In the beginning of the world there were not only many beautiful kinds of birds and trees and animals, there were also many hideous and nameless monsters. The worst of these were the Dragons, but there was also a mystery about the Dragons, and in a certain kind of way that we will probably never understand, they were also very good and sacred. The Dragons were not only crawling creatures like lizards and snakes, they were also giant sea-things, and they could fly too.

"In those ancient ancient times, millions and millions of

years ago, it is said that all the creatures had the power of speech and were gifted with intelligence. We are very foolish if we think we can say what this world was like a billion years ago. We can't even say for sure what's going on today. Personally, I can't comprehend numbers like billions and spaces like light-years. I don't think anyone can."

"Scientists," Grampa sneered. The Elders all nodded.

"But we can be pretty sure that there must have been disagreements among the beasts and birds, just like there are today. Geronimo once told a story about the birds and beasts going to war, and of the Chief Dragon who—"

"Yeah," Grampa interrupted again. "Geronimo was a Chiricahua of the Bedonkhoe clan. There's no such word as Apache. It's a white word for 'Enemy.' "

I took a big sigh and waited for him to finish. When it was quiet again, I resumed. "The Dragons could not be killed, because they were covered with four coats of horny scales, and arrows would not penetrate these. Eagles fought with arrows, before men appeared. That's where we learned about them. The eagles fought the beasts and won, allowing the light of their victory to enter the darkness whence the beasts had come from. That is why eagle feathers are still worn by man as emblems of wisdom, justice, and power. But they had not been able to kill the Chief Dragon, who was very wise and very powerful. He was like the black void of space, and he could swoop over the earth and moon with a single black cloud. His feathers are like cosmic interstellar gas clouds. He had become Death Itself. Where all his brother dragons had been slain by the growing light upon Mother Earth, He alone remained and grew with incomprehensible Power.

"He hated women who came upon the Earth, as a blessing out of Her womb, because She perpetuated Life. The Dragon wanted the Earth to be like the rest of the void of the universe—Dead and Cold. This first woman was called White Painted Woman, and she was blessed with many children, but these had always been destroyed by the Dragon."

Jane had a smart-aleck question. "Who was the daddy of the babies?"

"Water and Fire."

"Who was he? Where did he come from? If Mother Earth only created a woman, then—"

"She created a man too, okay?" Sky explained irritably. "Go on."

"He was a Spirit, a seed, like sunlight. His mother, White Painted Woman, felt that the Rain was his father, and that the sacred child was born to her, and she dug a deep cave to hide him from the Dragon. That's this cave right here."

"That one?" Sage asked, wide-eyed, pointing to the cave outside their house.

"Yes. The baby was called Child of the Water, since his father was Water and Fire. White Painted Woman closed the entrance to the cave, but over the spot she built a fire. She sat by the fire on the cliff above the cave, and in this way concealed the babe's hiding place and kept him warm. Every day she would descend into the cave, where the child's bed was made of reeds and sweet-rush root, to nurse him. Then she would return to her fire, because frequently the Dragon would come and question her, but she would say, 'I have no more children. You have eaten all of them.'"

"Why didn't the Dragon eat her?" Jennifer asked.

"He wanted to, but the Goddess of Life was becoming too powerful. His only hope was to kill off all hope of Her children, and therefore, eventually, the Earth. When Child of the Water got bigger he would not always stay in the cave, for he sometimes wanted to run and play. Once, the Dragon saw his tracks in the sand, right here by these same shores. Now this perplexed and enraged the old monster, for he could not find the hiding place of the boy. He roared and stomped around like a tornado, saying he would destroy the mother if she did not reveal the child's hiding place. But she wouldn't tell him. She just kept saying, 'I have no more children. You have eaten all of them.' When the boy grew up to be a man he liked to go hunting, and the eagles showed him how to make arrows out of the lightning, like their sharp beaks and talons.

"Then, one day, as it was bound to happen, the Dragon finally found him. The huge beast flew over the world and he was bigger than the whole sky. He was bigger than the galaxy! He made a sound that vibrated in the young man's ears but which was silent too. 'BOY!' the giant monster roared. 'YOU ARE NICE AND FAT! I AM GOING TO EAT YOUR BRAINS!' But then Child of the Water heard the Earth's Voice whisper in his ears, like faraway music, 'Don't Be Afraid.' She said. 'Fight the Monster and you will Slay Him.' So the young man said bravely, 'No, you will not eat my brains.' The Dragon stopped for a moment and said, 'I LIKE YOUR COURAGE, BUT YOU ARE FOOLISH. WHAT DO YOU THINK YOU CAN DO TO STOP ME?' 'Well,' the young man said, 'I can do enough to protect myself, as you may find out. I will fight you.' 'OH HO!' the Dragon roared, and laughed and laughed. 'FIGHT ME?! HA HA! NO ONE HAS EVER BEATEN ME! I HAVE EATEN EVERYTHING IN THE UNIVERSE!' 'We shall see,' the boy declared. Then he took up his quiver of the eagle's arrows and shot one into the outer fourth layer of the Dragon's horny scales, which were like armor. The arrow pierced the scales and they fell off. 'VERY GOOD!' roared the Dragon. 'NO ONE HAS EVER PENETRATED MY ARMOR! BUT I HAVE THREE MORE LAYERS. COME, LET ME EAT YOU NOW!' 'No!' roared the young man, reloading his bow. 'I don't want to die!' 'HA HA!' howled the Dragon. 'EVERYTHING HAS TO DIE!' The young man shot another arrow, and it pierced the second layer of the Dragon's horny, scaly armor. Then a third arrow, and a fourth. Each time the scales fell away, and at last the Dragon's heart was exposed. When that happened, do you know what?"

"What?" the kids and Elders all gasped in chorus.

"The Four Sacred Arrows flew up into a rainbow over the Dragon, and the brave young man escaped around the jaws of the Beast, and he was not killed! He was not eaten! He did not die! He became immortal, and today we call him Monster Slayer, for he was the first Great Chief to defy death and become a Holy Spirit. He travels around the galaxy riding on the head of that Dragon, who can't turn his mouth around to eat him. Monster Slayer didn't kill the Dragon, for you can never defeat Death. Most people die and are eaten. But a few sacred men and women over the aeons have found the courage and the wisdom to hear the

Voice of the Queen, as well as the vibration of the Dragon, and they have become Great Spirits."

Everyone listened in wonder as I took a breath and poured myself another cup of coffee. Jane smirked, and asked Violetta, "Aw, is that true?"

Violetta replied, almost inaudibly, "Yes."

"Sweet Medicine of the Cheyennes is another Great Spirit like Monster Slayer, and his story is similar. His body disappeared from Bear Butte and he was gone. A lot of people witnessed the ascension with their own eyes. He just burned up and was gone. Just like that. He disappeared."

11

HOW SPRING
SHOWS UP ON THE SCENE,
AND HOW
WINTER PASSES AWAY.

WHIRLWIND AND I WERE KICKING BACK ONE MORNING, EN-joying the warm sun on our faces and the cool, dry ground on our backs. He was grinning at it all like he was the only person in the world who knew that everything except Nature is crap. He was lounging like a lizard on a rock by the shore of the Rio Grande and yawned. "Almost spring."

"Yep," I replied. I wasn't too talkative. It was too nice a day.

"How do you get to be a Storyteller?" he asked out of the blue.

"Oh, you just gotta know how to tell big lies."

He grinned lazily. "I always wanted to be a Storyteller too."

"I know."

He stared thoughtfully at the sky. His big brown face was thinner now, almost handsome. He'd dropped forty or fifty pounds this winter, if you can believe it. Red Bird had had him on a pretty ruthless diet, and we'd done a lot of exercising on horseback and hunting and all. I personally don't think exercise is good for you. Look at all those joggers who drop dead of heart attacks. But Whirlwind was starting to look a little athletic in appearance. There was still a lot of flab here and there, but he was six feet and four inches tall, so he was getting to be a pretty impressive-looking god-damn Cheyenne Indian. Professional linemen in the National Football League are big, huge fat guys like that too, but everyone recognizes them as fine-tuned athletes and striking personalities. No one disputes their high quality of achievement, just because they look more like Neanderthals than modern homo sapiens. Whirlwind had his same old personality trait of being oblivious to most problems, and an air of distraction that comes with a lifetime of bad food, and bad education, but he was a pretty striking guy now. He had always been mammoth, but now . . . I don't know. He would raise the hackles on your back just to look at him, like one of them Hawgs on the front defensive line of the Chicago Bears. His voice could boom like a buffalo bull's, if he ever wanted it to. He was a helluva guy. Still dumber'n hell, but as nice as you could want. You could see that he grasped about one word out of every hundred that Arantzazu or Buddy said, but he was trying and he was sincere and he was getting better. He'd stopped drinking and smoking. He was definitely improving as a human being.

Some Indians floated down the shallow river just then on an old homemade log raft, and Buddy was sitting right there in the middle of them. "Afternoon."

"Well, I'll be danged. Look what debris just drifted past."

"Hau."

"Buenas días."

They pulled over to the banks in front of us. Another excursion cruiser followed the first schooner, but it wasn't exactly a birchbark canoe out of James Fenimore Cooper either. It was more like a rickety rowboat. They didn't exactly look like Hiawatha or Chief Winnetou either. More like a bunch of winos trying to dry out. They had pock-marked faces and bloated bellies and were wearing rags from various rescue missions. They grinned with mouths half empty of teeth and eyes that were used to despair most

141

of the time. They were all happy as hell to stroll ashore onto No Tongue's Paradise, and greet famous fellers like me and Whirlwind. It was an honor for them to know us.

Buddy told us, "These are some of the warriors we're gathering."

"Oh, all right."

Another pleasure craft or two floated in, and before you knew it there were several dozen new mystic Warriors of the Plains gathering around the stewpot as reinforcements for our embattled little hardcore group that had been riding out the winter. Everyone traded pleasantries.

"Where ya from?"

"Lame Deer."

"Hopi."

"Papago."

"Hau."

"Ho."

"Ignacio."

"Anadarko."

"Buenas tardes."

Whirlwind was particularly excited to hear that a few guys were Southern Cheyennes from Oklahoma, and I said hello to a Naskapi friend who knew a few of my long-lost Huron relatives in Quebec.

There were some Nakayes up from Mexico, and an old Nahuatl Elder named Tlakaelel showed up too. He had talked to me for weeks one time about Itzachitlatlan, the Land of the Red Giants of Atlantis. Oh, you wouldn't believe some of the yarns those old backwoods Skins would tell. We often got into arguments about the various curative powers of peyote and penicillin and aspirin. Did you know that aspirin is made from the salycylic acid from willow trees, which sprout in the month of April, the poet's month? And that's why I'm a poet 'cause I was born in April, and aspirin has always been really effective for me? Lots of things like that. Someone brought some *ghogthpi'e tiswin*, which is corn cider, non-alcoholic of course, and that stuff goes down smoother than black cherry Kool-Aid.

But this was not to be a good old-fashioned get-together in which we traded recipes and prowled for squaws. Nope.

Buddy slumped to the ground and leaned against a cedar tree. "Whoo-ee, am I tired."

"I'll bet," Whirlwind sympathized. "Whatcha been doin'?"

The Elders were all hurrying over, too, and we all just sorta lounged around the stewpot and munched on some pretzels somebody'd brought. Buddy said, in greeting to the others, "Hau. Long time no smell," he added, shaking Grampa's hand.

Grampa wrinkled his nose at the fragrance of the troops Buddy had brought with him. "Wheeow. Smells like a Coors brewery."

"They're all sober," Buddy hastened to explain.

Violetta frowned. "You could stay drunk for weeks just on the leftovers in their blood. What's goin' on?"

"A lot," Buddy replied. "We have to have a big council with all the Elders right now, including the ones I brought with me. There'll be more coming all day, by boat and horseback. Rabbit's bringing in supplies on truck and—"

"Where is Rabbit?" Red Bird asked, hurrying over. She gave her brother a hug.

"Well, who's this beautiful woman?" Buddy smiled, and hugged her back. "I wish we weren't related. Rabbit? Oh, she's just as muleheaded as ever. She's got a lot of news for you, and some mail from home. There's some Cheyennes who've come down to join us too. Have they got here yet?"

"No."

Buddy looked at Whirlwind. "Your uncle is here too. Whistling Hog."

"Uncle Fred?" Whirlwind asked wonderingly. "Down here?"

"Yeah. He's got some real interesting news for you. That's one of the things we've got to talk about."

Old Girl took charge. "Well, let's get some food going and find places for everybody . . . you kids stay out of the way for a while—"

Everybody started bustling around at once, and buzzing, and bumping into each other like bees in a hive. Another dozen kids had joined the army of enlisted personnel, and they all tore off into the trees to show the newcomers the owl's nest they'd found, and a secret silver mine, and a deep, dark pool where there were some huge fish just waiting to be caught. One girl was trampled in the stampede, but two other girls hoisted her up agreeably, tearing her arm out of its socket, but she was okay. A few other boys acted like they were mad and had gotten hurt but no one paid any attention to them so they went back to playing. A serious congestion developed around the outhouse off and on, as it was our only hole and the city planners hadn't anticipated such population growth and urban sprawl. A hundred Indians must have been crawling all up and down the river, and it was a mess.

Then Rabbit and El Cuartalejo showed up, and you never saw such a jam of horses and trucks and people then. I swear, they came riding in with dozens of old nags and beat-up trucks, and Grampa got pissed off to see that they had blown our cover completely. Buddy disputed the point. "Grampa, the Feds've known you guys were here for weeks. Whaddaya think this is, 1890?"

"What?" Grampa challenged. "You disrespectful young—"

Buddy poked his nose right up against the ornery old coot, going nose to nose with him. "An Indian ratted on you guys weeks ago. He went and told them every—"

"What? Who?"

"I don't know, some wino." Buddy sighed. "They waved a few bucks in his face. You know how it is."

The Elders all frowned at each other, and watched Rabbit pull in on an old 1959 Willys. She was wearing army camouflage fatigues. She skipped over the small talk and was all business. "The Feds are tracking every movement we make. Cop cars 'escorted' us all the way, with two or three patrol cars in front of our caravan, several more in between us, and more at the rear. And planes flying over, helicopters? Shit." She could only shake her head and almost smile, she was so jazzed about it. She spit on the ground.

We were up on the top of the cliff, and cars and horses were pulling in like they were going to a rodeo and this was the biggest powwow of the year. It was completely transforming our former tranquil pastoral idyll, and all we could do was watch in dismay.

Rabbit gave Buddy a big hug and patted him on the ass. "How about a long, deep, wet one?"

He blushed down to his shorts and looked at everyone, who pretended to disapprove of this dirty behavior. "Here?"

She threw her head back lustily and laughed. "I meant a kiss!"

Red Bird threw her arm around Whirlwind and laughed. "Hiya, Rabbit," she said.

Rabbit clapped her hands and giggled and jumped on Red Bird, wrapping her legs around her friend. "Oh ho! Hey there's my girl! Where's Jennifer?"

Red Bird joked, "As if you care. Some mother, you go away for—"

Jennifer was right there, though, and hugged her Mommy. She demanded angrily, not smiling, "Where have you been? You just abandon your little girl—"

"Oh, I'm sorry, Honey," Rabbit apologized. "I'm a completely worthless slut, you're right. I'm sorry. I was very busy. Thanks for taking care of her. How ya doin', Philbert?"

"His name is Whirlwind," Jennifer corrected, still mad.

"Oh, excuse me. Say, I hear you're a Chief?"

"No," Whirlwind replied.

Rabbit gave Buddy a strange look and said, "That ain't what I heard."

El Cuartalejo rode in with a dozen men on horses, and Buddy's eyes went wide. "Jimmy! Wolf Tooth! HO! HAU! Now we have some warriors!"

"HOKA HEY LET'S POWWOW!" a few of the warriors whooped as well. Whirlwind recognized them as Jimmy Campbell, from Pine Ridge in South Dakota, and Oliver Wolf Tooth, whom Protector had given a ride to Denver on their way down here to rescue Bonnie. They dismounted and greeted Whirlwind, calling him Philbert, and there was a lot of backslapping and disparaging remarks about each other's personality and general appearance. Jimmy was the famous soldier who had been held in a tiger's cage in North Vietnam for thirty-one months, and had slit four Vietcong throats to escape. He had damn near every medal there was. Wolf Tooth and Buddy had been with his detachment. El Cuartalejo had been a Marine LURP for two tours. He liked to spend his time in the highlands with the Montagnais tribesmen, who reminded him of Mountain Apaches. Buddy introduced them to the others, and Jimmy assured

145

him he was off the peppermint schnapps for good now, and didn't have the shakes anymore. The men still looked a little uncertain of their footing; but they also looked scarier'n hell, especially if you were a Fed watching with binoculars a few miles away.

El Cuartalejo was not unfamiliar with his newly acquired celebrity status. "We're already surrounded, Bud."

Wolf Tooth added. "I wouldn't doubt they'd call out the National Guard on us."

"You can count on it now," Grampa complained. "Why'd all you so-called 'warriors' come waltzing in here like this, like it was a picnic?"

"It was the only thing to do," Buddy countered.

"They were picking us off one at a time," El Cuartalejo added.

"Snipers," Jimmy said.

Buddy continued. "They've been rounding up our supporters one at a time, Grampa, here and there all over the country. The Secret Police. Picking 'em up for bogus traffic tickets and threatening their families."

"Lots of bullshit," Rabbit growled. "Every cockroach in the country who thinks they know what's best for Indians has been shooting off his mouth about what we're doing wrong here. 'Violence' and all those things the liberals knee-jerk about. God, I hate liberals."

Buddy continued. "The Rainbow Tribers in California yapping about how we have to let peace prevail, and Mother Nature will purify herself and—"

"We'd better get down to the cabin," Violetta commanded, looking around at the disorganized mob gathering on the top of the cliff. "Some kind of leadership is going to have to get this mess straightened out."

Jusepe shook his head. "I don't understand."

They started down the hill, when Whirlwind saw someone in the milling crowd. "Uncle Fred?"

A handsome old man with very black hair and very dark brown skin, almost black, grinned at him. "Crackers," he said affectionately, using the boyhood nickname of affection.

They embraced. Whirlwind had tears in his eyes. He has a lot of sentimental shortcomings like that.

A number of other folks gathered around them, and

spoke in a tongue the New Mexicans couldn't understand. It had a lot of *x*'s and *q*'s in it and glurpy intonations and foreign sounds. They were Cheyennes. They all looked at Whirlwind with a new look he had never seen. What was it? Respect?

To make a long story short, thousands of plot details careened around and in and out, people gathered and camped and made fires, and the Great Council of the Rio Grande convened inside No Tongue's cabin. There must have been fifty Elders vying for space, all demanding to be heard and lobbying for more dialogue and lines from the scriptwriter, but I'll have to exercise restraint and keep the jabber down to a minimum, as there is one helluva lot of action-packed suspense still to come.

After a lot of preliminary fights and questions, the nub of the plot boiled down to the presentation of one or two choices, and one or two consequent decisions. All good editors will tell you that good drama consists of choices and decisions.

"Then at least that much is settled," Buddy shouted over the uproar. Everyone calmed down and looked perplexed, at each other. What had been settled? "We have to go to Bear Butte in South Dakota. Red Bird and Whirlwind and Storyteller are determined on at least that much in common."

Red Bird nodded and they all looked at her. "Yes."

"It is our vision," Whirlwind smiled shyly, putting his arm around her.

"That's good enough for me," Jusepe said, and most of the other Elders there agreed.

Violetta added, "Yes. The northern visitors have come down here to help us, and now I think we should all ride north with them and help them."

El Cuartalejo seconded the motion. "Speaking for the warriors, I think, I can say we will help too. You will need our expertise of this country, if we're going horseback. There are a lot of people here who know every inch of this territory. Otherwise, you'll never make it cross-country to South Dakota."

"And there are Lakotas and Cheyennes who know Colorado and Nebraska and South Dakota when you get up there," Wolf Tooth declared.

147

"Why," asked one Elder, imposing a practical note into the insane proposition, "not drive? It's impossible to go from here to South Dakota on . . . are you saying to go by horse? That's crazy."

The impolite statement provoked another outburst in which everyone talked at once and disagreed with everyone else about just about everything. Questions about how they could possibly hope to go across the street, let alone a thousand miles, with every cop in the world watching them were raised, with no satisfactory answer. How, indeed, could they go on such an epic expedition in these anti-heroic times?

"Sure it's crazy!" Buddy shouted louder than everyone else, so they turned to look at him. "Sure it's hopeless! So what?! What else have we got going? The Americans don't give a shit about us anyway. They're slaughtering us anyway, ignoring us to death. At least this way we can make a statement, and maybe even unite the Indians between here and there along the way, a little bit. I'm willing to try. We've got nothing to lose."

Even though his statements should have cleared up the plot complications with good clean convenient simplicity, they didn't. Everybody disputed every little point he made, nitpicking about this and that, and other people nitpicked about other people's nitpicks, until the whole human circus erupted again and the clowns and dancing bears and sword swallowers ran out into the middle of the Three-Rings and the audience tried to follow it all. Finally, No Tongue pounded the table with a coyote jaw until he got everyone's attention, then he pointed to me.

I shrugged. "I think we need a Chief. One leader to decide."

I looked at Fred Whistling Hog, who stepped forward on cue. "I'm only a visitor here. I'm a fullblood from the Suhtaio clan, like Philbert Whirlwind here, who is my nephew. I've come down from Montana to bring you news of your family, Nephew. You never knew who your father was, and we decided not to tell you so no one would be jealous of you all these years and try to hurt you. I know you've had a hard time, but it's paid off. You're a warrior now, I can see that. Your father was Francis Little Whirlwind Dreamer, and he was the son of our great Sweet Medicine Chief,

Little Wolf. You are in the direct line of the greatest Cheyenne Chiefs going back thousands of years."

Red Bird burst into tears and hugged Whirlwind. She couldn't even see through her tears, she was so happy. "Oh, I knew it, I knew it! Somehow I just knew you were going to be a great man!"

Buddy put his hand on his best friend's shoulder. "The warriors will do what this man says."

Jusepe put his hand on Whirlwind's other shoulder. "I think I can speak for the Elders when I say we can trust Whirlwind to carry out the will of the Elders' Council, the new government of the people. We want you to be our Chief."

Dare I enter the heart of Whirlwind at this moment, the greatest moment of his life, and a moment few men experience in this world? Should I open myself to the ridicule of the rationalists out there who will discount this poem as the fantasy of a wild-eyed dreamer, a man who never 'grew up'? I have never been accused of being shy, or particularly reverent, but I acknowledge that there are such shy and reverent souls as Whirlwind in our world, and I give them their due. I recognize the greatness of men like Crazy Horse and Geronimo who lived only for their people, and died for them. You can say that I am only a storyteller and this is only a fictional fairy tale created in the imagination of a fool; and you are right. Whirlwind is only a man, and pathetic at that. That is why he was crying like a baby, and why it made everyone else cry like a baby too. The Powers enjoy humiliating us like this; and we are at our best when we acknowledge the humiliation and behave like fools.

After a lot of silly blubbering a general sense of relief settled over everyone, and they waited for the new Chief to say something. The new Chief didn't have the slightest idea what to say. He had practically no experience of chieftancy.

Whirlwind finally managed to ask Uncle Fred (and he sounded surprisingly like simple ol' Philbert), "My father was named Francis Little—"

"Little Whirlwind Dreamer, yes," Uncle Fred grinned. "You chose the same name, in a mysterious way."

Rabbit was amazed. "Far out."

Grampa decided to give him a hard time right away, without even a honeymoon. "This still doesn't solve what we're gonna do."

That irritated Buddy. "Well, if you Elders are the government, you tell us. Whirlwind? Just give the word."

Whirlwind knew this was the moment of his quietus; it would be the first of many such moments, he was afraid. Already the great weight of responsibility reared its ugly head. What should he do? He had to say something. "How does this work? Uh . . ."

Old Girl came to the rescue. "The Elders decide something and you carry it out."

"Do all the work in other words," Buddy remarked caustically.

"Yeah!" Rabbit laughed pleasantly at the realization. "Kind of like Congress and the President."

That brought a few minutes of relaxed hilarity, as the thought of the American Government in all its anarchy modeled on the ancient structure of Indian government was just too funny a picture in most of their minds. Unpatriotic comments about corruption and hypocrisy provoked further hilarity. Through it all, Whirlwind knew he was just being given a slight reprieve from his duties, and that he was going to have to provide some leadership, whether he liked it or not. Like countless great men who have had power and glory thrust unwillingly upon them, he would much rather have been out playing golf or hunting antelope or something, *anything* rather than this moment in the spotlight. Great men, I can assure you, hate their greatness. What if you screw up? Then those same people who adored you yesterday would be the first ones to nail your balls to the walls. The electorate are a pack of hyenas, mostly.

Red Bird saw his predicament, though (as all good women do who are the real power behind the Office), and she suggested, whispering in his ear, "I think you should name Buddy your War Chief."

"Huh?" (He could have sworn it was the same Goddess whispering in his ear whom he heard on his Vision Quest, of late.)

"A Chief," Grampa declared, clearing his throat as if he was going to make a big speech, "is no longer a man, he is a Chief. He must always put the good of the people before his own feelings. Always. Even if another man snatches away your wife, you don't kill him, or even rough him up. You let the bitch go. If a few old farts come around and make derogatory gestures about your eating habits and your general personal appearance, you agree with them. You especially treat wise old men, like, say—oh like, myself, just as an example—with tremendous awe and love. If we ever need any money, you give it to us, with a smile on your face. Always. That's what a Chief is. I know you understand all this, my Cheyenne friend. I will never forget the day you took us to see *The Son of King Kong*. That was the first time I knew you were special."

✓No one quite knew how to respond to such historic oratory. Indians have always been famous for their oratory, and poetic phrases. They are especially renowned as proponents of the advanced system of government of wise Elders' Councils and Warrior Societies. A fact that is not widely known is that Women's Councils really ran the society. Women determined whether there was war or peace, for example. Men like to pretend that they run things, but everyone knows the women are really in charge of everything, including the men. You can't find one man out of a hundred, red or white or black or brown, who really believes he makes the decisions. Only a fool would think that.

So Whirlwind made his first speech and first decision at the conclusion of that historic Rio Grande Council. "Uh . . . I guess Buddy should uh be uh in charge of the warriors, if you want? Like a War Chief, maybe?" It was an eloquent pronouncement, and everyone was deeply moved, especially Buddy and the warriors.

He nodded humbly. "Okay."

Rabbit exulted, "All right! Now we're cookin'!" She gave him a big smack right there in front of everyone, making it crystal clear who *really* ran his program.

"And?" Grampa pressed, not unlike certain aggressive Senators who over-usurp their station and think they can make the Commander-in-Chief rush into hasty decisions, for purely political motives.

But no, Chief Whirlwind was not a man to be rushed. Or confused. Like all great leaders, he kept one or two simple

151

goals in mind, and they guided all his actions. "I don't see how we can go anywhere, let alone to Bear Butte, but . . . I trust the Powers. Something will turn up."

That was it. The die was cast. A thousand details of their epic Escape were discussed over coffee and sweet rolls, but there were no disagreements anymore, to speak of. If it felt like ten million Gestapo and Schutzstaffel goons were just lying in wait to ruin everybody's day, then no one showed their concern. They acted like the script had already been written and things were going to happen how they were going to happen and there was nothing anybody could do about it anyway. What was that line in *Lawrence of Arabia?* It was written.

I won't go into too much detail about the chaotic preparations over the next few days. It was beyond belief. It surpassed French farce. There wasn't a single goddamn person there who thought the Indians would get five feet. Hundreds of highly trained SWAT teams and special Anti-terrorist Units were flown in from their subversive activities in El Salvador and Iraq and Libya, and lay in wait for these red fuckers. "Reds, yeah?" the wiseacres joked in the patriotic camps, around their warm trailers and full bellies. To the man, the soldiers had been brainwashed to believe anybody who didn't love AT&T and Jesus was a demon from hell. No doubt about it. They wouldn't show (and indeed, *haven't* ever shown) the slightest compunction in blowing away every fucking man, woman, and red baby who dared cross the lines of civilization. I kid you not.

Rabbit was in charge of Intelligence, and had portable telephones and CBs scattered out among her lieutenants in their pickups. She knew the Secret Police were the biggest danger to their survival. All the goody-goody grocery clerks and nicey-nicey folks on the streets were protected by the shitheads with guns and computers out there behind the facades of commerce and Christianity. Like the blitzkrieg panzers who rape and pillage, at the point of Civilization were the men who rape and hate women. They were only a very small minority, the rapists, but all the other men allowed it to happen so that women would be passive and docile. Most men pretended to be goody-goody and nicey-

nicey, but they all let the rapists go wild. The goody-goodies of the human race tolerated the mean fuckers so they could have a nice day for themselves. These were Rabbit's thoughts.

You and I both know there could never be such a Revolution in this country as our author is herein describing. Not in the good ol' U.S. of A. This ain't Czechoslovakia or Poland, where everyone wants to be fatass consumers like the Americans. No, this is America Itself! This is the land of the fatasses of fatasses! What could be better?! No, we'll never have the pleasure of a revolution here again. We can revere nutcakes like Sam Adams and Tom Paine, but boy, if they ever try to rear their ugly heads today, well, wow! Pow! Call me a Libyan, but I wasn't born yesterday. The human race is full of shit.

Chief Whirlwind hadn't arrived at such a cynical conclusion yet. He still believed in Spirits and Destiny, right? Right. Henceforth, our Tragedy commences. Forward Ho!

Because, you see, Indians have always produced a key tactical genius every now and then in their raggedy midst, and Jimmy Campbell was just such a genius. His idea was simple, and that's why Chief Whirlwind liked it. He could understand it, as a simple kind of guy himself. It was therefore implemented into a Battle Plan. All wars follow these basic patterns, and our Hannibal was a student of history. The plan was this (and it was discussed out among the trees, as the General Staff knew there were spies everywhere): Assumption #1—the Americans are predictable. They will expect the Indians to manipulate the running dogs in the liberal media to protect them—just as the Americans have been manipulating the (liberal?) media in their systematic way. So, do what they expect. Scream on the Evening News about the injustice done to Indians. Make the bleeding hearts cry with their guilt. Try to make this look like a publicity stunt.

And then, put Assumption #2 into operation—that Indians are sneaky sons of bitches and will do anything to overthrow the American way of life. Let a Plan leak to the sympathetic college professors keeping the Pure Flame of Truth alive in the Ivory Towers that the Indians are *really* going to sabotage a Nuclear Power Plant in Arizona. And

maybe burn down the Cathedral of St. Francis in Santa Fe.
And kidnap Joe Coors and James Watt and Dan Rather
and Bob Hope for good measure. The professors will blow
the secret cover, and the Secret Police will, hopefully, swing
into action and be decoyed.

For the real Ambush would come right here, simple and
easy. They would do what the Cheyennes did under Dull
Knife and Little Wolf back in 1878: they would leave their
fires burning in the camp, their tipis and campers in place,
their telephones and televisions humming, and the core
group of Hostiles would sneak through the enemy lines in
the dead of night. Hopefully, the Powers would protect
them, and the men, women, and children would be disci-
plined enough to move silently like Indians. Red Bird
would carry their Sacred Bundle at the center of the
multitribal nation, and the warriors would surround them
as the final line of defense. It would take a lot of luck and
a cloudy night.

They were ready on the appointed night. It was dark.

No Tongue stood with the leaders. He had supplemented
Jimmy Campbell's battle plan with a few maneuvers he had
learned when riding with Geronimo. Never surrender, he
advised. Even if you freeze and starve, freezing and starving is better than dying. Under the Americans you will die
if you surrender, No Tongue told them, through Jusepe as
a translator. Sooner or later, he said, they will get you with
fetal alcohol syndrome or the Bible or greed. It is better to
be pathetic out in the dirt like a worm than proud and
important.

On foot, and with only the worst horses they had, the
hardcore fools prepared to go into that gentle night with
only the rags on their backs and a few bites of pemmican
and cornmeal in their pockets. It was the way Indians have
had to go into the night since Christopher Columbus came.

It was the way of the Pipe, which they smoked in a final
desperate prayer. It was the way of the Myth, which Storyteller spoke, my words floating on the air like a spell of
magic, like the smoke from the Pipe. The Breath of the
people rose into the dark sky like music and vanished into
the ethereality that guides our Fate.

A few last-minute details popped up, like they always do when you have to pack up and move. Chief Whirlwind gathered all the children together in a circle around him, and he instructed them in his gentlest whisper. "Okay, Gang, this is the game: we're gonna sneak away from here and get away from the bloodthirsty savages, so you have to be quiet. We're gonna play 'no talking.' No giggling, or sneezing, or farting." They all laughed and squealed that they would be glad to play this game. It sounded fun. They all liked Whirlwind 'cause he played with them a lot.

The women knew better. It was after midnight when they hoisted the kids on the horses, fast asleep. Hopefully, they wouldn't stir.

Violetta asked Rabbit, suspiciously, "Where'd you all get the money to pay for all these things?"

Rabbit knew she was in a spot. If she lied that her drug contacts in Texas were investing in the operation, she'd get caught sooner or later; but if she didn't lie about it, she knew these conservative country folks would disapprove and they'd have a big fight. Rabbit was sure that they'd still be sitting back in Picuris with their fingers up their asses if she hadn't sprung loose twenty grand for gas and walkie-talkies and phone bills. A revolution can't run on spit. "Willie Nelson and Marlon Brando sent us some dough." So, she lied, so what?

Violetta was impressed. "Oh, Willie Nelson? I love his voice."

"Yeah."

That took care of that, and Rabbit went back to finishing up her taped voice on the CB. She had a whole tape of her and other troops as if they were talking back and forth. It would run for ninety minutes after they left, hopefully fooling the Feds long enough that she and the Intelligence Corps were still on the job. She looked at Buddy and Whirlwind, who were on their horses, Cimarron and Perdita. Everybody was just about ready. Rabbit clicked on her high-tech apparatus. "Breaker one-nine this is Pussy Leader bravo and roger. Pigs oinking at checkpoint seven-two-two-niner at oh-one-thirty hours—" and so on.

They were ready. If they weren't exactly wearing gorgeous buckskin and eagle headdresses and beaded moccasins, then that was okay too. Secondhand coats and crummy boots and cheap cotton gloves brought this magic poem down to reality. The kids were asleep. The horses were scruffy stupid old nags and young stupid geldings, and the tack was motheaten and tacky, but that was okay too. Red Bird sat on the best mare, a white beauty named Lady, with the Sacred Bundle on her back, at the head of the column. A dozen women surrounded her, including Rabbit and Violetta and Old Girl. Chief Whirlwind was up at the front near her, with Sky asleep on the saddle horn in front of him. Grampa was on his roan, Lupe, at the point, and the other elderly men surrounded the women around Red Bird, including Jusepe and Old Codger and Whistling Hog. The warriors waited outside of them, with four Mescalero scouts who had already ridden on ahead. Only five of the warriors had weapons: Buddy, El Cuartalejo, Jimmy Campbell, Wolf Tooth, and a young Paiute named Sanza. They had semi-automatics of foreign make, purchased in a gun store in Durango, Colorado. None of the other warriors had rifles, as the War Chief had been very specific he didn't want any "young hothead" endangering the people.

There were sixty-seven people in all: thirteen warriors, twenty-nine women, twenty children, and five elder men. The rest of the people whom they had not been able to trust implicitly, the winos and people who came drifting in from various agency villages and towns, had been given some money to go to Taos for supplies. It was a wild goose chase. They hated to send off Indians like that, and it wasn't that they didn't want to take everyone into their trust, but the Feds were everywhere, watching everything, and it was just too chancy to take a risk on anyone who couldn't be vouched for. They were okay folks, they just had a long way to go yet, to get back up on their feet. Later, they might be able to join the Hostiles, if they wanted, and if they proved themselves.

No Tongue held the reins on Whirlwind's horse. He said goodbye. Whirlwind acknowledged the farewell and thanked the old man for all his hospitality. Without any more ceremony than that, Whirlwind gave Perdita a slight kick and she started walking slowly to the north. The column lurched forward. They moved almost silently. Luck was with them: the sky was overcast and a breeze blew in their faces from the north.

Out across the horizon they could see the intimidating lights of Jeeps and searchlights and cooking stoves: the Enemy lines. They were only two miles away, in every direction. They had set up the siege because their commanders weren't quite sure what to do about this bizarre gang of Indians in New Mexico. They were waiting for the President to decide something. The President was waiting for the polls to come out before he could discern which way the political climate was blowing.

The scruffy mares and geldings stepped gingerly over the rocks hidden under the snow, and over sagebrushes loitering in the dark like huddled shapes on the ground. Luck had it that the horses didn't feel like talking or whinnying either. No show-off stud was looking for some tail tonight. The Elders led them skillfully, straining their tired brains to remember everything Granddaddy taught them about oldtime Indian sneaking.

No Tongue watched them disappear into the dark, following a gulley along the top of the eastern cliff above the Rio Grande which he had shown them earlier. They were making far too much noise.

He went back among the trailers and campers with their lights still blazing and turned on a couple of radios as loud as they could go. He threw a glass bottle of juice against a rock so that it made a loud crash. He walked hither and yon through the camp making as many loud and obnoxious noises of the modern times as he could. Then he sat at his drum and started banging away. He sang some old Apache songs to himself, and remembered the good Old Days, which had ended abruptly in 1886 when Geronimo surrendered at Skeleton Cañon. He tried not to remember when they were kept as Prisoners of War in the Military Reservation, Fort Sill, Oklahoma, for years. Or the deaths of great Warriors in Old Mexico like his father, Kladetahe. No Tongue thought of his real name, Sanza Niyokahe, and felt his three wounds from battles, especially the long scar in his throat which tore out his vocal cords. He got that at Bosque Redondo. Geronimo had seven wounds: shot in the right leg above the knee, and carried the bullet the rest of his life; shot through the left forearm; wounded in the right leg below the knee with a saber; wounded on top of the head with the butt of a musket; shot just below the outer corner of the left eye; shot in the left side; shot in the back. He was a great Chief. He always regretted surrendering, and said they should have fought to the last Warrior in the mountains rather than go in to the shameful state of a POW. His people were starved to death. The Apaches were almost gone.

But tonight, Sanza Niyokahe was proud of his people again. They were pathetic, but that was good. They were courageous. They were riding against impossible odds. He knew that there was no way they could win.

He stopped playing the drum and turned off the radios. He turned off the lights, as if the camp was finally going to sleep. He broke a few more bottles and glasses for good measure and went and stirred up the horses still in the corral. They cooperated and whinnied and stomped around and kicked the rotted old fence posts. He listened to Rabbit's tape playing in the communications tent and giggled. She was a feisty one. He felt himself getting half a hard-on and wished he could make a run to Juarez one last time.

But no, he was finished. He sat at his drum and played a sad song, his death-song.

The wind blew lightly and smelled of horse apples. A few leaves blew around the old man with his head on the drum, and his mind was on a time with a Yaqui woman one night eighty-five years ago, and it was good. This was his sanctuary. It was a good hideout. It was quiet and he could listen to the Powers. Yes, it was Spring now, you could smell it blowing in from the mountains. He closed his eyes for the final time and sighed, and passed on with Winter into the good land of white buffaloes and all his smiling ancestors.

12

HOW THE TERRORISTS CALLED FORTH THE POWERS OF DARKNESS, AND OF SOME FOUR-LEGGEDS WHO PARTICIPATED IN THE DECEIT.

THE HORSES WERE ANNOYED. THEY KEPT STUMBLING OVER little rocks in the dark and tripping on branches and bushes. One or two snorted irritably and were shushed for their trouble posthaste. They kept looking around at the two-leggeds for an explanation of this nonsense, but, as usual, the two-leggeds acted like they knew what they were doing and the four-leggeds had absolutely no rights at all. Where was the barn? Where was their hay? What the hell were they doing out here in the middle of the night!

They came up slowly on some lights and went single-file down a shallow arroyo. The horses liked that a little better; most horses, especially mares, like to stick their noses into other horses' asses and tails, especially geldings and stallions. Females of all species the world over are fond of such things. So they proceeded smoothly in this manner.

Two men crouched in the dark along the top of the little arroyo, on each side, and a few of the four-leggeds skittered a little when they heard the men click back those awful thunder-sticks they had in their hands. More than a few long brown ears, with their winter coats shaggy as dogs, went back in alarm. But all they got was kicked and shushed again for their trouble, until they straightened up their ears and behaved abnormally, which is all the two-leggeds ever wanted of them.

The column walked silently through a chink in the besiegers' armor as easy as you please. The warriors watched the sleeping crack soldiers in their tents and Armored Personnel Carriers. The soldiers and vigilantes couldn't see or hear a thing in that dark night. It also didn't hurt that it couldn't possibly have ever occurred to a man with any sense at all that sixty-seven people and forty-two horses would *want* to sneak past them. It was something beyond their comprehension; therefore, it was not possible. It *couldn't* be happening; therefore, it *wasn't* happening.

Mandy and Perdita waited beside their overweight cargo at the rear of the column, at the slight decline that led into the arroyo. They heard one of the two-leggeds muttering some strange Spell, which Perdita, in particular, was sure was a summons for Devils to come. Horses aren't dumb, you know. They're smart. They talk to each other. They know things. They have horse superstitions too. And indeed, there did seem to be a black protective shield cast over them, made out of my whispers. The Plot against America was just a matter of a few magic words.

Chief Whirlwind squatted beside me as the people passed. He helped adjust children on their horses when they were slipping off. Violetta had Jane and Jennifer both with her, on a good-tempered old gelding named Stewball. His presence calmed everyone as they walked or rode past.

Buddy walked back in the dark. "No problem yet. The Elders are watching up front, and two warriors are on each side."

The Chief was concerned about the guns. "I'm concerned about the guns," he whispered.

Buddy shook his head, but since it was dark, no one saw him do it. "That's only as a last resort. If they open up on us I don't want to be caught out here with just my dick in my hand."

They thought about that. It was indeed a very serious situation. You can say that Americans would never open fire on Indians, not in this day and age, not in New Mexico. But we know better. Whirlwind and Buddy Red Bird knew better. They'd been shot at in Sheridan, Wyoming, just last Christmas, for nothing; driving up and down some wrong-way streets and wrecking a Radio Shack and stealing a few dollars. And in Santa Fe for punching out an FBI agent and his Mafia friend. The American response to these minor infractions had been way out of proportion, so the boys knew it was always possible for gunfire to erupt. Americans are trigger-happy. The whole world knows that. They love their guns.

If there were more than just a few real pissed-off cops in those siege lines then that's no one's fault. So what that a few State Troopers and County Sheriffs and City Police-men had lost a few of their supercharged Patrol Cars in various accidental mishaps? And a few revolvers had accidentally discharged? They shouldn't go around blaming an innocent Indian or two who might have been standing nearby at the time. If a cop car or two had blown up and flipped out into a field and exploded, well, these things happen. It's no reason to go flying off the handle.

And where did the Federal boys get off, muscling in here out of their jurisdiction? Reports about international drug financing and arms shipments were none of their business. No one had gotten hurt. There weren't any laws broken, except maybe a few misdemeanors here and there concerning one or two semi-automatic machine guns from El Salvador and Cuba. But they were legal, the Second Amendment guaranteed the freedom to bear arms. Who was going to be picky about a simple failure to register a rifle here or there? Certainly the National Rifle Association would take exception to such flagrant violations of human rights. Criminals were going to find illegal weapons, anyway, anywhere they wanted to. So I don't know why the Feds were working themselves into such a lather about a few poor Indians.

Nevertheless, these things happen, and the poor dumb Indians snuck right through the Iron Curtain of America like they didn't know it couldn't be done, not in this day and age. I mean, didn't they *know* how many infrared lasers

and spy satellites and all sorts of other fancy high technological shit these rich bastards had trained on them? Why,
just the computers and smart bombs in one F-16A was
enough to intimidate the bejesus out of half the world, at
the cost of only $500 million per aircraft. That was a bar-
gain, for all the shit you could scare out of everybody. But
these Indians didn't know any better. Half of 'em probably
couldn't even read.

The horses clomping out of the arroyo were sure that
they had a helluva lot more sense than these idiotic two-
leggeds too. A jackrabbit would have more sense. Only a
dozen yards away they could smell the coffee and dough-
nuts. There was probably oatmeal somewhere close by too.
It was nerve-wracking. The big fat slobs crawled back on
Perdita and Mandy as the last refugee straggled by, and
Perdita stuck her nose in the last tail ahead of her. Dang,
it was only another mare, Hortense, who didn't have
enough of a brain to stop . . . she was so stupid she'd walk
into a fence if you let her. Clomp-clomp, stumble-stumble.
Chief Whirlwind shifted his weight on Perdita, and held his
breath. The Enemy didn't seem to hear us, or see us. It
was impossible. We were within spitting distance. But, no,
the Powers were with us. Maybe I really had cast a magic
protective spell over them, and all the soldiers were fast
asleep like in Sleeping Beauty when Maleficient comes in to
steal the sacred princess. I had explained the story to Whirlwind last night, in a simplified form, so that he and Sky
and Jane and the other kids could understand it. Maybe
such things really do happen, Whirlwind thought. I had a
smirk on my face, but it was dark so nobody could see it.

We rode off into the night. The lines of civilization
dimmed behind us, to the south now. Nothing stirred except our footsteps. It wasn't even too cold, so the sound
didn't crack like ice. A few horses sighed in exasperation,
and tried to get rid of the hated bits and halters in their
teeth, but it was quiet. They kept their complaints to themselves. They didn't want to be kicked anymore, was why.
They just had to get through this idiocy, somehow. Maybe
it would end soon. Anything was possible.

One mile turned into another mile, and the arroyo dis-
solved into a muddy gully, which went up a hill to a dry

plateau. It was silent and almost pitch-black, except for the light pollution from the sleeping army back to the south. Most of the adults got off their horses as they stumbled up a steep rise, holding the horses' reins. The horses didn't want to go and had to have their teeth pulled out before they'd go up, stubborn as mules. The children snored away, tied to the saddle horns. The plateau went down into another rocky draw, and then the horses got really pissed as they had to tiptoe through some cactus. They stopped and refused to go through a bramble patch, but they just got kicked in their guts again for their trouble and had to go forward anyway. So much for caution.

Up and down they went, around and over. The animals drew the final straw (of hay?!) when they came to a barbed wire fence. Grampa just chuckled and produced a handy-dandy pair of wire cutters and snapped it with one squeeze on each strand. Snap! Crackle! Pop! He didn't care if the horses (except for that stupid twat Hortense) hated to go near any wire, and their re-mounted riders didn't care, either, if they might step on the sharp metal. They just made those stupid clicking sounds with their mouths, and that stupid old gray mare Myrtle just did everything they told her, and the others followed like a bunch of Ninnies. It didn't do any good to protest against all this injustice.

There wasn't any water to drink. No oats. No rest. Not even a carrot. If you tried to take one bite of grass for one second you got persecuted for the effort. That gray gelding Galisteo tried to take a bite of his rider's leg but it didn't do any good. It was too bad he missed though. No apples. Just work. Drudgery. Keep walking. Walking. Walking. Not even a good trot was allowed, as the two-leggeds on foot couldn't have kept up. The bastards didn't care how much your back ached from the load. They didn't care how much you were sweating.

They went through another fence—the wire lying everywhere like snakes to bite at your hooves—and up onto a smooth surface. It was a gravel road. A few people in a few trucks were waiting for them, somehow, and they were getting some more poor four-leggeds and saddling 'em up. Cimarron recognized Raton and La Gorda from the old days.

Arantzazu sat in her son's pickup with the heater going. She handed Violetta a ten-gallon thermos of coffee and a sack of tortillas. "You're right on time."

"How'd you know we'd be here?" Violetta grinned, gratefully pouring herself a cup.

Red Bird dismounted and kissed the ancient old lady through the open window of the idling 1969 Ford Ranger. "She's an old witch, that's how."

Arantzazu giggled. "We brought you three more good families who want to go with you. The two men are honest hard workers. You can trust them."

"Bueno," Jusepe commented, looking at the new people saddling up.

"Do you know the way over the hills to Arroyo Hondo?" she asked.

"Of course," Grampa snapped. He pointed to the northeast in the truck's dim yellow lights, which was all they allowed themselves. The trucks had driven in the dark to meet them here with no lights on.

Arantzazu shook her head and pointed a good ten degrees farther east.

Grampa adjusted his calculation, and allowed, "That's what I said."

Without any further folderol we rode off into the dark again, and the pickups vanished away from the hasty rendezvous on down the side road.

No one asked the horses if they minded. They were just pointed across the pastures, which were lined with a few clumps of conifers and evergreen groves, like they were slaves with no rights or opinions of their own. Over fences and under tree branches. No water. No hay. They were getting ready to die, right out there in the middle of nothing.

This went on forever. The two-leggeds complained about sore rear ends and cold ears and tired children as if it was the horses' fault! You could see that one black stud Lobo was about to lead the rebellion in about one more minute when, all of a sudden, they came upon a little creek in the woods and stopped! The babbling brook was almost as sweet in their ears as the Chief's words, "We better camp here."

"Not a chance," Grampa argued.

"Well . . . there's water and everyone's tired."

"There's also a million soldiers," Jusepe argued. The other Elders nodded agreement.

"What about food?" a woman complained.

"And the horses are beat."

"They can drop dead for all I care," Grampa snarled. (Ah ha! the horses exclaimed! Now the truth comes out!) "We have to keep moving."

But a few sympathetic souls braved the barbarian's wrath and led the horses to drink. Oh, that spring water tasted good! After a few minutes the four-leggeds looked around for their hay. Where was it? Where were their oats? They looked at the Chief in the dim pre-dawn light.

The Chief looked back at everyone else. They were all looking at him. Thick white clouds raced overhead and reflected a pale light. Old Codger looked at the clouds. "Snow," he said.

"Oh great," someone complained. "That's all we need."

"You dern ignerant city people," Grampa cussed. "That's good. It might cover us when it gets light."

"We better pray for snow," Jusepe said quietly.

At that moment Chief Whirlwind wished he was pore dumb Philbert again, slouching obesely through the back alleys of Lame Deer. What was he doing here? He was freezing. What was he going to do? Seventy-seven people and forty-six horses looked at him for leadership. He saw Lobo perk up his ears suddenly, as the wind shifted from the northeast and blew a strong gust over them. The other horses smelled something suddenly too. It was the smell of other horses somewhere, and barns, and feed too! Where was it coming from?

Whirlwind said, "What's wrong with that black stud?"

"He smells something."

"Oh, ya know," one of the newly arrived relatives of Arantzazu realized, "they smell that dude resort over yonder."

"Dude resort?"

"*Si*. They got lots of them tourist horses and barns."

Grampa looked delectably at Whirlwind. "Horses?"

"Barns?"

"Feed?"

"Yep," the local guy replied. "There's probably a hundred saddlebreds over there, this time of year. It's a big damn place. Some rich Anglos from Texas—"

"A hundred horses?"

"Real beauties. There's even some thoroughbreds there."

Everyone stood around and perked up their ears. It was just light enough to keep riding a little ways more, maybe, enough for a man, or even a few men, to go for a ride somewhere and . . .

"No," Red Bird said.

"No what?" Whirlwind asked, understandably.

"You're not gonna go steal those horses. This isn't a game."

"Who said anything about stealing horses?"

"Whirlwind, I know you."

Grampa reassured her. "It never crossed our mind. But I think, as a representative of the Government, we could go ask for a few bags of feed, maybe."

"Yeah, real polite-like," another *hombre* suggested.

"It wouldn't be stealing."

"Just asking for any feed they got left over."

"Maybe."

The men were scared of the women, that was obvious. They were explaining their heads off. They looked at Whirlwind. "What do you think, Chief?" they re-directed pointedly.

The Chief looked imploringly at the women, and found a sympathetic smirk in Violetta. She relented. "I don't see anything wrong in us resting the kids here and making a cold breakfast, while the men go see if they can get some feed for the animals."

"There ain't much grass around," Old Girl explained to Red Bird.

"We gotta take care of the animals," Grampa added, lovingly petting his old mare Lucinda. (But she wasn't fooled. This was the same guy who'd said two minutes ago he didn't care if the horses dropped dead!)

The horses were all for the expedition. A few of 'em were actually chomping at the bit to go. Oats and barns were wafting strongly on the wind now. This was the first sensible idea they'd heard all night. Lobo wasn't going to wait much longer.

Whirlwind picked six men and six of the best horses to go on the polite visit over to the resort with him: Grampa, Buddy, Jimmy, El Cuartalejo, Sanza, and Wolf Tooth; and their horses. The women laid the sleeping children on old quilts and on a few down sleeping bags beside the creek. Rabbit hooked up her portable CB-Radio unit to listen to the police chatter. Sky and Jane were snoring, wrapped in each other's arms.

I watched the warriors trot away on their mounts. The mounts weren't at all reluctant now to hurry up their steps as they smelled the barn, dodging in and out and around the thick woods, and it was all the men could do to follow a bumpy four-wheel-drive trail through the forest, as the horses were anxious to break out into a full gallop and run and, it was obvious, kill their riders in the process. Whirlwind bounced wildly as Perdita changed her gait to a full run, and he was getting his balls smashed. Flop-flop went his big fat gut and tits! YA-HOO! They dodged around a few holes in the road, and over a few ruts in the snowy landscape. Flop-flop! They were sailing along at a pretty good clip in the dim light, and Grampa actually looked like he was enjoying himself, out in the lead. His old mare was faster than all the others. Whirlwind was sure his saddle was loose and he'd slip off and die any second. He had never ridden much in his life, you see, until this winter. BOUNCE-BOUNCE! BOUNCE-BOUNCE!

"YIPPEE HA!" Grampa whooped, unable to be quiet.

They came upon a dirt road, and Whirlwind couldn't control Perdita at all now. "WHOA!" he whispered fiercely in terror, pulling back on the reins as hard as he could. He was scared to death. But the evil animal just laid her ears back and ignored the stupid shit. "WHOA, YOU STUPID SON OF A BITCH!"

"YEEEE HA!" Grampa screamed. The others were all running at full speed now and didn't seem to be worried about it. Buddy was an especially picturesque equestrian and sat on Cimarron like he was part of the gelding.

The dirt road turned to paved road suddenly, and they were running through a long, beautiful line of elms and cypresses leading toward a row of lights and a complex of buildings ahead. Everything was happening so fast that Whirlwind couldn't follow it. All he could think about was how he was going to be trampled to death any second. He could see himself flying through the air and breaking his neck as he hit the irrigation ditch next to the trees and road. That paved road looked hard as Hell.

"Whoa. Oh, please, please whoa? Whoa? WHOOO-OOOOAAA!!"

The horses were blasting like mad slavering beasts and this was the fourth Race at Santa Fe Downs.

"CHHAAAAAAAAAAAAAAAAAAAAAAARR-GGE!!!"

It was Grampa, of course. Whirlwind hated him at that moment. Grampa was screaming and laughing maniacally, as they charged into the La Paloma Vacation Rancheria, past luxurious lawns and manicured gardens. A solar putting green was sheltered inside a plastic greenhouse, and duck ponds decorated dormant daffodil groves and pansy forests around the sculptured fountains, dry now in early spring. There were also several rows of long white barns and they could hear the horses calling inside; *they* knew something was up. The seven marauders could hear them kicking in their stalls and making a number of other noisy comments.

"WHOOOOOOOA!"

"CHHAAAAAAAAAAAAAAAAAAAAAAARR-GGEE!!!"

It was no use. The crazed Indian chased right through the open barn door and disappeared inside, not even slowing down. Whirlwind was sure he would never see Grampa alive again. Then the cacophony of dozens of horses going wild erupted from the barn and all hell broke loose.

The horses broke loose. They kicked out the doors of the stalls, or jumped over them, and tore after the Indians. Whirlwind found himself leaping a small fence as Perdita made a beeline for the oat silo. By some miracle he stayed on her. Expensive Pacers and Show Ponies followed her, and the others. Whirlwind couldn't see what was going on. He didn't know that sex-starved mares were raping stallions right and left, and that the dazed studs hadn't seen so many . . . well, you ten-year-olds know what I mean. It was a horse orgy. All the resentments of years of being whipped

168

and saddled and kicked by spoiled rich brats from Houston burst out of them and they wrecked one whole corral, pissed all over the hated saddle blankets and shit all over the tack shop, kicking down the door with their expensive shoes. Morgans kicked at rival saddlebreds, and jealous hacks took out years of spite on rival steeds.

Since there was really nothing the innocent Indians could do to stop the carnage, they went with it. The next time Whirlwind saw Grampa he burst out of another huge red barn driving a five-ton seed truck, loaded to the gills with oats.

"HOOOOOPOOO HOOOOOooOOOOOooO!!" He screamed.

A dozen horses picked up on the moving groceries and chased after him. Perdita took off with Whirlwind. The next thing he knew, he was off the evil animal and in the back of the truck shoveling oats out to more horses, as the truck raced past more barns and corrals (the La Paloma Vacation Rancheria was a really beautiful and big operation, it really was) and more horses stampeded over the gates and through the fences to catch the truck. Dozens of absolutely magnificent four-leggeds ran after the free lunch, and five other Indians on horseback flanked the truck and herded the animals in a tight pack behind it.

"Keep 'em together!" the impromptu wranglers shouted.

"Don't tip over, Grampa!"

But the ornery old horse-thief was oblivious to everything but the thrill of the moment and the glory of the chase. He couldn't stop screaming and whooping as he plowed off into the woods on the paved road. He gunned that baby up to eighty, and those horses kept right with him! He couldn't believe it!

The herd thundered off into the waning darkness, and a cloud of dust and mudclods splattered the expensive imported shrubbery along the foot of the elms and cypresses. White ranchers and cowboys and cooks and servants and dogs came running out of the houses back at La Paloma, but they couldn't see anything or anyone.

"WHAT'S GOING ON?!" they demanded of each other.

"I DUNNO!"

"Huh . . ."

"What?"

By the time they figured out that millions of dollars worth of insurance in damage and lost thoroughbred horseflesh was gone with the wind, the surprise attack was over. Later analyses of the attack determined it hadn't lasted more than ten minutes. Every single horse had run away.

Our raiders with their Grand Larceny roared and thundered back down the dirt road, to the four-wheel-drive trail, and back into the sheltering trees. Grampa slowed down, but not much. The horses were running happy as hell. They were free!

When the core of the guerrilla revolutionary army heard the pounding roar of a herd of horses, they naturally looked up from their cold cereal by the creek to see what was up. They were startled as about a hundred sleek beauties in the newly liberated brigade charged into an open clearing behind a giant seed truck painted red and with the emblem of some rich dude resort somewhere. Kids burst out of a dead sleep to see the truck fly over an unseen ridge and an old Indian leap out of the cab, screaming some ancient oath. He flew one way and the truck flew another way, and the horses stopped to watch in admiration as the truck arched twenty feet over a grove of cottonwoods, sailed over the creek, and crashed head-on into a small bluff on the other side. Dozens of trees were massacred and tons of oats flew hundreds of feet in every direction at the instant of the stupendous *CRASH!* The horses were undaunted by the explosion and tore into the oats—including the patient old nags with the army who had been wondering when some real chow was going to arrive. The truck just kind of crumpled and slid quietly to its death at the foot of the bluff. It didn't even burst into flames. The horses commenced grazing contentedly.

Grampa rolled down a nice soft snowy slope and giggled idiotically; because, it started to snow.

13

HOW AN ALLIANCE AMONG THE SPECIES WAS NEGOTIATED, AND OF A TREATY BETWEEN THE UNITED TRIBES.

THE HERD OF PONIES KICKED BACK TO DIGEST THEIR FEAST. A coat of lacy snowflakes wove its infinite pattern upon their shaggy winter coats, which were all the colors of the rainbow. Jack Frost festooned their manes to make them look like magical unicorns with icicles hanging from the tree branches over them like horns, and the snow hung heavily over them on the branches like wings stretching from Pegasus and Arion, Rosinante and Centaur.

The Indians lounged under the trees out of the snow and stared at the herd of ponies. It was a dream. The horses stared at them. There were no corrals in sight. Everyone stared at the Man-chief and the Horse-chief. She was a gorgeous pinto quarterhorse.

Chief Whirlwind walked bowlegged (his butt and nuts sore as hell) over to the waiting Pinto. She knew right away this two-legged was an amateur, but she also knew he was very kind. "Well," the thing said, "I see everybody has had breakfast."

She whinnied happily, and a dozen of her adjutants responded in kind. She ran around a little, kicking up the fluffy snow that was already masking their smell and tracks from those hated corrals at La Paloma Prison.

Neither side was quite sure what to do. The Elders enjoyed seeing the Chief put on the spot, and they said nothing. He'd have to learn sometime, they thought. He had shown enough initiative this morning to follow his instincts and make this fine oldtime Horse Raid, so they were glad to let him feel his way now. Maybe he'd come up with some new inspiration.

Red Bird came up to him instead, and she was mad. "I thought I told you not to go stealing horses!"

Uh-oh. The Elders cringed. They made themselves busy with a number of other chores that needed to be done.

"We didn't steal any horses," Whirlwind offered lamely.

"Oh?" she exclaimed angrily. "Then what are those? Do you see those animals over there, Whirlwind? What are they—camels? Look. Look at them! What are they?"

"Horses."

"About a hundred of them? Very expensive-looking horses too?"

"Yeah, I guess."

"So where'd they come from?"

Whirlwind looked beseechingly at Grampa, who only limped off into the trees to "relieve himself" as he muttered. The coward. "They . . . followed us home."

She stared at him with disbelief. "They 'followed you home'? He says 'they followed him home.' "

"They did."

"Do you know, approximately, how many policemen and soldiers are going to be swarming in here any second?"

"No."

She moaned. "We'll all be killed."

In his desperation, Whirlwind caught a glimpse of a white stallion thoroughbred taller than him, out of the corner of his eye. "I got that one for you."

She wheeled around to look. "What one?"

He pointed. She looked. She softened. The Pinto craftily appraised the situation at that moment as well—for she knew which side her oats were buttered on—and she ordered the big beautiful Hunk to go over to the Boss-lady and suck up to her. The big dummy pranced over obediently in his most charming manner, and nuzzled Red Bird. She tried to ignore the bribe, but everybody could tell she was eminently corruptible. She adjusted the straps on the heavy Bundle on her back, and petted the stallion. He gave her a gentle kiss.

The Pinto moved in on the Man-chief. He could see that she, unlike that goddamn old nag Perdita, would be a partner to him instead of a competitor. He wouldn't have to be afraid of her. She would be gentle with him. She was the classic black-and-white beauty of his dreams, a real Indian pony. Big and strong, too, with a steady intelligence in her soft black eyes. Whirlwind petted her nose. She responded to the foreplay by scratching her face on his back. All the other horses watched attentively, not one hoof moving. The Indians watched, too, even Grampa and the Elders coming back from their chores, not one finger twitching. It was poetry to see them together. They had obviously been destined for each other.

"Good morning," the man said. "It's good to see your family is well. Can I ride you today?"

She jerked and trotted away. Why is it that men always have to go too fast? Why can't they be patient with a girl, and wait to be invited? She was annoyed, but ... he was cute. So, after having made her point, she returned flirtatiously and poked him in the ass. Then she ran off again.

The courtship would have lasted interminably if Grampa hadn't stepped in. "This is enough, we have to get moving." He was anxious to rope a huge chestnut thoroughbred that had caught his eye. All the other horses and people were getting curious about each other as well. The dance could have lasted all night, but the Elders saw that it was okay to take command again. Red Bird had been completely won over by the white stallion. But when Grampa moved toward the four-leggeds with his rope and halter, Whirlwind stopped him.

He was just as surprised as Grampa. Before he knew what he was doing or saying, his arm jumped out and grabbed the old coot. He said, "Let's try it the old way."

"What? What old way?"

Whistling Hog moved in on cue. "I used to show Crackers, er, Whirlwind, pictures of the old warriors bareback with only a single little rope in their mouth on one side for a bridle."

"Oh, yeah," Grampa nodded. "I knew that."

"I've ridden rodeo parades like that," volunteered another Elder. He was one of the new guys who had just joined them.

"Yeah," several more Elders chimed in. They liked the sound of it.

The Pinto liked the looks of it. She watched the big guy hoist the bridles and saddles off the other old nags and throw them in a pile by the creek. Pretty soon, everyone had all the tack piled up. Curiously, she cantered over to have a closer look. Her tribe fell in behind her. Then, in another act of genius and inspiration, Chief Whirlwind unzipped his jeans (carefully avoiding the exposure of himself to the two-leggeds around behind him) and urinated on the hated saddles. The horses cheered. They whinnied wildly. Whirlwind urinated for a full minute, as he was wont to do first thing in the morning, and it splashed up everywhere. It was divine. The four-leggeds exulted. They ran around and around and around.

The Pinto came closer and admired the instrument of Man's Evolution. He coyly put It back in the Genie's Bottle, and she took a deep, satisfying breath. "You okay?" he asked, after the ritual was over. She felt good. He felt drained.

She nodded. In a flash, he mounted her before she knew what was happening. He was on top! Without a saddle or bridle or any other artificial contrivance!

She bolted, in her pleasure. He clung to her tightly, trying not to flop off and get bent in her frenzy. Females don't realize how rough they can be under such circumstances, and that men are frail and delicate flowers who must be fondled carefully. You cannot just thrash about willy-nilly as you are wont to do in these moments of distraction. You must realize that we can break in two, like a twig.

I'll dispense with any more erotica and relate to you that, eventually, the oldtime rope bits were hooked into the mouths of those animals who allowed such things to be

174

done to them orally, and everybody found the animal of their dreams. Grampa wrapped his arms and legs around the neck of the chestnut, and tears were actually seen to be in his eyes. "I've dreamed of having a horse like this all my life. I name you Betty Grable."

Whirlwind asked the Pinto if he could call her "Massaum," and she agreed to it. It meant Good Horse Medicine in Cheyenne.

Buddy stuck with Cimarron, but Sky had his eye on a sorrel mare and she let him call her "Hulk," after the wrestler Hulk Hogan. Jane admired a speckled Appaloosa and named him "Peckerhead," a word her Mommy often used. Rabbit, for her part, enjoyed the company of a plain brown mare with Morgan and thoroughbred blood whom she named "Emiliano Zapata." Red Bird dubbed her randy white stallion "Star." For my part, I accepted the partnership of a simple black saddle-bred stallion (which I learned months later was valued at $50,000) and named him "Gandalf," after the wizard in Tolkien's stories.

Oh, there were a thousand more things I could tell you about that enchanted snowy morning, but the Elders were anxious to get moving and I couldn't blame them. We were all a little nervous, naturally, about the specter of Red Bird's legionnaires coming to kill us all any second. So we put our affairs in order and trotted off through the trees, heading northeast toward Arroyo Hondo, wherever that was. The horses we had coerced into coming with us from No Tongue's Paradise were worn out and refused to carry another pound another foot. So they walked sulkily along behind us while we all rode our fresh new mounts. They were agreeable for the most part, except for a few recalcitrant mustangs who wanted to charge over hills and complain about everything. But Massaum and Whirlwind had forged a workable alliance, and most of the expensive new four-leggeds tagged along, as we had gathered the remaining oats in several dozen burlap bags (that had been stored in the destroyed truck) and they were very fond of oats. You may have noticed that a free lunch is often an ideal incentive to attract troops to an army.

It was snowing pretty good now, but a lot of people were foolishly bitching about it, as if being cold and wet and hungry was not a preferable alternative to being in jail or murdered. Just because it was about twenty degrees and the wind chill factor was making it more like twenty below zero, they had to act like we weren't having fun. They shivered and their teeth chattered when I can tell you for a fact that there have never been prettier canyons and forests and babbling brooks as we saw that day. There's no pleasing people.

Didn't they know the snow and wind were covering our tracks, and preventing Hueys and Cobras and Focke-Wulfs from swooping out of the sky and strafing us all in five seconds?

We rode into the radical village of Arroyo Hondo about midday, with about as much caution as you would exercise in the Easter Parade. Sometimes those Elders would sneak around and make a big fuss about one match or one word in the dark, and then another time they would act like we were invisible and could walk right smack into the middle of the White House and take a big dump in front of everybody. There we were, at least about eighty people and well over a hundred horses, waltzing right up to a cantina on the main street of a town like we'd done it every day of our lives.

People came out and stared at us like they'd been expecting us. Me, I expected ten thousand U.S. Army tanks to come roaring over the high hills along this deep river valley and blow us all to fuck. I was too freaked out about it that day to even remember the name of the nice creek running through the town and cañon. It was a remote little village all right, getting close to the Colorado border, but the main highway ran right through it. Usually, it would have been full of traffic, but today, the roads were icy and snow-packed, and travelers had been advised to stay home. So the highway was empty, except for snow and ice and a blizzard. It was almost too easy.

Arantzazu was there waiting for us, with a whole slew of other fellow travelers, and a feast of hot enchiladas and cocoa and *sopapillas* in the Bingo Hall. The whole town, it seemed, had turned out to entertain us. The *New York Times* might have described them, later, as "Chicanos" but they were just poor folks like us. Oh, there was a lot of talk about Land Grants and the Treaty of Guadalupe Hidalgo, but I had a cold and couldn't hear too well. I also don't speak Spanish too well. But they were good friendly folks and made the best damn gazpacho I ever had. A couple dozen even requested to join us, and the Elders held a quick council about it. Heavy coats and boots and mittens appeared out of nowhere for us, and frybread to go, and candy for the kids, and blankets for the horses. The Elders agreed to take on about half the village, and I could see this was burgeoning into something bigger than you or me.

Up we rode into the mountains, after wasting only a few hours in the warm town getting dry. We crossed the highway one clump at a time, with Arantzazu supervising from the warm cab of her son's pickup, and Violetta and Rabbit acting as her able assistants. It went smoothly, without a hitch. Only once did the warriors up on the hilltops signal an approaching vehicle, and we all disappeared into the woodwork. An ordinary Chevy or Buick would cruise by slowly, with Mom and Dad and Buddy and Sis inside ignoring the countryside. A beast-like eighteen-wheeler with COORS emblazoned on its semi-trailer tore past, too, but otherwise we had no interruptions in our progress.

The mountains rose mightily above us, wrapped in a thick green-and-white blanket of conifers and snow. We followed the creek, with locals as our guides and scouts scattered for miles around us. They protected us. It was beginning to feel safer. There must have been 150 people, at least, and the newcomers told us veterans that we had made the national news. They thought a lot more people would be coming to join us. It was incomprehensible. The outside world wasn't real, not up here in the high altitudes, where beavers built dams and bluejays argued about the weather. We just shivered and tried to make it to nightfall, when, hopefully, the Elders would let us sleep. We were exhausted.

But no, they only let us stop once on a high ridge overlooking the vast San Luis Valley off to the northwest. The thick clouds were clearing far off to the western horizon, over the mammoth San Juan Range that looked tiny in the distance, and the sun shone on us for a few precious minutes before it set. Red Bird rode over next to me and I said, "Colorado." It had finally stopped snowing, but it was three feet deep.

She wanted to smile and touch my cheek, but she was too cold and tired. Then Grampa barked, "Head 'em up! Move 'em out!"

We turned around and rode up, up toward the fourteen-thousand-foot peaks Coronado had nicknamed Culebra and Conejos and Cuchara.

14

OF THE TEDIUM AND
DISTRACTIONS OF DAILY
CAMP LIFE.

DIM LIGHT DRIFTED LIKE A GRAY CLOUD AROUND THE
light snowfall high in the Colorado mountains. The giant
pines and silver spruce had a dim gray coat of snow and
frost on every needle and branch, and clouds floated close
to the ground like ashen fog filling the world with an ominous obscurity. For this was where, according to the Utes
and Anasazi Hopis who had long claimed the Colorado Plateau as their own, the northernmost explorers of Ixtlan
(Atlantis) left repositories and libraries of their pre–Ice Age
culture in crystal caves. Between the Rio Grande and the
Colorado River lay the markers of the four corners of the
Kikmongwi and Nahuatl world, with such remnants as Mesa
Verde and Chaco Canyon and the Grand Canyon still waiting for our return. Famous shrines like the Sun Temple
and Long's Peak—the source of the sacred Rio Colorado—
should not have been tampered with by tourists and the
National Park Service. Indians have been bitching about it
for decades but are ignored.

179

These things and more I jabbered about to pass the time to Red Bird and Whirlwind. Big Windys helped take our minds off our frostbitten fingers and sore rumps. It may sound romantic to ride bareback through the scenic alpine meadows, but in reality, those mountains will freeze your nipples off. And as for riding bareback, well, it's like skiing without poles, or eating without silverware.

"I was born and raised in Colorado," I explained, to no one's interest, except maybe Red Bird's. She had taken to feeling sorry for me, I guess, and politely listened. "Long's Peak is a sacred mountain way up north on the Front Range, close to Wyoming. I climbed it three times when I was a kid at summer camp."

"Why is it sacred?" she asked, her lips turning blue at nine thousand feet above sea level.

"Don't know. It just comes into my dreams, and is the source where the Colorado River starts. My spirit is attracted to it. Don't ask me."

Buddy was sauntering along beside us, too, and shook his head with agreeable disdain and tolerance. Grampa slowed down beside us on Betty Grable too. Whirlwind surprised me with a question. "You're from here, Storyteller?"

" 'Fraid so. Used to be a pretty nice State."

They knew what I meant. Grampa spoke. "We better camp for a bit up here at dusk. Them little guys need it."

Whirlwind agreed. "Yep."

Buddy added. "The local Chicanos have scouted us a good spot, in a glen by that creek. Shouldn't be too visible from the air."

We had ridden all through that second night and again all the next day, which was where we were at now. The kids were crying and the snot was frozen on their cheeks. This wasn't any fun at all anymore, for them. It was nowhere near as good as going down the Giant Slide at Celebrity Sports Center in Denver, or the Man-made Surfing Ocean in Albuquerque; those were their ideas of a good time. Or renting seven videos and eating candy. *This* outdoor adventuring was for the birds.

So we set up a pretty ridiculous camp, hidden in the trees and rocks way the hell and gone at about 9,500 feet above anything. City folks would sneer at our hardy wilderness surviving, but that's the way things are. We crawled into crummy like makeshift tents of twigs and bushes so as not to be seen, with pathetic little fires to cook a few tortillas and try to thaw out—if you can call a couple of twigs and a few smoldering coals a fire. The horses were disgusted with it all, and munched their oats sullenly. We let them drift around in the trees as they willed. Massaum in particular was disappointed in these developments, and was holding an emergency conference with Star and Cimarron and Betty Grable and Gandalf. I was a little worried about a mutiny. But it was too goddamn cold to worry about anything for long, and I fell asleep in my tracks like everybody else did.

I woke up once or twice in the middle of the night to add a few twigs to my so-called fire, and El Cuartalejo actually expected *me* to help pull guard duty too. So I stomped around out there in the dark, trying to keep my toes from breaking off like icicles, watching for any imaginary enemies. It was stupid, and that night was a low point for a lot of us. It was pretty depressing out there, in the pitch black Timberline beneath mighty Culebra Peak. Maybe there were eagles soaring around her snow-capped summit, but I couldn't see them.

Oh, a few guys had brought along a few portable Coleman stoves and cooked some coffee and goat-stew, and someone else slipped me a Snickers, but for the most part it was a tough haul. There ain't nothing glamorous about starving and freezing in our own homegrown Sierra Madre as a revolutionary. Every revolutionary on earth would prefer to be home snug in bed with a big-titted redhead and no *federales* out there about to break down his door, I can testify to that for a fact. Nobody likes taking on the world. It's damned inconvenient.

Morning broke and more bad luck—it was absolutely gorgeous. You've never seen a bluer sky than there is in the American West, I guarantee it. It was breathtaking. The trees sagged under the tonnage of fresh snow as bright as milk, or ivory, and then I did see several golden eagles swooping for trout on the surface of a beaver pond. Otters splashed contentedly in the icewater and, I swear to Goddess, a herd of maybe twenty wapiti elk stood there grazing.

I watched Buddy Red Bird and Jimmy Campbell sneaking up on those delectable four-leggeds just like Indians, downwind, as perfect as you please. Jimmy pooped off two stags with his 30.06 he'd brought, and Buddy dropped another buck as they all scrambled up the cliffs. The gunshots woke everybody, and the women ran to skin and butcher breakfast. The Elders were already showing the kids how to catch some fish, and a few other troops had some potatoes frying and coffee boiling. I'll tell ya, it doesn't get any better than that. It was better'n a beer commercial.

However, there was a "downside" to all this perfection, as the suit-and-tie set would say. We'd had at least a dozen horse deserters in the night, and even two families of people had snuck back down the mountain. Nobody could blame them. One of the little girls in one of the families had a bad fever and cough; everybody, almost, was sniffling with a cold. Rabbit had a couple of gigantic bottles of vitamin C, and she regularly made a pest of herself going around forcing us all to choke down half a dozen of them twice a day. We tried to bundle up the kids as best we could, but as soon as you'd turn around they'd instantly lose their mittens, never to be found again. Women were knitting as fast as they could, but those younguns were losing their caps and socks as fast as they could too. Nobody had a $200 down parka or imported waterproof boots or electric underwear. We had to make do with our Arroyo Hondo specials from the Thrift Store and Salvation Army. Our horse blankets were moldy and stiff from sweat, too, and everybody yearned for the western saddles again, soaked in urine back at Oat Truck Creek.

Whirlwind took all the blame, and sat silently all morning while the elks were butchered and dozens of fat trout were brought in to be smoked and dried for later. Everyone was trying valiantly to forbear, but it was getting awfully tough. Too tough. Another family announced they had to go back, as the father had to be at his job at a welding shop in Questa, and their kids were sick too. They took five good horses with them. People were snapping at each other and not getting along too well. The horses were losing their optimism.

The Elders, mainly Violetta and Grampa and Whistling

Hog and Jusepe, announced halfheartedly that they should be moving again.

"Moving where?" Old Girl groused.

Old Codger retorted, "Well, why don't you tell us?"

"What does that mean?"

I could see Whirlwind wander dejectedly off toward our impromptu Rest Room—about as discouraging a cold and forlorn hole in the ground as you could imagine—the reverberation of the arguing Elders a sour song in his ears. I gave him a few minutes and then wandered off in his general direction too.

There he was, staring off at the magnificent scenic overlook to the north. It's hard to contemplate the great beauty of the moraines and buttes of the Rockies when you're scared, and cold, and on the run. The Sangre de Cristos and Spanish Peaks can be merciless.

He asked me, as I stood silently beside him, soaking up the warm sunshine and the view, "How far?"

"That's Mount Blanca up there to the north, a volcano Fourteener. We should cross the highway tonight if we can, and I think angle northeast through the Huerfano Valley and out into the warmer Plains, maybe follow the Arkansas River."

"That's close to where Cheyennes were massacred at Sand Creek."

"Yeah. It'll be warmer out there. The disadvantage is we'll be totally exposed. It's flat and treeless, mostly."

He was deep in memory. "Sand Creek. And Little Wolf ran through Kansas from Oklahoma, trying to get home, too, to Montana."

"Yep."

"We don't have a chance, do we?"

"Who knows?" I sighed. "We didn't have a chance going along the old way either."

"Everybody's mad at me. I never asked to be a Chief. The kids hate me."

"No they don't. They're just miserable."

"It's my fault. Red Bird's right, we shouldn't have taken those horses. We shouldn't have torn down the jail or robbed the money. I'm a flop, just like . . . Sky wants me to be his daddy. I'm not a . . . What's going to happen to us

183

Indians, Storyteller? This is crazy, out here. Everything we do is crazy. We'll never get home to Lame Deer, or Bear Butte, not like this. It's crazy. All I can think about as we're riding is when Dull Knife and Little Wolf, my great-grandfather, were running from the cavalry a hundred years ago. They were trying to get home, too, and most of 'em got wiped out. Women and children. What are we going to do if that happens? I could never forgive myself. We should surrender and give up. Maybe let Buddy and some lawyers . . . at least that way nobody'll get killed."

"Maybe."

"Or freeze or get sick. It breaks my heart to hear those little ones coughing."

I nodded. "Your great-grandfather was one of the Old Man Chiefs of the Suhtaio, as well as the Tsistsistas Cheyennes, the bearer of Sweet Medicine's Bundle."

"Not the Sacred Arrows, though, right?" he inquired, genuine interest returning to his face. That was my intention, to distract him. "The Arrows are our soul. They're the Mahuts of Maiyuneo Spirits. They're in Oklahoma with the Southern Cheyennes, last I heard. Issi'wun, the sacred Buffalo Hat, is in Montana with the Northern Cheyennes."

"Erect Horns brought the hat to the Suhtaio band," I added. "Yes. As to where they are now, well . . . I have a theory that you're not going to like, and I'm sure I'll catch a rash of shit from all the Cheyennes for saying it, but, Whirlwind, I have to. When Sweet Medicine was given the four Sacred Arrows at Bear Butte by the *maiyuns*, they were like the rainbow of deliverance, the same as Monster Slayer. The Arrows were not just shafts and arrowheads with feathers, they were . . . lightning. They were supernatural. And so was the Buffalo Hat brought by his profane twin Erect Horns."

Whistling Hog joined us just then. He looked concerned, as if he knew what we were talking about, but he said nothing. He stared at the vast panorama lying before us, and it was as if we were at the top of the world and our words were magic poems equal to the snow-capped peaks.

Whirlwind provided him some exposition. "We're talking about the Mahuts, Uncle Fred."

Whistling Hog gave me a penetrating stare. "I know."

I continued. "To make any of this even a little bit com-

184

prehensible for white people, you could say the Arrows were like the Ten Commandments given to Moses on another sacred mountain, Sinai. He, too, received divine revelation from the Thunder Beings and Lightning Spirits."

The other Cheyennes joined us, Red Bird and her brother, Buddy, and her children, Sky and Jane. Buddy asked, "What's up?"

I hurried to explain, "But there really isn't all that much similarity between Moses and Sweet Medicine. They were both great poets, yes, but your Ancestral Lawgiver did not lead armies against the Ethiopians like the Lawgiver of the Hebrews. No way. But they both came down from the Thunder Nation with supernatural power etched into history and language. Whatever the actual physical nature of the Tablets or the Arrows, well, that remains yet to be discovered, by holy men and women at Sinai and Bear Butte. The Jews should be concentrating on the meaning of their revelations instead of conquering territory and killing Ethiopians still. And the Cheyennes should stop acting like they know what they're doing. Fred, is there a Sweet Medicine Chief anymore, or a Sweet Medicine Society?"

Whistling Hog snorted in disgust. "No. No. A bunch of winos, that's all."

Buddy gasped. "Whooo . . . pretty strong statement."

"It's true," Fred snarled angrily. "They've let priests and soldiers in to see the Arrows, and the Chamber of Commerce in Sturgis, the closest town to Bear Butte, takes pictures of them! Unthinkable a hundred years ago."

"It went wrong long before that, Fred, I think," I added quietly. "When the men took the power away from the women. A woman should always carry the Buffalo Hat, to bring the buffalo. The buffalo cow goddess took away the economy of the Indians long before the whites came."

"What?" Whirlwind asked.

Buddy shook his head irritably. "That's stupid. I'm getting tired of all this—"

"They actually let an Episcopal Priest carry the Sacred Arrows back in the sixties!" Fred exclaimed suddenly. "A Christian!"

"There is a supernatural element to these things, Buddy, whether you believe it or not," I argued.

"Yeah, yeah, sure," Buddy snorted again. "That crap is what's killing us, not—"

"No, Buddy, you are wrong," Whirlwind said quietly.

Buddy was disgusted. "Forget it, forget it." He walked away.

Red Bird had a question. "The buffalo goddess?"

"Yes. That's why it's a good thing you are carrying a new kind of Bundle now."

"It is like a Renewal," Whirlwind realized suddenly, a new light on his face.

"Yeah—"

But just as a little ray of hope threatened to enter the dialogue, Jimmy Campbell came running toward Buddy and us. "Incoming choppers!" he screamed.

The horses were already running away. The warriors looked wildly at each other.

"Get the kids!" Whirlwind screamed, running.

"Grab the horses!"

A helicopter blasted out of the mists below and came straight at us, and then another one. The whirring of the blades blew the tops of the tree branches, and snow flew in clouds of crazy circles all around the monstrous olive-drab helicopters, with U.S. ARMY printed very clearly on them.

15

HOW THE ARSENAL
OF DEMOCRACY ENSURED THE
DOMESTIC TRANQUILLITY.

IF YOU'VE EVER BEEN UNDER ATTACK BY THE SPECIAL WEAP-
ons and tactics assault forces of the U.S. Government—and
a lot more people than you'd realize have had the thrill of
this unique experience—then you'll know how absolutely
amazing it is to feel the renewed excitement with which you
will run for cover from these well-paid troops of Democracy
and Freedom. The humdrum annoyances of daily camp life
were instantly forgotten in the light of this new element
introduced upon their boring routine. If you haven't experienced this kind of adventure, then it may have looked like
a lot of people and horses running around in panic, to you.
It may have looked like a lot of dirty terrorists hiding out
in the woods, and a lot of really fine young men in combat
fatigues jumping out of assault choppers to clean up this
renegade operation in the mountains. It would have made
your heart sing and your breast swell with patriotic pride
to see Our Boys mopping up this filthy Commie Nest of
anarchy and paganism.

But some people in this world are bleeding-heart Fellow
Travelers, and wish to see a story from another perspective.
It is sheer propaganda, of course; but, alas, the world is far
from a perfect place, yet. Someday, with the Grace of Our
Divine Father, the whole globe will swell with the purity of
the American Dream, but for now . . . let us look upon the
bloodthirsty sub-human terrorists and try to tell their one-
dimensional story. World opinion dictates.

Whirlwind ran toward Buddy, and Buddy waved for him
to go. "That way, Philbert! We'll cover you!"

"But—"

"Get the Bundle to safety!" Violetta screamed. The warriors and Elders were forming a protective circle around
their families and children, while the clean-cut boys from
Akron, Ohio, and Ukiah, California, approached by the
dozens through the trees, their automatic weapons and gas
masks and laser-radars (or whatever, I don't know anything
about armaments: I served with the Los Angeles Draft
Dodgers) drawn and ready. A few bullets zinged suddenly!

That brought home the seriousness of the situation, and
Massaum and Star dashed nakedly to the north, where Red
Bird and Uncle Fred were dashing with Sky and Jane in
their arms. Whirlwind saw the futility of his situation; and
also, he didn't know one end of a gun from the other. (He
had never served his Country either, utterly oblivious to the
Selective Service registration procedures, or anything else.)
Buddy and the warriors immediately returned the fire in
the trees and women screamed. A Congressional Panel in-
vestigating the "Incident" months later determined that
they could not determine who fired the first shot. Both
sides, of course, claimed the other fired first. Everyone, on
both sides, ducked. They all disappeared into the bushes
and snow. Bullets have a way of making cowards of us all,
that way.

Massaum took charge of the crisis and made it impera-
tively obvious that Whirlwind should just get on top so they
could get the hell out of there. Acrid gunsmoke in his nostrils convinced the Chief of the wisdom of her counsel. Star
followed them, and Uncle Fred hoisted Red Bird up on the
big white stallion—luckily Red Bird had the Bundle strapped

188

to her back—then he leapt behind her with Sky squeezed in between them. Whirlwind grabbed Jane by her armpit and threw her up behind him on Massaum, and they were off, rope bits in their mouths and fear drying their throats like sand!

The horses didn't have to be told twice that the best way to go was north, away from the gunsmoke and horrible noise of the helicopters, and that full-speed was the proper velocity. Massaum and Star ran through the snow and trees like they'd been doing it all their lives. Whirlwind tried to twist around and catch a glimpse of the village under attack, but he could only see Buddy and some of the warriors finding their own horses and putting up a retreating cover-fire for them. It was an awful, awful moment: to think that people might be getting killed. Even small arms fire has a way of punching the comedy completely out of a story.

How could these people, except for maybe Uncle Fred, who'd been mere amateurs when it came to bareback broken-field sprints and daredevil stunts only a few days and weeks ago, have stayed on those wild horses running down rocky mountain slopes and up rocky ravines? Some people might say it was because they were Cheyenne Indians and had it in their blood. Others might say they bounced and jounced and held on to the manes in about as ugly a style and as desperate a manner as you could ask for. Albeit, they were scared and the children were crying. This was no fun at all anymore, for them. They ran suddenly into a little glade and right through a line of soldiers, with their faces painted in olive-drab camouflage, who were cordoning off the perimeter.

"Hey!"

"Watch out!"

"Halt!"

As fast as the horsepeople appeared, they disappeared. The crack infantry stared at the silent trees. Had it been real?

Back at the village a dozen warriors had ridden off after the Sacred Center of their nation to protect Her, and two dozen riderless horses had fanned out in a brilliant recon-noitering counter-flanking retreat strategy. But the rest of the hapless sub-humans were captured by the cavalry (or is it calvary? I get those mixed up) and had their hands up. There were no injuries on either side, thank God.

The cavalry pointed dozens of firearms, capable of firing thousands of rounds of ammunition as fast as you could say Jack Robinson, at the dangerous old men and little children. They were frisked for hand grenades and other forms of plastic explosives. The cavalrymen had been instructed in all the devious arts these foreigners were capable of, and all the insidious new technological terror they imported from North Korea and South Chicago.

A Commander, with a plainclothes political operative beside him, barked, "FBI! You're under arrest!"

Just last night he had been briefed about the reports, confirmed by Intelligence, of Libyan infiltrators coming into the country across the Canadian and Mexican borders. Their objective: to knock out all the power and light of the land by hitting key power plants. Knock out the electricity of industry and, in a matter of hours, the country would be paralyzed, destroyed. These were the shock troops of the infiltrators, the Commander had been assured.

"Hands up!"

One old fart snarled, "Why don't you frisk the horses, too, while you're at it?"

The plainclothesman looked suspiciously at the dozens of thoroughbreds trapped up into a small rocky box canyon, terrified of the whirlybirds. He motioned for his men to read the horses their rights too. They were put under heavy guard.

"Feet apart!"

"You have the right to remain silent . . ."

The four-leggeds stopped kicking and screaming, and stared curiously. They did what they were told. They trembled as they were frisked for weapons. The ground forces took them into custody, employing the same old hated iron bridles in their mouths. O why didn't they heed the advice of No Tongue and Geronimo when they had the chance? They should never have let the coppers take them alive! It looked like the Slammer for them. They tried to look penitent, and gave the two-legged Indians dirty looks. It was all *their* fault, Your Honor!

A lieutenant colonel, expertly trained in Materiel Observation Techniques, inspected the dirty dishes on the ground in front of an abandoned wickiup made of bushes, next to a small black firepit. A major with Special Forces analyzed a grimy cooking pot.

"Yep, they were here."

"Yes, Sir."

They looked off across the mountains to the far meadows where the remaining fugitives had flown. "Reconnoiter the perimeter, Mister."

"Squadron leaders assure me the cordon is secure, SIR!"

"Very good. Airlift the Jeeps and dune buggies in here for good measure, and alert the infrared surveillance units."

"Yes, Sir!"

"They can't get far. We'll cordon off the perimeter. We'll secure the demilitarized zone. We'll—"

"Yes, Sir!"

The lieutenant colonel gave the major an annoyed look.

The major wasn't sure what he'd done wrong. "I mean, NO SIR!"

Helicopters whup-whup-whupped everywhere, just like in *Apocalypse Now*. Buddy watched them, hidden under a huge silver spruce. "Saigon. Shit."

Massaum and Star tore down a forgotten four-wheel-drive trail ten miles away already, and dashed suddenly across a major highway running east and west. A monstrous Coors semi-truck blasted its horns and swerved wildly to miss the fucking horses that came out of nowhere. The driver was a good ol' boy from Golden, Colorado, who was sure that Coors Beer was the best thing since peach ice cream. He jackknifed and slid like a ruptured dinosaur sideways into the borrow ditch on the side of the road, splattering two thousand cases of Silver Bullet in cans which blew a hole in the side of the truck like a cannon going off. If you've ever shaken a beer can and then popped it open, you know the tremendous concussion that could result, and which indeed *did* result, from thousands of such grenades going off at once. Residents of nearby Fort Garland later testified that they thought Mount Blanca was erupting, but people tend to exaggerate about these things. The good ol'

191

boy did, however, take a lot of razzing for weeks afterward from his fellow employees about the comical predicament he was extricated from at the site of the accident. It took several firemen from Alamosa to cut him loose from the tons of beer cans with a welding torch. Accusations that he'd drunk all the beer himself were hurled; and no one believed his wild story about Indians riding bareback on thoroughbreds across the road in front of him.

Be that as it may, the Indians riding barebacked on the two thoroughbreds (well, yeah, Massaum was only a Morgan quarterhorse valued at only about, oh, on today's market, $25,000) were way the hell and gone past the La Veta Pass highway and rounding around the eastern slope of Mount Blanca. It was already starting to get dark and they were beat. The horses were beat.

They walked up yet another rocky slope on another high divide, in the open. In plain sight of the whole world.

"Look!" Red Bird exclaimed, crawling off her horse. She was sure she had no ass or legs left. She pointed back down the slope to the timberline below them. They were up at about eleven thousand feet.

The others looked, and were sure they must have been hallucinating in the thin oxygen. But no, it did look like Buddy and Jimmy and the others were following them, in a broad half-circle. Whirlwind couldn't believe how great they were. "They're covering our retreat," Uncle Fred commented, like it was the most ordinary thing in the world.

And, just as commonplace in this day and age, an AWAC C-130 approached from the southwest over a distant ridge. "Run!" Sky screamed, pointing to it. Kids these days are very knowledgeable about advanced aeronautics. "Radar aircraft!"

"Where?" Whirlwind wondered aloud.

Uncle Fred spotted a cave ahead of them. "Over here!"

They crawled over a pile of rubble and boulder fields toward the cave, which was braced up by old timbers hewn by hardy pioneers a hundred years ago, it looked like.

"It's a gold mine," Jane declared.

"Let's all get in it."

"Why?"

Red Bird hesitated. "It might be dangerous."

192

The horses, again, decided what to do. If you left things up to two-leggeds, they'd still be back in New Mexico debating whether to turn right or left. Massaum and Star stumbled into the shelter and took their passengers with them. It was dank and dark immediately, but warmer. The four-leggeds then realized how tired they were, and lathered up. It had been a brilliant run. The two-leggeds had bruises over their entire bodies, but no one had fallen off, not once. Sky had almost enjoyed the wild chase. It was better'n a movie.

Red Bird was scared of the cave. "What if there are snakes in here? What if it collapses? What if—"

"Quiet," Uncle Fred warned irritably. He pointed up.

The huge airplane flew right over them. It sounded like an avalanche.

"Why do we have to whisper?" Jane whispered. "It can't hear us."

The plane was gone in a few more seconds and Whirlwind peeked carefully outside. It was getting dark. "It's gone."

"We won't know if they saw us until the Army pokes its nose in here," Uncle Fred said, sitting down. "God, I'm tired."

"I wonder what happened to everybody, else," Whirlwind wondered, collapsing on the dank rocky ground, too, and leaning against the musty wall.

Sky was exploring, "Maybe there's some gold in here, and we can pay back the police what we took, and they'll let us go."

For some reason that made Red Bird start crying, and she hugged him. "Oh, my darling little boy! C'mere, Jane. I'm so sorry to put you in this." She hugged them, and got mushy, the way Moms do. Kids just learn to endure it.

The horses found some water trickling down the walls and licked the rocks greedily. They were heaving and panting and smelled to the high heavens.

Everyone was pretty ripe, for that matter. Whirlwind sat by the door and watched it get dark outside, turning the tailings from the gold mine sulphuric yellow. They were all too tired and hungry and frozen and scared to talk. Red Bird carefully undid the Bundle from her back and laid it on the ground next to her. She felt like Frodo Baggins carrying the Ring of Power to Mordor. It got heavier with every step she took towards the Mount of Doom. She rocked her children in her arms, and they fell fast asleep, a lot more tired than they were willing to admit, like all kids. She hoped Buddy and the others were okay outside. She had come to know her brother better over these last few months than she had during her entire life. He was a hero, to her. She had always looked up to him, as a football star first, and then for his intelligence and the way he had always believed in their people and stood up for them. Sure, he was an asshole, but so are all men. At least he was a brave asshole. Their parents had always favored him over her, as most parents usually favor their sons over their daughters, and she had rebelled against the neglect. She also rebelled against having to live up to their ideas of what a daughter should be—a cutesy girly-girl playing with dolls all her life, and ribbons, and all those things that supposedly made you "feminine." She hated that. Where were Mom and Dad now? At home, she guessed, watching *Wheel of Fortune* on TV, or going to Mass at St. Andrew's.

Whirlwind came over and sat beside her, giving her a big, gentle bear hug. "Ohh, that's just what I needed," she cooed, and rested her head on his chest. He was getting lean and strong, and she closed her eyes. In a few seconds she was asleep, and the kids readjusted in their sleep to find a few pillows on Whirlwind's ample girth.

He let them all snooze. He felt horrible for them. What kind of man lets his woman and children come to this mess? "What kind of fool am I?" he sang softly, remembering an old song lyric. These oddball tunes run through us all, irrationally, at times. He couldn't remember any more of the words. He was embarrassed to be singing, and listened anxiously in the pitch darkness to hear what kind of deprecating remark Uncle Fred would have for him. But Uncle Fred was snoring like a bear. Even the horses sounded like they were snoring.

Yep, a bear, he thought. That's me. That's us, a whole bear clan with cubs and sows and boars. Hibernating in a gold mine.

He heard another engine fly over outside. It sounded more like a helicopter, and a shiver of horror ran through him. They'd found us! But it passed in a moment, and all was silent and dark again. He knew that he would fight them now; no one was going to harm his people anymore. Not here, not now.

It was not history. Colorado had been a very great mining State, you know; much of its glory began in the halcyon days when *Pike's Peak or Bust* resounded on every American lip. It had been as great as other mottoes like *The Oregon Trail* and *Forty Acres and a Mule* which helped Win the West too. And Colorado is still a very great mining State. Molybdenum is very big, and so are coal and oil shale—or at least they would be, if Congress would be patriotic and instill some price supports and protection against the foreign trade deficit. You'll be glad to hear there is also a fair amount of silver and gold mining still going on, though, and there are lots of uranium holes and . . . well, it's all really quite wonderful. Lots of good-paying jobs and high-quality folks are just pouring into the Columbine State.

The bears in their caves cowered. One of them, a big boar with his family, remembered how his fellows had once huddled like this after another mopping-up operation 125 years ago at a place out close to the Kansas border called Sand Creek. Whirlwind put a name to the sub-human creatures—Cheyennes—and a word to describe it that was pure propaganda—Massacre. That's Colorado history, too, but . . . well, it's negative and unpleasant, so let's forget it and concentrate on the good things.

"Not even the great President Lincoln cared," Whirlwind thought. I'm sorry to report that there are still such people with such chips on their shoulders, even today. It's absurd. He was in a bitter state of mind, for some reason. "They gave those butchers a victory parade down Larimer Street in Denver. And Custer killed every male Cheyenne over ten on the Washita River in 1868. Lieutenant Henely hacked up Cheyenne babies on the Sappa in Kansas in 1875, under a white flag of surrender and truce." He sobbed suddenly, convulsions shaking his great chest. Had he dozed off? Did he see piles of burning Indians in his sleep?

He jerked back to reality. John Wayne wasn't standing over him with his army. He was still in his black subconscious cave, warm, the fires in his memory still hot.

Sky was awake. "What's the matter, Daddy?"

It was a stupid question, but well meant. Daddy hugged his little boy desperately. "Nothing. Go back to sleep."

The horses made a few emotional sounds, too, and their hooves clomped on the rocks. Maybe they were dreaming about rodeos and racetracks and dog food slaughterhouses.

"What are you thinking about?" Sky asked. He sounded wide awake.

Whirlwind marveled at the thoughtfulness, and balance, of this boy. He was always on an even keel, it seemed. Sky was always right there with him, loyal and true and loving. "Did you know that General Custer had a Cheyenne boy?"

"No. Who was Custer?"

"An evil man who was a great American general."

"Oh, yeah, okay." That explained it clearly for him.

"The boy's name was Yellow Swallow. He was a light-haired boy. After Custer rode in one time in Oklahoma and slaughtered our Cheyenne people on the Washita River he took a young girl into his bed, named Monasetah."

"Why did he do that?"

"Because men like to be mean to women. He killed her whole family first. He kept her with him all winter and spring, and she bore him a son in the fall."

"Yellow Swallow," Sky said.

"Yes. It's a well-known story." Whirlwind shifted uncomfortably on the hard sharp rocks.

"Why was he called Yellow Swallow?"

"Because he had yellow hair like his father. He was with Dull Knife, who was called Morning Star later in his life, and Little Wolf, my great-grandfather, when they ran through the whole U.S. Army from Oklahoma to Nebraska a hundred years ago."

"Like us," Sky added, perceptively.

"Yes." Whirlwind gulped, profound sadness flooding over him. "Fort Robinson, Nebraska, 1879. Most of Dull Knife's band were butchered there, like cattle, in the snow."

"Yellow Swallow too?"

196

"No. Some people heard he died in a hole beside War-
bonnet Creek, with . . . a pile . . . of . . . Indian women and
. . . babies . . ." He choked and couldn't continue. He
couldn't help it.

Uncle Fred spoke in the dark. Whirlwind became vaguely
aware that Red Bird and Jane were awake, too, and embracing him. Everyone had been listening. (How much time had
passed? Maybe he had been asleep after all.) "The soldiers
found over twenty Cheyennes trying to hide in some breast-
works in a ditch. They surrounded them and mowed them
down. They tried to claw their way into the earth, and seventeen men were dead on top trying to protect the others.
Down the next layer were four women with two small children dead in their arms. Under them were seven more
women and children, alive but wounded, one woman mor-
tally. Hog was a Chief, and he had a beautiful daughter
there who was still alive, bloody, haggard and wild, her neck
drawn tight against her bullet-torn shoulder. And deep in
the bottom, under everything that the thunderous barrage
of guns had missed, was a pile of dried deer meat they had
three feet high, standing in a pool of the blood that the
frozen earth refused."

"Oh! Oh!" the Cheyennes in that cave sobbed.

Uncle Fred managed to continue, for he wanted the children to know, and never forget. "One soldier, he was nicknamed Little Dutchman by the Cheyennes who knew him
from the Fort, was so ashamed, he shoved aside the other
men and crawled into the bloody ditch, when it was over.
He picked up a little six-year-old girl named Lame Girl,
who recognized him through all the blood and was holding
out her arms to him to help her. As he picked her up, he
felt a stickiness under her arm, a gunshot wound in her
side. Two 45-70 Springfield bullets had torn into her. Little
Dutchman raged at the other soldiers, 'See what you have
done?! You brave men have murdered a little girl!' And
he carried her all the way back to Fort Robinson, where
she died in his arms. The Indians always remembered
Little Dutchman as their friend, even though he had to
obey orders and fight our warriors."

"So there are . . . some good Americans?" Sky asked quietly, after a while.

"Yes," his mother replied simply, blowing her nose, and stroking his hair.

"But what happened to Yellow Swallow?" Jane asked.

"He was taken back to Oklahoma, to the hot, dry Indian Territory the Northern Cheyennes hated so much. He lived until he was seventeen. But he got sick from starving when they wouldn't feed the Indians, and bad diseases, and seeing his mother murdered, too, so he died."

They were all silent for a long time, lost in their thoughts and feelings. It was warm in that cave, too, about fifty degrees or so, which made them reluctant to come back to grips with reality and their present strait. They could see a shower of bright silvery stars decorating the black sky outside.

"Hello?" someone shouted outside. It was a familiar voice, cracking through the silence like a gunshot almost.

Whirlwind crawled over to the entrance. "Buddy? Up here."

"HO!" the War Chief shouted, and in a minute he came walking into the doorway. "I thought you guys were up here. How ya doin'?"

"Okay," Whirlwind replied simply. The two friends embraced each other fiercely right then, for some reason. It wasn't practical.

Massaum and Star re-emerged, too, signaling a change of venue.

"We'd better get down to a lower altitude," Uncle Fred decided. "It's way too cold up here."

"You're right."

The horses led them down the boulder fields, everyone walking. Seven warriors joined them in the dark, walking their exhausted horses too. No one said it, but the children needed food and warmth badly. Surrender occurred privately to all of them, including the horses, but no one dared mutter the awful word, not even the children. Visions of little girls with sticky blood under their arms silenced Jane and Sky. It was much colder outside than it had been in the cave, and the stars were much brighter and far more numerous than they had been inside the earth. They filled the universe like diamonds.

"Look!" Jane exclaimed loudly.

"SHHHHHHHH!" they all warned at once.

"I saw a shooting star," she whispered.

The steep slope was slippery with the loose tailings. The horses stumbled badly. Rocks rolled down the ridge that was barren of trees, which had all been used to prop up the mines. The whole area was excavated and eerie, dead, ugly.

And it was ice cold.

They slid and fell and scratched and cut their stiff hands. It was painful for everyone, and getting colder by the minute. It was unbearable.

But still they had to go on, putting one painful foot in front of another, because there was nothing else to do. The dim moonless light of the stars cast a pale pale glow over the evening, and meteor showers shot across the dark blue kettle of the canopy over them. The pitiful wretches on the ground far below, closer to the sky than anywhere on the continent, kept moving.

They got to a level slope finally, at the bottom of the vast mine fields, and lifted themselves up on the warm horses with the last shreds of their energy. The horses showed their breeding and behaved with splendid equanimity. They pitied these sad two-leggeds. Maybe they were even growing in virtue and wisdom.

They rode down into the sheltering timbers and found another old four-wheel-drive track. The horses took the loose reins and led the way. Even the warriors let down their guard a little and lay limply on their backs. They all worried about the others. Where was Grampa? How was Violetta? What about Jusepe? El Cuartalejo had been separated from his wife and children when he chose to protect Red Bird and the Sacred Bundle. A dozen riderless animals escorted them too. A black pony nudged the little boy, once, when he started to slide off a bay mare that was carrying him now. Hulk was long gone somewhere. Jane missed Peckerhead too. And where was Storyteller? Massaum nuzzled Whirlwind's leg when he started to slide off, too, and he jerked awake violently. They couldn't go to sleep out here, not now, or it would be death. They'd never wake up.

The horses walked steadily, descending on the trail and

finding another descent through the trees at every opportunity. It was important to lose some altitude, and to go east, east toward the Plains and out of the mountains. East into the broad open Huerfano Valley above Walsenburg, Colorado, but well south still of the polluted metropolis of Pueblo.

Miles passed effortlessly, it seemed, under the steady gait of the fast walking horses. They were definitely superior stock. It makes a big difference to have the right kind of horsepower under the hood, when you need it. You never know when you might need just that little extra bit of power if you get in a tight squeeze on the Powwow Superhighway.

And then, as fast as you can snap your fingers, a dog came out of nowhere and barked ferociously at the trespassers.

"YOW YOW YOW YOW YOW!"

The horses freaked. ""HEEEE   HEEEEE   HEEEEE HEEEEEEEEEEEEEEEE!"

Several of the more immature smart alecks of the four-leggeds actually started to buck, and even Massaum laid her ears back and wondered what the hell was going on.

"YOW YOW YOW YOW YOW YOW YOW YOW!!"

"HEEEEEEEEEEEEEEEEEE! HEEEEE!"

To add to this startling new chaos, an explosion of bright lights burst out of the darkness suddenly. It was like the weirdest damn object you ever saw and it seemed to be coming at them right out of the trees! It blazed like a midnight sun, and flashed all kinds of blinding spotlights in green and orange and blue colors as pretty as a Christmas tree.

16

OF EXTRATERRESTRIALS AND OTHER NON-TRADITIONAL LIFE-FORMS.

WHIRLWIND WOKE UP LATE THE NEXT MORNING IN A DIF-
ferent place, or at least he thought he woke up. He took
one look around and went back to sleep, or maybe that was
when he woke up. He couldn't be sure of anything anymore. He thought he saw the weirdest damn room he'd
ever been in in his life, and he didn't want to think about
where he was. He didn't want to remember. It had looked
exactly like a room in a Flying Saucer, and he couldn't face
up to that, not yet. Maybe tomorrow. In his delirium, he
thought he remembered taking off from his dearly beloved
planet and that they were well on their way to the center
of the Milky Way Galaxy. They were flying beyond the
speed of light, he heard one of the Aliens mutter as if in
a dream. They were flying at *The Speed of Thought*. Nope,
he had to be dreaming.

Did a Space Woman wake him up in the middle of the
night and say, "Here, take this."

He struggled to get away from the spoon of puke-green liquid. "No! What is it? No!"

"It's good," she lied. "It's a basil-and-dill-seed emetic with lemon." Then she shoved it down his throat.

He was sure he was poisoned, but they had him. He'd been abducted, like he'd read about a lady in *National Enquirer* taken up into a Spaceship and they'd done hideous experiments on her. The Space Woman woke him up again and forced him to eat "some nice falafel and mushroom soup. It's good for your fever." She was a cruel, sadistic tortureress. She even had Red Bird hypnotized, and they both sat at his bedside soaking his forehead in cold compresses.

His bed wiggled and wobbled, and he tried valiantly once to break free, but they held him down. "No! No! Let me go back to Earth! HELP!"

He woke up another time, and sunlight was filling the room. It was probably simulated sunlight, or from some Sun in another solar system with two red moons around it and purple rings. The room had whirlybobs floating around in the air and thingamajigs bouncing on a table. His bed gurgled, and waves rolled back and forth over him if he moved. It was a foul dungeon. He raised himself feebly to his elbows and wondered where the children were. Had they been dissected already and fed to man-eating plants? He thought he heard bizarre noises in other chambers of the Ship, but his head swirled again and he fell backward. Yes, he had been poisoned. He was under some insidious sedation.

He woke up another time in the dark and felt awful. He was dying. All was lost. He was alone. All his fellow earthlings were gone, and he would be next.

In a dream that was closer to any reality he had ever known, he saw Sweet Medicine smiling at him, and a rainbow rose out of the cone of Bear Butte. It was beautiful. Then Red Bird was beside him, in her wedding dress of white doeskin. It all switched to total night suddenly, and the Milky Way showered out of the cone of Bear Butte and filled the world with knowledge and poetry and art.

His eyes popped open as suddenly as the sunrise. Consciousness returned. New awareness arrived. It was like he was just being born. Everything was new. He was on a waterbed in a Flying Saucer, traveling at the speed of thought, and the Space Woman was holding some food in front of him again. But he had been tranquilized and smiled. He was no longer a hostile alien, but a good robot now. They had operated on his brain in the night, and he would be a good docile android from now on.

"Feeling better?" she asked.

"Yes," he replied sweetly, obediently.

She felt his forehead. "Yes, your fever's broken. We were worried about you. Here's the marjoram cream pie you asked for last night."

"Oh, thank you," he replied politely, accepting the simulated food. He ate it greedily. It even tasted good.

Red Bird and Buddy and the kids all came in the room, with a Space Man, who had made himself look like an ordinary bald earthling with an earring. His family almost looked normal too. It was amazing what advanced science could do. Red Bird knelt on the waterbed beside him and gave him a kiss. "You okay?" Her lips even felt real.

"Yes. I'm fine. How are you?"

"Fine," she replied courteously.

"Fine." Sky spoke happily, and kissed him too.

Everyone was fine. The Aliens were introduced as Sparky and Moonbeam, and this was their home, a geodesic dome. Yes, Whirlwind replied, for he was ready to believe anything now.

After an appropriate interlude, they all tiptoed out to leave him alone to take a shower, if he wanted, and to dress. Yes, he replied, that would be pleasant. Moonbeam showed him his new clothes on a table. She was wearing a Japanese satin kimono with a tiger on it, and she was very beautiful, with blond hair, and when she leaned over she showed him her large breasts as if there was nothing wrong with that. She showed him a beaded buckskin tunic someone had brought for him. It was very old, she said, and the designs were probably Cheyenne. He thought that they were. They were of old green Hudson's Bay beads. It was an authentic traditional tunic, exactly the kind he had always dreamed of. It was just his size. Everything was perfect, of course, in this fantasy world. Moonbeam was perfect. She kissed his cheek and led him to a gorgeous bathroom with a huge porcelain tub in the middle of a huge room with gorgeous azure Mexican tiles on the walls and floor, with designs of the Feathered Serpent on them. She ran his water and helped him undress. She wasn't embarrassed at all to see him naked, and he was passive about it too. Nothing was real anymore, so why pretend to be modest? It wasn't natural. Oh, he was coming to realize this wasn't *really* a Flying Saucer, anymore, and Moonbeam wasn't *really* a Space Woman. Probably. Well, maybe she was a little spacey, but . . . She gave him some natural emollients and unguents for his bath, and left him alone to bathe.

Ah, yes, this was the life. He eased down into the giant tub and it was the first such contrivance he had ever found in his life that was big enough for him. The water was hot enough. The sunroof above showed the blue sky.

After a long soak Red Bird came in the bathroom and sat on the edge of the tub. "You going to stay in here all day?"

"Yes."

"Even when the best omelet you've ever had in your life is going on the stove in a minute?"

Moonbeam and another beautiful white woman came in the bathroom and sat around on the edge of the tub too. The women were all wearing beautiful satin robes from far-off foreign places somewhere, and pretty jewelry from Africa or somewhere. The other woman was introduced as Carmenta. "She's a psychic," Red Bird explained to him. (They could all see his dork clearly in the water . . .)

"I knew you were coming," Carmenta said.

"Beg your pardon?"

Red Bird giggled. "She saw us all in a channeled trance, Whirlwind. She described us exactly."

"And we support you completely in what you're doing," Moonbeam added.

"We've been on television and everything," Red Bird bubbled. "Oh, it's just unbelievable. Buddy and Rabbit have a press conference planned for this afternoon and they want me to be there too—"

"Red Bird is definitely a Channel," Carmenta declared.

"It is the fulfillment of the Prophecies of Anathoth that she is the reincarnation of Queen Caelestis—"

"What . . . how did we get here?" he struggled to ask, hoping they didn't notice he was getting half a hard-on.

"Well, my goodness." Red Bird giggled. "I see our Chief is coming back to life!" The others all looked at his dick and smiled.

He could have died. "Uh . . . how is Rabbit and the others?"

"Fine," Red Bird replied blithely. "The lawyers have everyone bailed out and—"

"Grampa and—"

"Yes, Whirlwind," Carmenta answered. "No one was hurt in the shooting. It was not meant to be."

Moonbeam and Red Bird looked at Carmenta adoringly. Whirlwind went limp, thankfully. "Oh, good. Everyone's all right then?"

"Yes."

"Thank the Powers," he prayed.

"Amen," Carmenta added. "Marduk and the Legions of the Ashtar Command told me it would come to pass exactly like this. And you are a Great Chief, too, Whirlwind Dreamer, from the center of the galaxy, where the Antares system has forged an alliance with the Benevolent Forces of the Pleiades to—"

"See?" Red Bird commented proudly. "She even knew your name."

"—to enact the coming of the Spirit Guide who rules the Bird Clans of the Ongwhehonwhe."

"Oh yeah?" he wondered. He had a question for Red Bird. "Where's the Sacred Bundle?"

"Oh! AHH! The Sacred Bundle!" Carmenta rejoiced ecstatically.

"Hanging over our bed, where it's supposed to be," Red Bird answered. "Now stand up and we'll dry you off."

He was shocked. "Whaa?" And blushed crimson down to his roots.

"C'mon, stand up, don't be shy," Red Bird exhorted. "These are my priestesses."

"Your . . . what?"

Moonbeam explained. "Red Bird is the High Priestess of the Goddess, and we have been honored to—"

"Chosen," Carmenta corrected.

Moonbeam stood corrected. "Chosen, to be her priestesses in the service of Our Lady."

"And you are Her King," Carmenta added, "the Sacred Chief."

"Don't be shy." Moonbeam smiled and kissed his cheek. "You have no secrets from Woman. We saw you naked when you came into life. There is nothing to be ashamed of."

"I'm not . . ." he stuttered, and looked imploringly at Red Bird. "I can dry myself off, okay? Maybe—"

Red Bird laughed and stood up. "Oh, it's okay, you're not ready. Let's go, Ladies, and make him breakfast."

They all laughed and gave him various and sundry lascivious glances and left, with Carmenta explaining as they went out the door and up the stairs, "It is very proper that you have the Sacred Bundle hanging over your nuptial bed. That—"

He shook his head to clear it of the cobwebs. Nothing was comprehensible. He had understood the Spider Trickster's pranks back at No Tongue's better than he did these foreign discussions. He stood up, and water flowed from him like a walrus. He was pink from the hot water, and wrinkled like a prune. Two large towels dried him, and he stood in front of a wall of full-length mirrors, bordered in gold from Egypt. His clothes were laid out for him on a dressing table. He left puddles on the parquet tile floor, gleaming like glass. He couldn't believe the buckskins laid out for him, with beaded moccasins, too, and a bear fur cape! Moonbeam had even laid out a beaded knife sheath for him, with a huge elkbone-handled knife for it! His tunic fit him perfectly, making him look almost slender and very, very tall. He brushed his hair as he stepped outside through sliding French doors. What a magnificent panorama! The whole Valley lay at his feet. His long black hair blew freely and cleanly in the warm spring air! How could the world be so good!

So why didn't he feel too well?

He wasn't sick anymore, the women had assured him, as

he stepped back inside, putting on his soft moccasins with hard soles. He wasn't queasy anymore, although he was very hungry. He knew he had lost a lot of weight in the last few days, and all winter. He was getting in shape from his long horseback ride, and fasting, and dieting.

His horse! Where was Massaum?

He went out the door and up the stairs.

Only to emerge into another kaleidoscopic chamber of the strange geodesic craft these people called home. Triangular windows with stained glass cast eerie shapes and colorful patterns on the round walls and angular corners. A feast of unfamiliar sights filled his brain, and he had to close his eyes and shake his head, then open his eyes again. It was all still there, and more kaleidoscopic than ever.

For starters, Sky was entrenched in the middle of several television and computer screens, and playing a Nintendo game of *Teenage Mutant Ninja Turtles* while flicking the channels on the thirty-six-inch TV. He waved hello.

"Daddy! You know what? Sparky has a satellite dish and he gets a *Thousand Channels*! And he has hundreds of videos and every Nintendo and Atari video game *ever made!*"

"Oh," Whirlwind answered. Sky was obviously hysterical and in a complete trance in Kid Heaven. His eyes were bugging out of his head.

Red Bird and Carmenta and Moonbeam and three or four other beautiful white women in exotic clothes and scarves and headbands and jewelry turned to look at him. They all exclaimed rapturously at once. "OH! AHH! You look *FABULOUS!!* Absolutely *GORGEOUS! MAGNIFICENT!* Oooooo! Ahhh! You lucky GIRL!"

His scrotum got hard and sent another crimson body rush from the top of his head to his toenails. His testicles actually turned hard as rocks and his zygotes solidified.

The women swarmed all over him, each begging to let her braid his hair, and perfume him, and tie eagle feathers in his scalplock. He completely forgot what he was going to ask them. They led him to the kitchen, explaining about the fresh spinach they'd picked for the omelet, and the real chestnuts, and a lot of herbs he'd never heard of. One of them poured him freshly ground Nicaraguan coffee (Ah ha! The CIA exclaimed) into a cup a local potter had made, shaped like a blue duck with feet. They sat him at a glass table made of an old pioneer wagon wheel, and Jane set the handmade clay plates in front of him, giving him a kiss. She was dressed like all the other women, and proud of it. One beautiful blond woman of about forty braided his hair while another got him fresh goat cream and organic sugar, and another fixed a black buffalo bone choker around his neck.

Meanwhile, Sparky and a few long-haired men, also in their late thirties and forties, were talking in a side room among a lot of other machinery piled up to the crooked wooden ceiling. A lot of red computer lights were bleeping and blue dials too-too-tooing, and Whirlwind caught a few words. "If the perpetual motion centrifuge . . ." and "But doesn't that preclude the solar generators from . . ." and ". . . my satellite motor won't take that much voltage unless we . . ." They were passing around a glass bong several feet long with a lot of weird-colored tubes running in and out of it, and smoking from the thing. It smelled sweet and strong, but for some reason Whirlwind didn't accept a puff when they came over and politely offered him one. None of the women accepted either. They were too busy with breakfast and hair and talk.

Whirlwind grasped a few words Red Bird was saying to him. "You'll look *fantastic* for the press conference."

He gulped down a huge bite of the omelet, dripping with three kinds of cheese and a garden's worth of vegetables. "Me? Press conference?"

"That is"—Moonbeam fretted over him—"if the poor Darling is up to it. How are you feeling?"

"Oh, uh . . . okay. But I don't want . . . I can't . . ."

"Don't worry, Whirlwind." Red Bird leaned over and kissed him. She had the faint odor of . . . beer . . . on her breath? It couldn't be. "You'll just have to sit there. You won't have to say anything."

"He won't have to," a beautiful black woman sighed seductively in front of him.

"Buddy will do most of the talking," Red Bird explained further. "I don't want to, either, but—"

"You should definitely be the main speaker," Carmenta

argued. "Your sacred presence is far more important than a man's call to use weapons and politics to—"

"Oh, I just hate guns," another woman complained.

"And politics," another declared. "We have to change ourselves from within, not by trying to force other people to—"

"The real revolution will be in our individual transformation and awareness, not—"

"I read in Lynn Andrews in *Jaguar Woman* where—"

"Starhawk says—"

"Oh, I went to a Shirley MacLaine seminar, and I don't care what anybody says about her, she is very charismatic and sincere."

"I agree that we have to focus our energy a lot more on our personal lives rather than trying to change the world."

"And a career is important."

"Absolutely."

"It's naive to think you can go through this life without some security. I see no contradiction whatsoever in having the finer things of life and pursuing a spiritual path. The Spirit—"

The house became a cacophony of whirling thingamabobs and swirling philosophies for Whirlwind, and he excused himself for a moment. He tried to find a bathroom. He passed Sky, who was flipping channels like a maniac. He watched for a second.

"—we need the Extra-panoramic Foundation," a bodiless head exorted. Another bodiless head argued with it. "You'll have to communicate telepathically with the Twins first. Jack and Walt must be kept alive, even if one is growing older and the other is growing younger. You'll need to go to the Star System Gargantua to find—"

Sky punched the remote control and another channel flashed on. It was a woman interviewing a man on a talk show. They both wore suits and ties and had short hair and no makeup. "Life after death is not just a parapsychological phenomenon, based on religious preconceptions. When I say that light is darkness I mean—"

He flipped again, to a science documentary, discussing a closeup of a huge computer complex. "—this is the TR-80

Model 16. It can run three jobs, such as billing, inventory, and order entry, simultaneously using common data files on hard disk—"

Whirlwind searched for a toilet. He paused as he went by the men. "Mushrooms are big business. Not only do you have to—"

"Uh, excuse me," he said. "I'm sorry to interrupt. Where's the rest room?"

They smiled indulgently at him, and Sparky put his hand on his shoulder. "I'll show you. Out here. Have you ever seen one of these babies before? It's a compost toilet with no chemicals or water."

"Oh yeah?"

"Enjoy."

Whirlwind relaxed on the sleek, ultra-modern throne. The bathroom had a computer in it. The screen said: PUSH RETURN. As he sat, he found the RETURN and pushed it. It clicked on to Sky's central television complex.

A voice was speaking as atomic bombs were going off in various special effects and negative colors. "—and now there are some fifty thousand warheads in the world, possessing the explosive yield of roughly twenty billion tons of TNT, or one million six hundred thousand times the yield of the bomb that was dropped by the United States on the city of Nagasaki in Japan—"

Whirlwind watched the channels flip in a quick succession of commercials. It was a surreal cavalcade of cars and sexy woman and beer and douches and cars and more beer and AT&T. Bible shows flashed by, fishing programs, another dozen commercials, and Whirlwind punched OFF on his intercom.

As he pulled up his boxer shorts he heard a woman exhorting in the hallway. "There's nothing wrong with a good Australian lager, once in a while. I mean, goodness sakes. It's a cliche to say Indians are drunks just because there's an alcohol problem on some of the reservations. Why should you be denied—"

Whirlwind came out of the bathroom to see Red Bird taking another drink from a crystal goblet full of beer. She looked guiltily at him. He said nothing. The redheaded woman who had been talking took a drink of her beer too.

210

"Hi. We were just discussing the stereotype of Indians and alcoholism. Don't you think that's a racist—"

"I don't know." He shrugged, and walked past them.

"One or two good lagers," the women continued, "with no artificial preservatives are actually healthy and good for you."

The house was hot. It felt oppressive. He saw Buddy and the other warriors arriving out on the patio, with at least another dozen white and black people, mostly men. He walked out to them.

Buddy was dressed to the teeth in Indian buckskins, and looked great too. He saw Whirlwind and looked relieved. "Hey, Partner, how ya feeling?"

"Okay. You?"

"Fine. We're staying down at another Dome down the hill. This is a whole commune here, they own over a thousand acres, did you know that?"

"No."

"It's really something. Did Bonnie tell you about the press conference?"

"Uh . . ."

Several aggressive men of their age started talking to Buddy again, and the whole cacophony was repeated again, only they were outside on a huge cantilevered porch hanging over a cliff. The view of the mountains they had crossed, back to their west now, was spectacular. The sky was blue and gigantic. It was probably sixty degrees, above average for April. Only a few clouds added some contrast to the vast azure dome at the top of the world.

Buddy broke away from everyone demanding his time and attention to address Whirlwind again. "Everyone's out on bail now, did they tell ya?"

"Uh, yeah, sort of. They're okay, huh?"

"Amazingly, yes. We're meeting everybody over at Mount Blanca for a big hookup. The TV Networks are all gonna be there and—"

"The backdrop should be spectacular," one white man with a beard explained.

An expressive black man reached over and shook his hand, while Buddy introduced Whirlwind to everybody, none of whose names he remembered. "It's an honor,

Chief," the black man said. "Jesse Jackson has sent a tele-
gram of support for you."

"And H. Ross Perot wants to give you a million dollars,"
the bearded white man said in awe.

Buddy smirked. "A lot of big celebrities are with us. It's
a national movement now, Philbert. You're famous. We're
going to have to figure out what to do with—"

Whirlwind shook his head. "You do the press conference,
Buddy. I don't know what to say. I don't know anything
about politics."

"Politics, My Friend," the bearded know-it-all said patron-
izingly, putting his arm around Whirlwind's shoulders, "is
the price of bread."

Red Bird and her coterie of courtesans emerged out onto
the porch and confronted the men with their petitions
about how the press conference should be run, and how the
money should be spent, and how the government should be
organized after the triumph of the Popular Revolution.
They were drinking beer and smoking dope. Whirlwind
stayed in the background, squeezing over by the railing and
looking out at the horizon, toward the east and north,
toward Lame Deer and Bear Butte. Home. Jane was in
front of him at one point, carrying around a silver platter
full of liver canapés, and Whirlwind asked her, "Where's
Uncle Fred, do you know?"

"He went to do that peyote ceremony," she replied, and
moved on busily about her task. There were a hundred
things to do.

Peyote? Whirlwind thought. Yeah, Uncle Fred had always
been into that. He would have to try it himself someday,
he told himself. Who knows? He felt very inadequate. He
knew none of these things everyone was talking about. He
was an ignorant man. He couldn't lead anybody out of a
paper bag, let alone into the Renewal like they had been
discussing. He was a ship without a rudder. He missed Storyteller. Red Bird walked past him once, and he asked her,
"Has anybody heard from Storyteller?"

She stopped to think, and frowned. "No, now that you
mention it. I'll go ask the others. You sure you don't want
anything?"

"No."

She couldn't understand why he had a pained expression on his face; she thought she was just imagining it. She was a little tipsy. Oh, it felt good to be human again. She asked around, "Have you seen Storyteller?"

"Who?"

Bits of conversations drifted in and out of Whirlwind's ears and brain, but very little registered.

"—it's like the Baltic States in Eastern Europe right now. Estonia and Latvia and Lithuania already got their sovereign independence too."

"Exactly like the Navahos and Sioux and—"

"Exactly."

"They want to go the way East Germany and Hungary and Czechoslovakia have—"

"Yeah, but the Soviet hard-liners will never grant Estonia or Latvia the same freedom they allowed in Bulgaria and Czechoslovakia."

"That's right."

"It would tear Russia apart, to have all those 'ethnic minorities' go free, just like honoring the Indian Treaties here would never be permitted. The Sioux are a sovereign nation, absolutely, but try to tell that to the white people of South Dakota, or Arizona around the Navahos and Hopis and—"

"It's within the internal borders is why."

Then Whirlwind remembered what he'd forgotten hours ago. Massaum! Where were the horses? "Where are the horses?" he asked Sparky, whose eyes were glazed over with some kind of drug. Whirlwind felt suddenly like he wanted to get as far away from there as possible.

"Oh, Man, they're cool. We got a righteous stable and corral with plenty of fresh—"

"Where?"

"Down the hill, that way. They are in Horse Heaven."

"Thanks."

He worked his way through the party. He felt dizzy again, and almost nauseous. A whole bar with bottles of whisky and gin and wine was set up on one end of the lovely porch. He heard Buddy expounding.

213

"We need adequate defense weapons, I'm sorry. These people will *never* give up their guns, let alone their missiles and tanks and bombers and—"

"That's right, the whole American economy has come to be totally dependent on war."

"Guns and drugs," Buddy continued. Whirlwind walked off the porch and down the dirt driveway. No one paid him any attention. He could hear Buddy's words fading in the wind. "I'm not going to leave my people at their mercy anymore. These guys would slaughter Indians again tomorrow if their pocketbook was threatened. Don't kid yourself. Indians have to re-arm if we are ever going to be able to—"

Whirlwind walked away. With every step he felt more and more alone. The sun was revolving around to the southwest in the early afternoon, and a fairly strong breeze blew from the northwest. He was sore from all the riding, and his gut was a little queasy, but he was glad to have the beautiful buckskins and bear cape Moonbeam had given him. He knew it was foolish to be leaving all those beautiful people. He didn't understand what he was doing or where he was going. He was surprised that he didn't stop and turn back. He felt stupid and muleheaded. What was he doing? But he kept walking and looking back. The party was noisy and busy, and no one noticed him. He felt warm in his animal clothes. His moccasins felt good on the hard, dry earth.

"DADDY!" Sky shouted out of the breeze behind him. The boy was leaning over the rails on the porch. "WHERE ARE YOU GOING?"

"NOWHERE!" Whirlwind shouted back, as a few people looked curiously at him. "GO BACK TO YOUR TV!"

"BUT WHERE ARE YOU GOING?"

"I DON'T KNOW. TO CHECK THE HORSES."

"Oh, okay," Sky replied, and went back in the house.

A pang of regret shot through the Sacred Chief, for he knew now that he couldn't go back in that place. He wasn't sure why; everybody was really nice, but . . . he belonged out here. He wanted to feel the sun and wind on his face. He wanted to ride his pony.

He followed the driveway trail down around a steep incline. It was the same road they had come in the other night, when the dogs barked at them. He saw the dogs chasing around in the fields below, down the steep incline. Sparky's Dome was up on a steep ledge overlooking a broad, flat valley.

He walked, and the kinks worked themselves out. He saw the corral in the aspens ahead. Massaum saw him, and she was mad. She was in a corral. She couldn't run free anywhere she wanted. When Whirlwind got there he apologized. "I'm sorry, Sister. I didn't know they'd kept you in here."

She pouted and stomped away from him to the other end of the corral. Many of the other wonderful horses were in there, too, and they were even madder than she was. He opened the gate, and that got their interest. "Go," he said. "You're all free to go. No horses of mine will ever be penned up again. I will open the whole world to wild game."

The four-leggeds hurried out to where the pastures were greener. Massaum respected what he did and stood by him. She scratched her face roughly on his back, almost lifting him off his feet. "Well," he said, his voice full of self-pity, "it's good somebody's glad to see me."

He found the simple rope bit and she let him hook it into her mouth. He lay on her back and wiggled up on top of her. She felt thinner from her long ride and run over the mountains. He had been too hard on her. He let her take the reins and she turned east, down the slope, toward the warmer pastures she could see across the valley below them. He let her go. A whiteman watched them ride and he waved. "Taking her out for a spin?" he asked.

Whirlwind nodded assent.

Massaum found a gravel road and they walked slowly on the hard packed dirt. Her shoes felt harder on it, and she took the softer sand and grass along the sides, stopping often to eat the grass. He let her do what she wanted. He didn't feel he had the right to tell anyone or anything what to do. He felt like the dumbest man in the world. He was leaving all the people he loved more dearly than anyone he had ever known. Sky and Jane were almost like his children, but they were better off here. They had all the things they wanted. Buddy was his best friend, but Whirlwind couldn't

215

keep up with him, not by a fraction. And Red Bird? His heart constricted in pain, but he couldn't be around her when she was drinking. There was something mean and bad about it. He had no right to judge her, he knew. He'd been the biggest drunk and dopehead around for years. He had no room to talk.

Massaum wandered slowly eastward, from patch of grass to patch of grass. She drank from an irrigation ditch. She examined the fence along the road, and was startled when a coven of western wood pee-wees flew out of a nest in a clump of huckleberry bushes. The sun was getting low in the southwest off behind his right shoulder. Thin white clouds showed that the air was warm, and strong gusts of wind blew to show that the rapid changes in temperature were upsetting the weather. It was a nice spring afternoon in the foothills.

A few cars passed by on a paved road off to his right, maybe a mile away. They walked past some farmhouses back down long dirt driveways, but no one paid him much attention. They looked twice, from their gardens or garages, to see a huge Indian in buckskins walk past on a gorgeous Pinto, but they went back to work. There was hay to be put in and fences to be mended. People minded their own business out here.

Whirlwind felt himself sinking into an irrational despair. He was filling himself full of self-pity. He wanted to cry. He wanted to die. All was lost. He hated himself. He was so stupid. He knew Red Bird hated his fat stomach. His body was embarrassing. He had been forced into being some kind of "Chief," and almost got everybody killed. They were hiding in a cave only two or three nights ago! Frozen, starving, sick, terrified. It was the end.

17

OF CONTRARY FORCES,
AND OTHER PREVAILING
BREEZES.

JUST AS THE BIG FAT DUMB SHIT WAS SLUMPING OVER AND
ready to fall off the merry-go-round of life, his nose picked
up a strange fragrance. What was it? He felt his mind and
senses about to fall into the abyss of despair and self-
loathing, where almost all the losers of the world go when
they look at themselves in the cosmic mirror, when the most
sacred odor in all the world literally lifted him back up by
his moccasin straps. Where . . . ?

He saw a jackass grazing near a lone cedar tree on a little
knoll. There were no farmhouses around anymore, nor did
the sound of cars and trucks from the road intrude on this
little glen. Another mule was also grazing in the fine pasture nearby. Whirlwind slipped off Massaum, and she
gladly joined the jacks in the grassy pasture, flipping the
halter out of her mouth.

The air was filled with a perfume finer than any mixture
made by women, save the Great Lady Herself. It was . . .

sweetgrass! Burning sweetgrass! He floated toward the source.

"Saved by a nose," a voice said. The big red Indian nose looked unto where and whence the disembodied voice had come, and saw me grinning at him, leaning against the cedar tree. A little altar of sweetgrass was burning in front of me. Dozens of the braided green stalks were stacked against the embers, with thick white smoke rising into the prevailing breeze which was blowing Indian-ward.

"Storyteller?"

He saw that I looked different though. A lot different. My face was painted red and I was wearing a very strange ornament on my forehead, tied around my head by a bright red cloth. I had on a long, thick robe made of six bright colors. I pointed to a flat area near the lone cedar tree and Whirlwind followed my finger.

The Cheyenne Indian froze, for he saw an ancient half-circle of sage with a buffalo skull placed on the earth at the opening of the half-moon circle. It stirred vague semi-recollections of old, old Indian times almost forgotten. What was it? Whirlwind couldn't move. He stared at the scene in front of him.

I laughed and stood up, grunting comically as I did so. "There is your Contrary Bow," I said.

"What?" Whirlwind whispered. It was more of a gasp. "Contrary Bow?" It wasn't possible, he thought. It was sacrilegious to even mention such sacred things. There hadn't been a Contrary Bow among the Cheyennes since they surrendered to the whites in 1877. He looked, and when I pointed again he saw that there were, indeed, two tall Staffs standing in the middle of the half-circle behind the skull.

I casually walked counterclockwise around the circle from behind and stood facing the skull. "The buffalo is facing, oh, approximately north by northeast toward the Sacred Mountain. C'mon."

Whirlwind came over to the circle, walking around behind it as I had done, and we stood facing the skull. Then I broke into a Cheyenne song that made Whirlwind break into sobs:

Hohnuhk'e piva!
Hohnuhk'e piva Zezestas
Suhtaio Maheo Mahuts!
Hohnuhk'e Nowah'wus
Issi'wun ah ya yi Mutsuv'iu'i'v!

I was singing about all the sacred things and people and places of the Cheyenne Nation since their creation. Whirlwind felt as if the whole universe was pouring through his soul again, and that it was being carried on the sweetgrass smoke through his nostrils. I led him into the half-circle, around the buffalo skull, and we looked at the two Staffs.

"This one"—I pointed to the one on the left—"is my Thunder Lance." It was about six feet tall, and the bottom four or five feet were made of wood, it looked like; stripped of bark with a mosaic of natural wood designs inherent in it. Tied to the top of it was another rod wrapped in buffalo fur with a huge crystal on top, and a smaller one on bottom. Eagle feathers and a medicine wheel made of porcupine quill was tied to it. "Only a few priestesses on the Sacred Mountain have ever seen this Lance. It is made of spruce wood that was struck by lightning, and has given me power over the great *maiyun* whose supernatural names can never be spoken, not by such fools as we are."

I quickly grabbed the Lance and held it to the sky, and shouted with a voice that echoed up and down the valley, "Hau Thunder Beings and Lightning Spirits! I no longer fear your noise and terror! HAU! HO!"

Whirlwind gulped. His mouth was dry. He waited to be struck dead by a thunderbolt any moment at this blasphemy. He wanted to get away from such a crazy man as fast as he could: my hair blowing wildly and my face painted a ghoulish red, and the long robe waving all around me on the hilltop. My long Lance did look magnificent against the great Colorado sky, though. It was really a pretty impressive picture.

I lowered the Lance and smiled casually at Whirlwind. "See, no thunderbolts. I am a Contrary too. We are sacred clowns, Brother. We have been given a great honor and courage, but great shame also. Our thunder visions and dreams give us a lot of power, but we have to pay for it. We have to look ridiculous before the world."

"You . . . are a Contrary Hohnuhk'e?"

"So are you, Chief Whirlwind. Look, this is your Contrary Bow. No Tongue gave it to me before he died, to give it to you.

"No Tongue died?"

"Not really. They didn't find his body, like Monster Slayer's."

Whirlwind's mouth was as dry as dirt. He looked at the second Staff wedged in the ground between rocks. They were stuck in a crack in a rock in the ground. In the old days, a Contrary was given a dream of thunder and lightning, and he had to perform his dream in public or die. He had to be awakened to a fearsome and terrible responsibility. His would be an almost unbearable burden. Indeed, the duties were so demanding that there were only three or four Contraries among all the Cheyennes in the period during the Custer Battle when they were at their height as a warrior society. When they were penned up on the Reservations, the Contrary Bows lost all their power. The people lost all their power.

"Without a Contrary Chief," I explained, "there will never be a renewal of the Zezestas and Suhtaio Nations."

Whirlwind stared at the Contrary Bow standing in front of him. It was a tall staff of wood, too, about six feet tall, but curved like a bow, whereas my Lance was straight. There were no decorations or any designs or feathers on it at all. He blushed, for he knew he should grasp it and make it his own, and decorate it according to the medicine signs given to him in dreams, but he couldn't. He felt that it would burn him alive if he touched it. He would be struck by lightning.

I tried to persuade him. "I know it is dangerous, Brother. I know. But you have to do it, or you will die in an even more terrible way. Your spirit will be taken off to the center of the galaxy and you will never find your way home. Never. Not for all eternity. You must obey the Powers. You have no choice."

"But I . . . I don't understand any of it."

"You're not meant to. Neither do I. We just take orders. We are Contraries, Whirlwind."

220

"We should smoke the pipe before we do any of this."

"Of course. My pipe is at the Sacred Mountain. Do you have yours with you?"

Whirlwind looked desperately at the man beside him, who had a crazy look on his weird face. "No. I don't have a pipe."

I giggled, shaking my head. "Contraries to the last! No pipes! Ha ha!"

Whirlwind stared at the Bow. Sweet Medicine himself had such a Bow. He was a Contrary too. He had to live alone all his life, and do everything differently. Soldiers were always looking for him, too, to kill him for doing everything against the law and everything else. Sweet Medicine never did anything like he was supposed to. He had no respect for anything. And today he is revered as if he was the most respectable and distingushed gentleman who ever lived. There's no figuring people.

The Contrary Bow beckoned, but Whirlwind could not accept his moment of truth. He knew that he should take it and string it with two strings of buffalo gut, and tie a stone of some sort to its top, never letting the top touch Mother Earth. The skin of a tanager, and the feathers of an owl, hawk, and eagle, would sure look good on there. He would repair it and renew it at the same time the renewing ceremonies would be held for Mahuts, the sacred Arrows of Sweet Medicine.

"Yep, ol' Sweet Medicine, he was an ornery sort too," I said, as if I could read Whirlwind's thoughts. "Wandering willy-nilly here and there, doing anything he wanted in the most irresponsible manner possible. He would probably just lounge around all day and eat plums off a tree if he felt like it, and stare at the clouds and think. A complete bum. He would wave his Contrary Bow and make it rain if the land needed moisture, not giving the slightest thought to the heresy of his actions. He probably made fun of God and little babies too."

The Contrary Bow was not actually a weapon. It was carried into battle, but was used only for counting coup—not for killing an enemy. When its bearer shifted the Bow to his right hand, he could never retreat. Armed with that sacred lance, a Contrary Warrior was the bravest of a brave people. During a battle, he charged the enemy alone, since he had to ride along the flank of the other fighting men. A Contrary, Whirlwind remembered, could court death with recklessness, because the power of the Contrary Bow would protect him.

He knew, suddenly, that his true Protector was this memory and this power evoked by this piece of wood in front of him. It was his power inside himself, his immortal spirit, that the *maiyun* wished to summon forth. Only by holding the external world in his hand could he hope to bring the truth back to his people. He reached out and took the Power.

"HAU! HO! HOO! WOO WOOOOOOOOOOOOO OOOOOOOOOOOOOOOOOOOOOO!!"

The two men whooped wildly unto the heavens and jumped up and down like wild savages! They screamed like animals, intoxicated by the goddess! They sounded like wolves howling in the primeval canyons of our mind; echoes reverberating back from the prehistoric knowledge long buried by rockslides of reason and mudslides of respectability!

They danced on the bed of sage and sang hymns to the sunset, grasping their power in their hands like mighty tree trunks thousands of years old. Finally, as the crescent moon shone on their crescent temple, and Venus danced with her Sister's daughter, they waltzed out of the circle and said goodnight to the buffalo skull.

I said, "I borrowed some pork chops at the store in town. Dollar eighty-nine a pound, can you believe the price of meat? You hungry?"

Whirlwind's stomach growled like a grizzly bear, in reply.

I hopped right to work, building a campfire and pulling out some pots and pans and a grocery sack. "Got some coffee and beans and maple longjohns too. Oh, you want half this Snickers? It's one of them extra large size for a dollar. Can you believe that?"

"Thanks."

We ate the Snickers and cooked dinner. We checked the animals, who were fine. "What happened to Gandalf?" Whirlwind asked, sipping some coffee as a few trillion stars came out.

"Oh, he was too much horseflesh for me. I found a jackass waiting and figured it would be more humble for me to be seen on him. Gandalf ran back to La Paloma or somewhere. I got this other mule I borrowed out of a field and stored up on salt and pepper and cooking utensils for our long ride. You got a sleeping bag? I picked up another one for you in the store. Down, good to forty below. And some groundcloths and a change of shorts."

Whirlwind allowed as how he'd appreciate having the sleeping bag, as he splashed a puddle of ketchup on his pork chops in his tin plate. We didn't talk for a while, and only interrupted our progress to stir the fire and heat up the longjohns. We built a real fire for a change, as if we didn't have a million worries in the world and warrants out for us coast-to-coast.

"What's that doo-dad you got tied on your forehead?" Whirlwind asked conversationally. It was the time of pleasant after-dinner repartee.

I fondled my Lance with my left hand. I always held It in my left hand. The Lance was propped securely against a rock next to his bed. "Oh, just a bronze brooch of a Jinni I got in North Africa."

"I like it," Whirlwind commented courteously.

"Yeah? I think it makes me look scary, like a wizard or something."

"Yeah, it's great. What's that big robe you're wearing?"

"Oh, the Irish ollave-wizards used to wear them, after they mastered the nineteen-year course at the Poetic College. They were the only ones allowed to wear six colors, beside the Queen, because dye was so expensive and hard to get."

"Oh."

"It was like a thing of honor. People used to respect Poets."

We nodded and sipped our coffee, and gazed at the Contrary Bows framed against the cedar tree and the night sky. It was a pretty picture, all right, and we closed our eyes contentedly, not even worrying about the fire or the horses or anything. The Powers would take care of it all.

18

HOW CHIEF WHIRLWIND WAS
FORCED TO BECOME AN
EXISTENTIAL HERO, IN
SPITE OF HIMSELF.

WE HIT THE TRAIL THE NEXT MORNING, RIGHT AFTER PAN-
cakes and eggs and bacon and a bucket of coffee, of course.
We did the dishes in an irrigation ditch, scrubbing the
grime with sand. The four-leggeds preferred to stay in the
pasture, but the plot wouldn't allow them their natural pref-
erences so they were persuaded to see what was over the
next hill. They followed their noses, with the big red fullblood Indian nose out in front, as if he could smell trouble
brewing ten miles away. Not only was his nose a particularly
bright red this morning, but so was the rest of his face and
body, as I had loaned him some red body makeup, which
had been loaned to me by a drug store in the last town.
Nature always provides.

"I'd of paid for it all," I explained, "if I'd had any money.
It's not my fault I'm broke. It's the economy."

We held our Bows by our sides and looked, generally,
like the goddamnedest outlaws who'd ever ridden, at least
since the days of Billy the Kid and Hopalong Cassidy.

Smeared with paint and chapped by wind, we actually scared a little old lady who was out in her yard feeding her cats, and she ran back inside her trailer yowling.

You might have wished that your heroes had gotten up before dawn and stolen a cattle herd by now, but, as has been pointed out too often, we were lazy, worthless bums who didn't care about anything. If it was pushing nine o'clock before we finished our leisurely petit-fours and sipped the last of our café-au-laits in demi-tasses, then you can't blame us. We didn't have a clock. If the Three Musketeers meant no more to us than a candy bar, it's not our fault. They've tried to educate us in the proper procedures of etiquette.

But there we were, sauntering down the road in the bright, warm daylight without a care in the world. So naturally, every care in the world had to come descending down on top of us like a ton of bricks.

Sky galloped after us on his horse, Hulk, as the first brick thrown from the outside world. "DADDY! DADDY!" the boy screamed, as if he hadn't heard him the first time.

"What?" Whirlwind halted. "Sky?"

Hulk charged up to us, and splattered slobber and lather all over us as he pulled up to a quick stop. "You're getting to be quite a horseman, Sky," I said in a very complimentary fashion.

Sky rudely ignored the compliment, for he was hysterical. "WHY'D you leave me?! WHERE are you going?!"

"Uh . . ."

The boy jumped off the horse, and he looked very small all of a sudden, standing at the bottom of the very big (and very hot) horse. "The man back at the commune said you went this way, so I came out after you this morning when we couldn't find you and I've been riding all morning, scared that the cops got you and you were hurt or—"

"Okay, okay, slow down," Whirlwind said soothingly, getting off Massaum, and holding his Bow. "What—"

"OH!" the boy exclaimed wildly, and jumped in his arms, embracing him fiercely. "DON'T LEAVE ME, DADDY! Oh, I'm sorry if you're mad at me for playing video games too much and I—"

"You followed us all this way?"

"—yeah, yeah—I was running so fast and I know Hulk isn't but I couldn't so oh, yeah, yeah—"

Whirlwind hugged the boy, and looked up at me, embarrassed, and touched, and, if you want to know the truth of his heart, thrilled with such affection and love from another person. There was something about children that he really liked. The boy hugged him ferociously, squeezing him tightly, his tears wet on the man's cheek and smearing his red paint. "I thought you liked it back there, with all the games and TV and—"

"I WANT YOU!" the boy sobbed wildly. There was no hesitation in his mind, or doubt. Then his mood broke just as quickly and impulsively, and he stared at Whirlwind's face. "Why are you wearing makeup?"

"Uh . . . it's a long story."

"I'll tell ya about it later," I said.

"But for now," Whirlwind cross-examined, "does your mother know where you are? She'll be worried—"

"Mommy's been crying all night. Everybody's been out looking for you."

"For me?"

"YES! WHERE HAVE YOU BEEN? WHAT ARE YOU DOING?!"

"I'm . . . we're . . . going home. To Bear Butte."

"Can I go with you?" Sky sniffled. "I won't be any trouble. I don't have to eat much or—"

It was Whirlwind's turn to break into tears and start jabbering a bunch of nonsense, and kissing, and hugging. "Oh, no. You don't have to, of course. You can go with me—I just didn't think you wanted to leave all those nice things and toys when I didn't have any money and the soldiers were trying to kill us and we were cold in the cave and—"

"Okay, okay, Guys," I interjected, trying to reinstate a little pace in the plot. "Let's ride. We haven't got all day."

Whirlwind hoisted Sky up on Massaum in front of him, explaining that he shouldn't touch his Contrary Bow, and he told the boy about our Contrary Ceremony as we rode off. Hulk wandered along beside us, eating every blade of grass he saw, and trying not to drink the irrigation ditch dry. It's a horse myth that a horse will drink himself to death if you let him. Four-leggeds weren't born yesterday. That's horse-ism.

We went another mile or so on that convenient road, which ran due east out toward the looming prairie, when another interruption forced itself upon our peaceful stroll.

Buddy and about ten warriors came galloping down upon us from a side road, at an intersection. They were waving wildly and shouting the usual questions about what the hell did we think we were doing, and how could we leave everybody in the lurch like that, etc. etc. etc. I was getting tired of having to account to everybody for my actions. I didn't ask them what they were doing every second of the day, so where did they get off interrogating us?

Whirlwind was a little more disconcerted about it though. He tried to explain that he didn't want to talk at a press conference, and they acted like they couldn't understand that. Didn't he know he was important? The debate continued as the horses just kind of wandered on down the road.

I leapt into the breach and explained something. Actors don't always understand the motivation of their characters and need some direction, once in a while. "We're going home, Buddy."

"Home?" Buddy smirked. "Where's that? Oh, you mean Bear Butte. Well, I don't see how we can do it. It's, what, maybe eight hundred miles and all the cops in the world after us? It's impossible."

Whirlwind nodded and just kept riding. The horses just kept walking, when they weren't stopping every ten seconds to graze.

Uncle Fred pulled up right then at another intersection, with a few of his peyote compeers I guessed, riding some stray animals from somewhere. They had saddles, like Buddy and his Warrior Society. Uncle Fred took one look at Whirlwind and me up at the head of the column, in our paint and holding our Bows in our left hands and said, "That's a Contrary Bow. Where'd you get it?"

Buddy and the warriors looked with renewed interest, as they, too, had noticed our strange get-up and paraphernalia. They even looked a little skittish about us. Whirlwind and I didn't answer, choosing to heighten the aura of mystery that was starting to surround us. It's always good to develop a myth around yourself like that. People leave you alone.

On an impulse I switched my Thunder Lance over to my right hand. "Uncle Fred, do you remember what it meant when a Contrary Bow was put in a Hohnuhk'e's right hand?"

"Hohnuhk'e?" Uncle Fred gasped, and looked incredulous at his fellow peyote-heads.

Even Massaum stopped and looked around at me. Her passenger asked in a tremulous whisper, "You . . . it means we can never retreat?"

"That's right," I replied. "No retreat, no surrender. Victory or death, all the way to Nowah'wus."

We were all just standing in the middle of the world on the edge of the Colorado foothills, where they blend into the limitless Prairie beyond, and looking stupidly at each other. I couldn't think of anything else to do to tie up the story and get it over with. There didn't seem to be anything else to do, not in this day and age.

On another irresponsible impulse, Whirlwind swung his Contrary Bow over Sky's head and put it in his right hand. He looked like he was ready to be struck dead by lightning any moment.

Uncle Fred, too, appeared to be waiting for all of us to be fried to a crisp. Not even the horses were distracted by the green grass, for a few seconds. It was a simple occurrence in the middle of a gravel road in the middle of some alfalfa fields. As Indians, everybody there knew, vaguely, what a Contrary used to be. They were a little spooked by us. My Jackass and accompanying pack mule took the initiative and stepped on down the road. Massaum took her cue and joined Jackass. The other horses and men followed, at a safe distance. It was all unspoken, as these sacred story lines at their supreme best have always been.

The West is full of such inexplicable legends as these, and Indians especially are full of it. We have given up hope of ever being able to explain to the whiteman our instinctual journeys. We just go. Whirlwind and the boys just went. After about ten minutes Buddy's brain began to clear and his worries began to race. "If we're gonna do this, there's a million things we've got to plan."

Whirlwind and I nodded quietly, above the ordinary details of daily life. Buddy and two or three of his guys took a detour at the next intersection to find a telephone and call Rabbit, alert the troops, send out the smoke signals, whatever. I, personally, wasn't up to the myriad of plot complications still to come, and I don't think my listeners around the campfire were either. I know you much prefer to go deep inside the esoterica of the human personality, don't you? Yes, I thought so. A good liar always knows his audience. Why, for instance, didn't Buddy and the others already know we were going to light out across the open prairie and make plans accordingly? How many times do these clear stylistic intentions have to be expounded upon? How many of you out there want this thing to drag on for another hundred chapters? One, two, three, four, five . . . ten. I thought so.

We rode, and people fanned out all over the countryside, and the sun moved across the sky. Indians didn't have to think twice about what to do. They pulled up beside us in campers and horse trailers, saddled up, and fell in behind the procession. The call had gone out all winter, and troublemakers were pouring in from Oklahoma, Washington State, Minnesota, even as far away as Manitoba and Guatemala. There's no way to analyze these things, not in a rational way. If you want a realistic plot, go read John Steinbeck or Mark Twain or somebody. Don't come around bothering Indians. We got our own problems.

A big crossroads along this newfangled River of Huckleberry Finn's appeared just ahead in the form of Interstate 25. It cut right across our tranquil horizon. We came down over a few dirt hills and there they were: probably hundreds of real pissed-off motorists going north and south stopped in their vital progress by a few scruffy malcontents blocking traffic both ways. It was like the Panama Canal waiting for us to cross, and there was Rabbit and her Corps of Chicanas and Watusis. Television mobile vans crowded around to see, and lit up the late afternoon with huge kleig lights, and there were plenty of cops there, too, you can bet. And plenty more Indians saddling up out of their horse trailers with Arizona and Texas plates. Rabbit had some dilapidated Rezz Cars laid horizontally across the vertical highway, and monstrous eighteen-wheelers with SAFEWAY and ALLIED ELECTRONICS and BUDWEISER graphics smeared artistically across their vast bellies, like logos printed on the scales of diesel-dragons, and I was reminded of *The Grapes of Wrath,* for some reason. There *were* a lot of Okies in the parade, and even some earnest California refugees too.

We were delighted to see Grampa waiting for us, and he was more than delighted to produce a shiny new pair of wire cutters, which he promptly employed upon a barbed wire fence which had the temerity to lay directly in the path of the Chief. The walls of Jericho came tumbling down and, I'll tell ya, even I got a little excited when we broke into a trot and clomp-clomped right through the Canal and over the asphalt layers of intercontinental America! A scruffier army of Myrmidons has never been seen, at least not since the days of Leonidas of Athens, or Cincinnatus of Tuscany!

"HO! HAU! HAU! WOOOOOOOOOOOOOOOO!!" Grampa screamed wildly, and leapt onto Betty Grable, waiting at his side. He trotted right in behind the Chief, laughing his ass off and crying and carrying on in a pretty embarrassing manner.

Everybody was setting up quite a racket. "HO! WOO! WOO! YA-TA-HAY KEMOSABE! YOOOOOOOOO OOOOO!!"

I wouldn't have been surprised to see a symphony orchestra just about then, blasting out the *1812 Overture,* there was such a mixture of noises. A whole slew of Indian Elders from everywhere pranced right in around us, and a lot of other pretty disreputable characters from just about everywhere. A skeptical person might have thought they'd emptied the prisons. I expected Prussian cannons to start going off any second, and maybe Napoleon come riding over the horizon at Austerlitz. A squadron of Highway Patrolmen tried to detain the Chief at the ditch in between the north-south lanes, but Massaum had no respect at all for the Badge and she just rode around them. You could tell the boys in blue hated to be flanked like that, but there were so many goddamn TV cameras everywhere, they'd have to wait until later when it was dark to blow these terrorists to Kingdom Come. It was preposterous, of course, but I was there and I can testify that it all happened exactly as I am relating to you now. I'll even sign a deposition if you want me to.

On Interstate 25 northbound, an even more dramatic scene was unfolding. Red Bird stood in the road ahead of Whirlwind. The fact that dozens, maybe hundreds, of cars were honking madly behind her didn't seem to distract her from her lonely vigil. Whirlwind cantered on Massaum up and out of the ditch in between the one-way lanes to nowhere and, I couldn't see his face because I was trying to stay on Jack a few feet behind him, so I can't say what expression he might have had. His face was still painted red, though, and you could see Red Bird was a little startled by his appearance. He was really right out there in front of everybody and just about as impressive as a man can be in this life, short of the movies. I could tell she'd been crying, though. And she had her coterie of Moonbeam and Carmenta behind her, and her Sacred Bundle strapped on her back. She was also wearing a gorgeous white traditional doeskin dress, and her face had vermilion coloring on it too. But still, she looked pale and upset, to me. She looked imploringly at Whirlwind as he approached.

Whether he might have slowed down a little, I can't say. I heard him say to her, though, "Hi."

Did she smile a little? I couldn't tell. TV lights were in my eyes, and headlights from the trucks flashing angrily from low to high beam, but I think it might have been a little encouraging to her. She looked penitent enough to me.

But, you have to understand, in the heat of history and Contrariness, some men on the pinnacle of world events have greater responsibilities to their nations that preclude personal considerations. Chief Whirlwind was no longer the big fat dumb shit in Chapter Sixteen who just wanted to sleep with his lady and play with his children and go home. No, he'd accepted the Staff of Power and so he could never look back. He had to ride. No retreat. The Powers demand total obedience that way, a fact to which I, to my sorrow, can personally testify.

He went on by Red Bird and trotted over another cut fence on the eastern side of the Interstate and disappeared into the unlit twilight descending upon the Plains beyond. Cheyenne Land lay to the flat sagebrush ahead. I smiled at Red Bird as I passed her, but she only turned around to Rabbit beside her, and I think she might have been crying. She might have even been sobbing. But I had to ride, too, alone; even though hundreds of Indians had fallen in behind us.

I saw the warriors under Buddy's able leadership protecting us in a broad circle, with Elders around the inside of them. I turned on Jack to see Red Bird mounting Star and falling in behind, too, on the innermost circle of the Nation. It was the way things had to be, for now. She was surrounded by the women on their horses, and the children. Sky had rejoined Hulk before we hit the Highway and, like dozens of other kids, was having the time of his life.

Reporters from everywhere shouted questions, but we answered none of them. We had no answers. Rabbit organized her corps of TV cameras and joined the warriors on the outermost perimeter, and I'm sure the Chief was glad to see there were no guns anywhere. He was down on guns, everybody knew. And drugs, which includes booze. He was pretty unreasonable about it too. So they had cameras now, to shoot at the armies of the night that surely lay ahead of us. They had microphones and Walkman headsets, too, and CBs and portable telephones and who knew what all else. I didn't ask. I didn't want to know where they got the money for all those things, either, or for the pack horses laden with tents and tipis and travoises with tipi poles. Pickups and rows of old DeSotos and Studebakers were fanning out in every direction around us, too, on whatever roads they could find close by. It was becoming a real army now, and I, for one, never volunteered for the Service. I have no experience in these logistical maneuvers, so I can't say as to what order the Divisions and Brigades and Platoons were divided. But I was proud and excited, like everybody else, to see so many people in this world who cared enough to get up and off their butts and go out there and cause some trouble, for the good of the future generations.

Whirlwind rode alone, off a little ways from the main contingent. So did I. Everyone stayed away from us too, as the word spread like wildfire that we were Contraries and any close contact with us would probably get you frizzled by lightning for your trouble. We were oddballs, Whirlwind and me. Yes, there is a sadness surrounding all such Warriors, but it is not self-pity. Nor is it self-importance. We are often accused of feeling superior for our visions and sublime power and exquisite talents, and looking down on the rest of mankind as a bunch of sniveling cowards and common ordinary mortals, but I can assure you I don't think I'm better than you.

Buddy Red Bird wasn't too afraid of Whirlwind. He galloped over to him as it was getting dark and explained that a nice creek bottom was ahead about two miles and that it would be a good place for everyone to camp for the night, if that was okay with him? Whirlwind agreed that it was okay with him, and that he wouldn't mind having some buffalo ribs somebody'd remembered to bring along.

I won't bother you with too many details about setting up camp, and fanning the herd of four-leggeds out to their grazing tasks, because I know how impatient most audiences are with such trivia. Suffice it to say that everybody found something to eat and somewhere to sleep, and Whirlwind went off alone on a hill away from everybody and kept his private thoughts to himself. So did I. I can tell you, however, that I was content to appear scary to the children, and let the rumors spread far and wide that I was a Great and Terrible Wizard with a lot of black and white magic power at my fingertips, and that if anybody betrayed the integrity of our army or the purity of our intent, I would personally cook their brains in a sorceror's stew and hurl their souls out into the galaxy for all eternity. It's always good to keep people in line with a few such supernatural threats. It helps the discipline.

19

HOW KING ARTHUR
RESTORED PEACE UNTO THE
REALM, AND HOW HIS LADY
COMMANDED HIS FEALTY.

THE REVOLUTIONARY GUERRILLA ARMY RODE FOR FOUR
days at a stretch and then let the four-leggeds graze for
three. It was a time-tested pattern for armies who foraged
off the countryside, ever since Julius Caesar and U.S.
Grant perfected the technique. There are many things
like this which Indians have learned from western civilization. So if a few farmers griped about a few soybean fields
being trampled and a few potatoes stolen from their
barns, they weren't students of their own culture. They
should have realized that it was patriotic to have their
fences cut and winter wheat eaten down to the roots by
marauding bands. It was a healthy symptom of demo-
cratic ideals. Disgruntled ranchers who found a few cow
ponds drunk bone-dry should have studied agronomical
science better when they were in school, instead of running off after girls all the time.

Oh sure, there were a lot of complaints filed against the
horde of naturalists who shoplifted their way through the

little towns of Fowler and Rocky Ford and La Junta on the Arkansas River. People will always be selfish like that. It's human nature. And a lot of lawless citizens even tried to take the Law into their own hands and form vigilante posses to go after the innocent pastoralists. These things have to be expected. Fortunately, Anarchy was avoided when every deputy from the five-state area was brought in to protect the tourists from disgruntled locals.

And I'm happy to report there was a strong minority of farmers and merchants who were living in danger of foreclosure and bankruptcy who were actually glad to assist in the re-distribution and re-organization of the economy. Most country folks are very friendly that way, and will always give a passing traveler a helping hand when in need. More than one cowboy was glad to see the Indians. The rest of the country may have been thriving, but in Lamar and Limon the inflation rate was sky high and the price of corn rock bottom. It took a real pessimist to see that the dwindling aquifers did not portend good times ahead, but farmers have always been a pessimistic lot, on the whole. A few unhappy hayseeds even helped the Vandals cut their own fences! They drove their tractors into Eads and Kit Carson behind the guerrilla army, and there is even a documented case of one terrorist in overalls driving his Allis-Chalmers right through the front window of the Bank! It was a sad day, for most Americans, to learn of these negative fits of pique.

The army made about twenty miles a day, four days a week or so. They tried to find Recreation Areas and Reservoirs for the herd of animals to graze and fatten up, and were often told, to their sorrow, by frantic Game and Parks Rangers that everything they were doing was illegal and extremely detrimental to the environment. Sadly, they looked upon the ravaged river bottoms the Army Corps of Engineers stripped to make dams for new golf courses and more drinking water for Denver. They looked upon the alkali in the soil that hadn't been there a hundred years ago before the cows and oil wells replaced the unprofitable herds of Bison. They looked upon the power lines and roads which shot up the price of real estate and shot down the value of the sub-soil moisture at the same time.

Yes, there was no doubt Whirlwind's legions were as un-
popular with the bankers and corporate executives as King
Arthur's Knights of the Round Table had been with the
Saxons when they purged Britain of its great civil war raging beneath the surface of poverty and ignorance. The
Great American West may have *looked* like it was prosperous
with a chicken in every pot, but all you had to do was
scratch the surface and you'd find a helluva lot of griping
and disgruntlement going on around the kitchen tables. I've
personally never heard so much bitching about corruption
in the government and unfairness between rich and poor
and poor quality on television as I've heard in Hugo, Colorado, and elsewhere. New York and Washington, D.C., may
be going to great pains to proclaim that everything is great
Out There in the Heartland, but as far as I can tell there's
a Civil War raging underneath the surface. The politicians
and network anchormen haven't been out on the streets
lately if they think everything is hunky-dory. But then I'm
just the progeny of Cowboys and Indians and don't have
the sense God gave a chicken.

Whirlwind, as usual, went his merry way as if the whole
world wasn't watching his every step. He went miles out of
our way to stop at the site of the Sand Creek Massacre, for
instance. We stayed there four days and prayed for the
slaughtered Cheyennes who waved the peace flag in 1864.
They were unarmed too. We looked at the police cars who
looked at us from every direction too. They had their sirens
and lights flashing all day and night, in front of us, behind
us, in the middle of us. Helicopters and search planes flew
over routinely and regularly.

Whirlwind helped the Cheyenne and Arapaho relatives
of Black Kettle and Left Hand, who were the peace chiefs
butchered at Sand Creek, to set up some ceremonies in
remembrance. Seven sweat lodges and seven great bonfires
were kept going for four nights in a circle around that
horrible place. It was like Auschwitz to us. There were no
markers or memorials there, and heads of foreign governments never came here to lay wreaths at Indian tombs in
the semi-arid prairie. Whirlwind had decorated his Contrary Bow by now with eagle feathers given to him by the
Arapahoes, and a porcupine medicine wheel he made him-

self, and his buffalo skull was painted yellow and had sage stuck in the eyeholes. The horns were painted by hailstones and black thundercloud circles from his vision. He fasted for four days out there, alone most of the time.

I know he was remembering, as we all were, that bad day in 1864 when Colorado Governor Evans sent the volunteer Colorado Regiments against the unarmed peace camp. They were too cowardly to fight armed warriors, either Indian or Confederates. They rode in with four twelve-pounder mountain howitzers and blew 105 Indian women and children to hell, and 28 men. Chiefs White Antelope, One-eye, and War Bonnet were assassinated.

Most of the media people who surrounded us, along with a lot of politicians and bureaucrats, thought it was just a big PR stunt. Buddy held a press conference and informed them in no uncertain terms that it was anything but. Whirlwind surprised everybody by coming in to the conference, out in the open on a nice May morning, and sitting quietly at the table beside Buddy. He said nothing; he didn't have to. He was about the most impressive Indian most of the Honkies there had ever seen, dangerous-looking and mean. Of course, as you and I know herewith from this authenticated history, Whirlwind was about the un-meanest fella who ever walked the earth, like Black Kettle.

"Evans is still honored in Colorado history," Buddy was concluding. "Counties and national forests and schools and libraries and streets are named after him all over the State."

Whirlwind got up and stormed out, not even a pleasant look on his big red-painted face. His picture made the cover of *Time* magazine that week.

He didn't give a damn about that, I knew, as we hit the trail again the next morning. He was thinking about the handwriting on the wall. As strong as our army was, we still didn't have a chance. As Buddy said at the press conference, "Democracy is a bitter joke to Indians. The vast majority of Americans have never given a rat's ass about us, and they never will." For all our efforts and all the help and contributions pouring in from the world, polls in every American newspaper and on every television station showed a strong majority of Americans "disapproved of the lawlessness" of Whirlwind's army. For every farmer who fed

us a barbecue of beef and buttermilk along the way there
were ten farmers who hated us. And our army was getting
more ragtag as our situation got more perilous. A lot of
black people came to join us from the cities, ravaged by
crack and AIDS and other plagues that hadn't even been
heard of ten years ago. Whirlwind accepted all the tired
and hungry and poor, whose legions were swelling more
and more every year in the land of plenty.

One afternoon suddenly, right after April showers had
turned to May flowers, Whirlwind stopped out in the middle of a vast open treeless expanse where he was riding, as
usual, alone and a little ways off to the side from the main
contingent. He just stopped and turned around and looked.
He saw the main body with Red Bird in the middle, her
Sacred Bundle in her middle. Someone had donated a
beautiful buffalo-hide tipi and it was set up every night in
the middle of the seven circles of the nation, which Red
Bird and the Sacred Bundle stayed in. Dozens of other tipis,
mostly canvas, had sprouted up around it, and more than
a few aging Hippies had added a great deal of their accul-
turation to our renewal. Most of the druggies and drinkers
were gone, and there were still a lot of ex-winos and sick
and homeless folks struggling to keep up with us, as always,
but mostly it had been developing into a fairly well organized society. The Elders loved to argue into the night
about the re-organization of the government, and they almost always set up a caterwauling with drums and singing
and dancing until dawn, on the days when we weren't traveling especially, enough to drive a rational man crazy.

Although he was the acknowledged Chief, and greatly
revered and respected, Whirlwind knew better than anyone
that the women were the nation, and the children. He saw
that it was good. He did not feel threatened anymore. He
did not have that evil anger that rises in men, for he felt
the gentle music of Mother Earth all around him, and that
violence and resentment are stupid attributes of men,
mostly. Sure, women and children can be raging assholes,
too, plenty, but he thought of a conversation he overheard
one night between Rabbit and the other women. Rabbit had
said, "I don't know any woman who isn't afraid of men.

Most women have been threatened with rape at least once in their lives. Every woman has a story about a man being cruel to her, and ninety-nine percent of the Lesbians I've known said they were abused by their fathers or brothers, or some man."

Whirlwind dismounted and Massaum picked at some grass. He waited for the center of the Nation to catch up with him. His heart was broken, you see, without his Lady. He was sure that she hated him now, for his long, stubborn silence with which he had been trying to punish her, for some stupid damn reason. Maybe it was because he was afraid of her, afraid that he couldn't please her sexually well enough, afraid that he was exposed too much for the fool he was, naked and vulnerable.

She approached on Star, looking thinner and sadder than ever. She had suffered too. Women feel everything in their bones, in their blood. The emotions burst out of them like wind and weather bursting from the atmosphere and the oceans. Bonnie Red Bird had always felt things deeply, too deeply, so that she went out of balance often and needed to take a drink, smoke, chase her pleasures wantonly wherever she could find them.

Whirlwind waited for her, and when she stopped in front of him, the whole Nation watching, he bowed his head before her in supplication. He said, "I'm sorry."

"So am I," she said, and got off her horse.

They looked at each other. He whispered, "I don't know what to say. I was mad at you for drinking and finding something I couldn't give you. I was jealous."

"It's okay," she replied, and smiled. He was grateful. Oh, where would we be without the zillions of times women have forgiven men? Back in the slime, probably. Like a baby, he reached out, and his arms asked for a hug. They moved into each other and there wasn't a dry female eye for miles around. Even a few male tear ducts went into operation, including mine.

Impractically, they fell to their knees, still wrapped up tightly into each other. We could all see that we weren't going anywhere else today, so we set up camp around them. The women put up the buffalo tipi around them. Whirlwind broke his clinch only long enough to stand his Contrary Bow out in the front of the lodge, with the door closed, indicating they didn't want any visitors tonight.

It was a quiet night, with very little visiting back and forth or singing. Most everyone stayed in with their sweethearts, if they had one, and communed with nature. The flowers were bursting around everywhere, after all, and the trees were budding and the foals were foaling. On May Eve I had celebrated my own birthday, smelling the wild yellow roses and feasting my eyes on the cherry blossoms.

Without going into too much detail, we hit the trail again the next morning, this time with Chief Whirlwind and Red Bird riding side by side at the head of the Nation. Buddy and I flanked them, and the Elders flanked us, with the women and children inside the circles behind us. The warriors and scouts scoured the countryside around us for food and signs of danger.

The signs were plentiful. We were approaching the east-west artery of Interstate 70 at Limon and, the scouts informed us, "National Guard tanks and APCs as far as the eye can see, coming from Denver."

We came over a rise a few miles to the south of Limon, and were shocked. The superhighway was jammed with cars and trucks and military vehicles for miles, over the horizon to the west toward the distant line of the Front Range. It was getting close to dark, and Whirlwind and Buddy looked at each other. Whirlwind decided, "Let's go." Massaum took the lead and Red Bird dropped back inside the protective custody of the women and children. She had to protect the Sacred Bundle at all costs: it was the power of the people and the spirits. She could not jeopardize it. This is not to say plenty of women didn't ride out in front with the warriors, because Rabbit and her warrior society especially were never the ones to be left out of anything; but mostly the men were challenged by this impending war. Young men especially need to exercise their muscles and prove their courage, if only to themselves. Rabbit tended to argue with this fact of nature by saying, "Horse apples! Women need to learn how to be bold just as much as men." Nobody argued with her. We were too afraid.

Massaum broke into a trot, and Whirlwind stayed right

with her, armed only with his Contrary Bow. Buddy and I followed close behind, with our sub-chiefs El Cuartalejo and Jimmy Campbell exhorting the other Warriors to stay close, and be brave. Maybe you'll say I'm exaggerating that there were hundreds of warriors with us by then, and I would be the first to agree with you that most, if not all, of us were pretty sloppy excuses for warriors, in our raggedy blue jeans and an apparel that was a pretty mixed bag of buckskins and blue jeans and beaded rosettes and a few eagle feathers and turkey feathers here and there. The smart soldiers waiting ahead for us would certainly have looked down on us, at least for appearances' sake. They waited in their expensive Armored Personnel Carriers and Jeeps and vans with radar dishes on top and all the electronic gadgetry the bloated Pentagon budget could provide.

✓Thousands of good citizens waited on the roads and hilltops for miles around, too, having their picnics and hoping to witness the triumph of democracy. Oh, I suppose there might have been one or two well-wishers for our "Cause," too, but they cowered back in the mob. The media was there in force and pretended, as always, to be concerned about journalistic objectivity, whereas, in truth, their advertisers called all the shots, and their advertisers had determined in a number of nationwide surveys that marauding armies foraging across the profitable landscape of commerce were bad for busyness. Therefore, a subtle shift in the media bias in recent weeks showed we really "didn't represent the vast majority of law-abiding Indians" and "that it was always more constructive to make changes from within the System" than "to go around screaming 'Nazis' from the rooftops." One sage in New York advised us "to read the Federalist Papers." Ha, I wanted to reply. Nobody hated democracy more than Thomas Jefferson and James Madison.

Be that as it may, Propaganda Ministries aside, Whirlwind was charging; and I don't mean he was using American Express. A general waited directly ahead in our path, on the paved road approaching the junction of Interstate transportation. You could see that he was confident Divine Providence was on his side. So were all the guns in the world. You never saw such a mob of M-16s and .50-calibers

241

and what-all. I expected squadrons of fighter-bombers to appear out of the patriarchal Heavens at any moment, and annihilate us transgressors for our sins. General Patton held up his hand as if he wanted to talk, but Massaum was faster than he or Radar anticipated, and Whirlwind crazier than the CIA had determined, and before anybody knew it, Whirlwind was on top of the General and bonked him over the head with his Contrary Bow.

"COUP!" the Chief whooped. "WOO WOO WOO WOO!!"

The General crumpled over on the ground next to his twenty-first century Jeep and sat there like an idiot, with stars and little birdies flying around his head. Panic immediately seized his troops, as the chain of command had been interrupted and none of his subordinates dared take charge and risk court-martial. Without effective leadership, the fucking savages swooped through the tanks and APCs and Cadillacs, and pandemonium erupted. It reminded Grampa, as he screamed and counted coup on a rent-a-cop, of the Battle of the Bulge, in which he had participated forty-eight years ago. Vietnam Vets were reminded of Saigon on a Saturday night. Korean Vets thought of the DMZ.

With sublime orderliness, the anarchists followed their Chief through the U.S. Army, over Interstate 70, and disappeared into the dark a minute and a half later. Before anybody knew it, it was over—like a Heavyweight Boxing Match. Dozens, maybe hundreds of cheering fans decided on the spur of the moment to switch their allegiance to the Underdogs, and were glad to see them getting away. Once again Indians had foiled the well-laid plans of mice and men.

The Chief slowed to a fast trot and kept right on going into the wilderness. Everybody stayed with him. It was fun to win one.

Grampa was having a good-natured argument with Buddy, as they trotted along across the fields of victory. "It was like hitting the Commies at Inchon. I was there in 1950, or was it '51?"

"Nobody hates the Commies more'n me," Buddy countered, knowing he could get a rise out of the cantankerous old boy.

"I hate 'em more'n you, you disrespectful young—"

"Aw, what do you old farts know about Communism anyway?"

"I know enough to kick you on your butt!"

"I drove hordes of Reds back at Khe Sahn and Da Nang."

"I get sick of hearing about Vietnam!" Grampa cussed. "Vietnam! Hell, that wasn't a war! W W Two, now there was a war!"

The warriors were recounting all the coups they'd struck, just like in the old days. They had left the enemy disorganized and devastated, there was no doubt about it.

Under their bear robes later that night, Red Bird felt the sadness of her Warrior-Chief. It was in his tension, and quietness. "What's the matter?" she asked, as countless women have asked over the centuries.

"Nothing," he shrugged, as countless men have lied over the centuries.

Weeks of steady slow walking passed over the land. The debate raged upon the flames Buddy had fanned in yet another press conference. "Total revolution is the only answer," he had declared simplistically.

The Indians stopped to hold ceremonies at one massacre site after another: Summit Springs, and then the Sappa in Kansas, and the Blue Water in Nebraska. Whirlwind made a point of going out of his way to pay homage to the slaughtered Cheyennes at every site, much to the embarrassment and annoyance of historians and journalists. He was, they often reiterated in the gin joints of Julesburg, Colorado, and Oglala, Nebraska, kicking a dead horse. But Whirlwind and the Elders told the children about how women were thrown alive in big piles and burned to death. About babies hacked to pieces by bayonets. Girls raped repeatedly. All the grisly horror stories that Hollywood ignored. All the hatred and racism and starvation and cruelty of the cruelest race of people ever to walk the earth. Buddy was going way overboard when he said, "Not even the Mongols, the Russians, the Romans set about with a deliberate national policy to eradicate fifty million buffalo from a continent. The mass genocide of a whole economy of a whole race of people. Not even Stalin, not even Hitler, not even Pol Pot systematically wiped out twenty million Indians in Mexico, countless tens of millions in South America, countless millions right here between the borders of the United States."

The liberals anguished in guilt and torment, while the patriots screamed foul. "It is past," they declared, while they called for law and order. "It is over," they decided, and passed emergency legislation for a pay raise for Congress and another $50 billion to bail out the banks.

Laymen like Whirlwind couldn't see that anything was over, not as he rode through the sand hills of Nebraska. The water was brackish, the sun shone unnaturally hot in the depleted ozone, the soil was blowing away. The Elders lamented that they couldn't tell too many signs of nature from all the plants lost to pesticides. Lakotas rode down to join them, and Blackfeet from Montana, and Crees from Canada. The story was the same everywhere. Pollution was worldwide and practically irreversible now. The rich got richer and the propaganda against the poor grew more virulent. Indians arrived daily with tales of fetal alcohol syndrome, sterilization of women, jails bursting with Indians and blacks and Asians. And always, more and more fences to be cut, more and more roads, dams, power lines, cattle full of chemicals and cancer.

Insects were the only ones prospering from the global cloud of insecticides.

Then one day in June, Whirlwind stopped in his tracks. He got off his hungry, thin animal and stared to the north. Red Bird looked too. We all did. It was still a very beautiful sight.

"The Black Hills," the Chief said simply.

They shone like a solemn black-and-blue line across the wide horizon, shimmering like a mirage in the late spring heat.

"The Holy Land."

20

CHEYENNE SPRING.

THERE WERE A FEW MORE MASSACRE SITES TO RIDE PAST
first, before they could go into the sacred burial grounds
and vision places the Lakota Sioux called H'e Sapa. Fort
Robinson on the southern fringe of the Black Hills was the
site of the massacre of Dull Knife's band, at the conclusion
of another Cheyenne outbreak, back in 1879. Seventy-one
Indians had been killed in the ice. The great Crazy Horse
had been deliberately assassinated here in 1877, because he,
like Buddy Red Bird, didn't go along with the treaty chiefs
who could always be found to kiss the whiteman's . . . bill-
fold. Tribal councilmen they called them these days, and
Bureau of Indian Affairs people.

The traditionalists smoked their pipes and burned their
sweat lodge rocks for four more days, and a great keening
and mourning went up from the women. It is a curse to
have a memory, if you are a Lakota or a Cheyenne in
America.

Anger was rising all across the land at this inconvenient

criticism and discontent in their midst. World opinion was turning against the Leader of the Free World as all this dead and forgotten history was drudged up. Buddy Red Bird was not a hereditary chief, like Crazy Horse, but he was a fearless and charismatic and articulate war leader, and that made him just as hated and despised as the great Contrary Sioux of yore. Buddy was not a Contrary or a Thunder Clown, but he *was* a war hero with three bronze medals and a Purple Heart, so no one could say with any conscience or truth that he was a traitor or a coward. Many members of the VFW, if it were ever known, secretly admired him. He stood up for what he believed in, even if what he believed in was a pile of crap. It was every American's god-given right, they felt, to believe anything he wanted, even if it was total horseshit. You'd be surprised how many Americans still fall for that line and *really* think it's the way things are in this country.

Nevertheless, as has been too amply illustrated in this fiction of our times, the tides of history were rising against our embattled anti-heroes, not to mention the tides of human anger and jealousy and ignorance. I know how you wish upon a star that all your dreams will come true, and that there will be a happy ending and we will all live happily ever after, but . . . that ain't reality, as I have been reminded too many times. This story is a fantasy, many great and wise scholars have pointed out. It couldn't possibly happen. We're only allowed *one* Revolutionary War per country.

The remnants of Little Wolf's band escaped around Fort Robinson in 1879 and fled north through the Black Hills; and so did the remnants of his great-grandson's band in the 1990s (to keep the Time and Place generic). If nine out of ten landlords and homeowners in the picturesque bastion of Mount Rushmore and Flintstone's Village in South Dakota didn't welcome the invasion of these amateur historians, then you can't blame them. They had lived here for several generations, some of them going back a hundred years! They had put down roots, not to mention memento and overpriced curio shops for the tourists in quaintly named towns like Custer and Deadwood. Gambling had been reinstated here, to revive old, old traditions that went back, oh, fifty years! Or even seventy-five years! It was smug for Indians to point out that their roots went back thousands of years. White historians could always be found to point out that the Sioux only came here two hundred years ago. For tens of thousands of years there was no record of the buffalo hunters in this area, so, of course, there couldn't have been anybody around, not if there wasn't an anthropologist right there to record it. It just wasn't reasonable to make assumptions that wandering tribes or occasional individual drifters would have stumbled on such a beautiful and lush and bounteous outcropping of water and game and trees as the Black Hills. Nope, there was no archaeological evidence of the Sioux being here before the Spanish brought the horse or the French brought the iron beaver traps, so the only intelligent conclusion to make was that it was a home where only the buffalo and the antelope roamed. If there were, oh, yeah, a few strange pictographs on the cliffs, and some suspicious tipi rings of stone going back tens of thousands of years, well, those were probably made by Neanderthal Men from Europe. So, really, Europeans were probably the *first* people here, if you care to study the scientific facts of it. A lot of scholarly studies, indeed, were coming out with some pretty conclusive circumstantial evidence that the original Natives here may well have been the mysterious Cro-Magnons! Of Germany! Indians were really Whitemen!!!! Or maybe the Lost Tribes of *ISRAEL!!!!!* Alleluja!

So it really shouldn't be so surprising that gunshots started to go off in the direction of the Philistines, from snipers along the scenic roads of the National Park. The rednecks and other guardians of the monotheism of the ancient judeo-christian tradition had no other choice but to oppose the polytheism of the Sumerians. There were more than enough quotations to be found in Holy Scripture justifying imperialistic conquest. Hadn't Abraham come unto Kir'iath-arba and declared to the Hittites, "Entreat for me Ephron the son of Zohar, that he may give me the cave of Mach-pelah"? What more justification than that to kill Palestinians and Pawnees, I ask you? A few redskins were hit, too, by the random gunfire in the nights. Regardless of the Intifada, unarmed except for bows and arrows and lances and rocks, incursions upon Sacred Writ could not be tolerated. Even the Holy Roman Emperor had come out against such heresy.

Thus, in like manner since the days when Apollo and Jehovah burned the pagan Temples of Athena and Baal, all the shit of the world came down on the Indians of America. Injuries from sniper-fire increased. Cops busted small groups of Crows or Bannocks when they stopped at the Gas-o-Mart in Hill City. Outstanding warrants were found for Mohawks and Rappahannocks when they tried to take a shower at Trout World.

In the end, the War would reach its inevitable conclusion in Heaven, where gods and goddesses dispute for the loyalties of men and women. Whirlwind and Red Bird reached the ridges overlooking Sturgis, South Dakota; and beyond, rose the volcanic cone of the Sacred Mountain.

Did it look like Mount Sinai to the wandering Hebrews? Slaves emerging from the deserts and civilization of Egypt? Bear Butte sat off alone from the rest of Her Sisters, like a Contrary Queen, lovely and stern and pitiless. She was the goal of all Thunder Dreamers, whether they were named Moses or Dionysus or Sweet Medicine. She was full of secret passages and wellsprings of mysterious knowledge. Maybe, in our fondest dreams, she would bestow upon us once every few thousand years a Tablet or two of Truth, a Sacred Arrow shot from Thunder Nation lighting the darkness with a glimpse of the secrets of Power. But, to be sure, as Rabbit pointed out succinctly, "We don't need a Savior to tell us about it, anymore."

"Nowah'wus," the Cheyennes prayed.

"Mato Paha," the Sioux prayed.

Whence these sacred mountains and creation myths of all the religions of the world? "Bear Butte," a few whites prayed.

The armies of the night gathered before them, to prevent at all costs the Return of the Queen and her Sacred Knowledge. The Great Dragon rose out of the limitless American sky and Minuteman II Intercontinental Ballistic Missile silos surrounded the Mountain, in the name of God. B-1Bs flew low overhead, and Comsats high overhead, and hundreds of camouflaged National Guard tanks and APCs and dozens of other baby dragons prowled along the roads in between the legions of the Goddess and Her Home. There would be no cutesy-cutesy counting of coups on this afternoon of the Summer Solstice. There would be no jokes of the Trickster upon the veteran troops bivouacked for dozens of miles in every direction today. No pompous weekend general commanded these troops, but a hardened West Point man and a good Presbyterian. The soldiers quickly moved into a pre-arranged maneuver to surround the guerrillas, moving in tighter on them in a pincer movement.

Whirlwind and Buddy Red Bird saw they didn't have a chance. It was hopeless. Five miles away from Bear Butte, so close and yet so far. To have come a thousand miles and to fail. A loudspeaker boomed at them, "This is an illegal assembly and you are all under arrest! I repeat, you are all under arrest! Lay down your weapons and put up your hands!"

Thousands of Marines, National Guardsmen, and Guardswomen closed in with automatic weapons and gas masks. They looked like Martians. Dozens of attack helicopters swarmed overhead in hostile posture. It was unbelievable! It was awful! It couldn't be happening, not here, not in America in this day and age!

"YOU ARE ALL UNDER ARREST! LAY DOWN YOUR WEAPONS AND COME OUT WITH YOUR HANDS UP, OR WE WILL OPEN FIRE!"

Red Bird looked at Storyteller. "I thought you said it would be a happy ending?!"

Storyteller rose above them all on a little rocky ledge, and waved his Thunder Lance at the gathering storm clouds, which were racing in from the west. Awesome thunderclaps and lightning-bolts exploded from the Beast hidden within all Nature. A thunderbolt struck him suddenly and he disappeared totally!

Everyone was gone. Day had become night. Fact had become fiction. Everything was reversed, as it is in the creator's imaginary Spirit World.

I sat on the rock overlooking Bear Butte, where I live, and I had driven the armies of the daylight away. The Sacred King and Queen were safe, and their marriage was assured in the bright moonlight and starlight, invisible to the watching eyes of our enemies. All was calm on this holy night at the Solstice. Everything was good.

Cynics might say that not one word of this story was true. None of it happened. It is not a true picture of our world, they say.

11-17-92
B+T
11.00